The Bond of Black

The Bond of Black

William Le Queux

Originally published in 1899.

Published by Wildside Press.

Visit us online at wildsidepress.com.

Introduction
Karl Wurf

William Le Queux's *The Bond of Black* first appeared in 1899, at a moment when London seemed both bright and shadowed—electric lights in the West End, moral panics in the press, and an eager taste for sensation. Le Queux, already well known for topical thrillers, set his story in that uneasy border where clubland confidence meets the city's secret life.

The novel opens with a simple rescue. A gentleman helps a young woman who is lost and frightened; soon after, a sacred object in his rooms turns to ash, an eerie sign that hints at powers moving behind polite doors. The shock leads to questions, and those questions lead to a death: a popular member of Parliament is found lifeless, with no clear cause the doctors can name. The mystery is not only "who," but "how," and why the signs point toward a creed that feeds on stolen holy things and fear.

Le Queux builds his plot along two tracks that often meet in his work: modern investigation and ancient dread. The settings are crisp—clubs, chapels, quiet streets after midnight—yet what drives the action is belief, or the loss of it. A charismatic preacher stands near the heart of the story, and the book keeps asking what faith means when evil hides behind ritual and fine words.

As a journalist-novelist, Le Queux wrote fast, close to the day's headlines, and loved to frame danger as a public warning. Elsewhere he tilted toward spy scares and invasion tales; here he treats London itself as the threatened territory, with a secret order at work inside it. That mix of civic alarm and narrative drive was his signature, and it helps explain why his books reached wide audiences on both sides of the Atlantic.

Today the book reads as a brisk, curious blend of crime story and occult thriller. It captures a moment when a confident city worried about what it could not see, and when fiction tried to name those fears. Read it for the puzzle, for the mood of gaslit streets, and for the way Le Queux turns private vows and public lives into one tight, troubling knot.

Author's Note.

In this story I have dealt with an extraordinary phase of modern life in London, which to the majority will come as a startling revelation.

Some will, perhaps, declare that no such amazing state of things exists in this, the most enlightened age the world has known. To such, I can only assert that in this decadent civilisation of ours the things which I have described actually take place in secret, as certain facts in my possession indisputably show.

It is no unhealthy problem of sex, or of the ethics of divorce; no story of woman's faithlessness or man's misplaced confidence, but a subject upon which I believe no English author has yet touched, and one which I anticipate will prove interesting, and point a wholesome moral. It may not be out of place to add that I have been compelled to touch the subject with as light a hand as the purpose of the story will allow, in respect for the susceptibilities of the reader, and because it is furthest from my intention to sow evil broadcast.

Chapter One.
London's Delight.

IT IS A REMARKABLE sequence of events, a story which in these days of high civilisation is so extraordinary as to almost stagger belief. Yet the higher the civilisation the more refined are its evil-doers, the more ingenious is the innate devilry of man, the more skilful are those who act with malice aforethought.

In replacing this strange drama of present-day life before the reader—a drama of love, of self-sacrifice, of evil passions, and of all uncharitableness—I, Clifton Cleeve, am compelled to speak of myself; to recount the strange adventures which befell me, and to expose to the public gaze the undercurrents of a curious phase of society, of the existence of which few dream. If, therefore, I am forced to the constant use of the first person singular, it is in no egotistical sense, but merely in order that my strange story should be properly understood, and that the blame which rightly attaches to me should not be borne by others. In this narrative of curious circumstances are facts that will astound, perhaps even terrify; nevertheless be it recollected that I myself was an unwilling actor in this drama, and that I only relate that which. I saw with my own eyes and heard with my own ears.

Even now, as I recall the past, there are scenes before me as vivid in every detail as though the events occurred but an hour ago; scenes which could not fail to leave a life-long impression upon the mind of any man, so unusual, so striking, so utterly extraordinary were they.

A little more than two years have now elapsed since that well-remembered night when the prologue was enacted. Yet the months that have gone by have seemed a veritable century of time, for have I not trodden the path of life overburdened by a weight of weariness, my youth sapped by vain longings and heart-sickening disappointment, my natural desire for existence blunted by an ever-recurring sorrow, and a constant, irritating, soul-maddening mystery, which lay unsolved, a barrier between myself and happiness. I am no faint-heart, yet as I live again those breathless months of anxiety, of fascination and of terror, I am again seized by that same fear which two years ago consumed me, and held me dumbfounded.

I was not feeling well. Having risen late after a dance, I had spent the afternoon over a book, dined at home in my chambers in Charing Cross Mansions, and had afterwards gone out for an idle stroll across Leicester Square and up Piccadilly. The night was moonless, but brilliant for October, yet the atmosphere was of that artificial clearness which in London renders the street-lamps unusually bright, and is always precursory of rain. At the corner of Park Lane I turned back, hesitating whether to turn into the Naval and Military for a gossip, or spend an hour at a theatre.

London had finished its long and toilsome day. Tired Hammersmith and jaded Notting Hill crowded into the omnibuses, eager to get to their homes without a moment's delay, while gay Belgravia and Kensington were starting forth upon their night of delight, to be spent within that little area of half a mile around Charing Cross, wherein centres all the life and diversion of the giant metropolis. Gay London is very concentrated.

A brazen-lunged man pushed the special *Standard* under my nose, saying—

"'Ere y'are, sir. All the winners!"

But I uttered one word, expressive though not polite, and strode on; for, truth to tell, I had read the paper an hour before, and by it discovered to my chagrin that I had been rather hard hit over a race. Therefore, a list of the winners being pushed into my face by this man was an unintentional insult. Yes, I was decidedly out of sorts.

Self-absorbed, a trifle melancholy, and undecided where to spend the evening, I was passing the corner of Bond Street, when I felt a hand upon my arm, as a voice exclaimed—

"Hullo, Clifton, old fellow! You in town? How long have you been back from Tixover?"

I looked up quickly and saw one of my oldest and closest friends, Roddy Morgan, or, to be more exact, the Honourable Roderick Morgan, a tall, smart, good-looking man about my own age, thirty, or perhaps a couple of years my senior, with dark eyes and hair, well-cut features and a merry, amused expression which did not belie his natural temperament. Roddy was a younger son who had gone the pace as rapidly as most men, until he had suddenly found himself with a sufficient quantity of writs and judgment summonses to paper his room with, and in a very fair way to becoming a bankrupt. But of judgment summonses the ever-merry Roddy had once laughingly declared that "no home was complete without them;" and at the critical juncture a generous maternal uncle, who was likewise a Duke, had very considerately placed the easy-going Roddy on his legs again. And not only this, but he had induced Roddy, who was an excellent speaker, to stand for a county constituency, and paid his election expenses, with the result that he now found himself representing the important division of South-West Sussex in the House.

We clasped hands heartily, and as I explained how three days ago I had come up from Tixover, my father's place in the country, he strode on at my side, gossiping about our mutual friends, and telling me the latest amusing story from the House.

"Ah! my dear fellow," he said, "a chap in Parliament has a pretty hard time of it in these days when the Opposition papers in his constituency keep their eye upon him, ready at any moment to fling mud, to charge him with negligence if he refuses to ask some ridiculous question of the Government, or to comment sarcastically if he chances to miss a division."

"But you like it," I said. "At Oxford you were always to the forefront at the Union. Everybody, from the 'Honourable George Nathaniel' downwards, prophesied that you'd some day place your silk hat on a bench in the House."

"I know, I know," he answered, rather impatiently, "but the truth is I only allowed myself to be put up because my old uncle pressed me. He made me a present of a neat ten thou', so what could I do? I was simply led as a lamb to the slaughter, and nowadays I get deputations waiting upon me, headed by the butcher of Little Twaddlington, and consisting of the inn-keeper and the tinker of that rural centre of civilisation. I'm civil to them, of course, but hang it, old man, I can't promise to ask all their foolish questions. I'm not built that way. When I make a promise, I keep it. Members nowadays, however, will promise anything on earth, from obtaining an autograph for the butcher's wife's collection to the bringing down of manna from above."

I saw that Roddy was discontented, and was considerably surprised. His Parliamentary honours weighed heavily upon him. He had joined the St. Stephen's Club in the manner of all staunch Conservative members, and I attributed some of his dissatisfaction to the fact that he was nightly compelled to dine with the old fogies there, so as to be within reach for divisions. The Club is only across the road from the House, standing at the corner of the Embankment, and connected with Palace Yard by a subterranean passage. When the division-bell rings in the House it also rings in the club dining-room, and anxious members leave their soup, dash through the tunnel and vote, and come back to finish it. Indeed, it is no uncommon thing for this to be repeated several times in the course of dinner, causing much puffing and grumbling on the part of the stout and gouty members who, overtaken in this helter-skelter to vote, are very often shut out and find they have had their scramble for nothing. Then on returning to table they have to withstand the chaff of the younger and more active legislators, of whom Roddy was a very fair specimen.

"Going down to the House tonight?" I inquired.

"No. It's Wednesday, thank Heaven! I've been down there this afternoon, but we rose at six. Where are you toddling?"

"Anywhere," I answered. "I want to look in at the Naval and Military for a letter first."

"From a charmer, eh?" he asked, with a merry twinkle.

"No," I answered briefly.

"You're a rum chap, Clifton," he said. "You never seem to take girls up the river, to the theatre, or to the races, as other men do. I'm beginning to think that you don't like womankind."

"Well, I don't know. I fancy I've had as many little affairs of the heart as most men," I answered.

"Somebody was saying the other day that you were likely to be engaged to May Symonds. Is it true?"

"Whoever said so is certainly premature," I laughed. "Then you don't deny it, old chap?"

I shrugged my shoulders, smiled, and together we ascended the club steps.

After a drink we lit cigars and went forth again, strolling along to the Empire, where in the lounge we idled about, chatting with many men we knew, watching the acrobats, the conjurors, the eccentric singers, the ballet, and the other variety items which went to make up the attractive programme.

Leaning upon the plush-covered backs of the circle seats, we smoked and chatted as we watched the ballet, and subsequently entered the bar, where there had congregated about a dozen men all more or less known to me. We joined them, my friend the irrepressible young Tory Member being hailed by a youthful sprig of the Stock Exchange as "The Prime Minister," whereat there was a round of hearty laughter.

We had chatted for some moments when suddenly Roddy started as if he had encountered some one whose presence was disagreeable in the extreme, and turning to me, said in a hurried half-whisper—

"I'm off, old chap. Forgot I have another engagement. Good night."

And ere I could reply he had slipped away, and was lost in the chattering crowd.

At the time it struck me that this action was strange, for I felt sure he had seen somebody he did not wish to meet, and reflected that perhaps it was some unwelcome creditor or other. I continued chatting with the other men, until some twenty minutes later I left them and crossed to the little bar where cigars are sold, in order to get something to smoke. The lounge was then so crowded that locomotion was difficult. I was forced to elbow my way to the end of the promenade.

The curtain had fallen upon the ballet, the orchestra was playing the National Anthem, and the place was congested by people coming from their seats in the grand circle, and making their way to the exit. The air was heavy with tobacco-smoke mingled with the odour of a thousand perfumes, for the chiffons of each woman who passed seemed to exhale a different scent, from the nauseous patchouli to the latest patent of the ingenious Parisian perfumer.

Having bought my cigar and lit it, I stood chatting with another man I knew while the theatre emptied, then parting from him, I returned to the bar, only to find my group of friends had dispersed.

I wandered out to the vestibule, and as I stood glancing round, thinking it unusual that Roddy should have left in so mysterious a manner, my gaze encountered that of an extraordinarily pretty girl.

A pair of wistful blue eyes with a half-frightened expression gazed out of a face which was beautiful in its every line, a face saintly in its expression of innocence and youth. As far as I could judge she was about twenty, the paleness of her cheeks showing that no artificial colouring had been added to tinge them, like those of the women about her, while from beneath her hat a mass of fair hair strayed upon her brow, imparting an almost childlike softness to her face; her blue eyes were clear and wide-open, as if in wonder, and her mouth half-parted showed an even row of perfect teeth, while her dimpled chin was pointed and altogether charming.

About her figure was a grace of outline too seldom seen in London women, a suppleness of the hips that seemed almost foreign; yet the face was pure, sweet and winning, an altogether typical English face, refined, with a complexion perfect. In her dress was nothing startling, nothing calculated to arrest the attention of the sterner sex, nothing vulgar nor loud, for it was of dead black grenadine, relieved by a little white lace at the throat and cuffs—an almost funereal robe in contrast with the gay-coloured silks and daring ornamentation of the loud-tongued women who swept past her with inquiring glance and chattering gaily as they made their way out.

I looked at her a second time, for I confess to being attracted by her quietness of dress, her natural dignity, and the agitation within her which she was trying in vain to conceal. Demure and unaffected, she was so utterly out of place in that centre of, London gaiety that I could not help pausing to watch her. Those of her sex who passed looked somewhat askance at her and smiled among themselves, while more than one man ogled her through his monocle. But not a single glance did she bestow upon any in return save myself.

In dismay she looked slowly around the well-lit vestibule and out into the street, where cabs and carriages were driving off. Then she gazed about her, evidently hesitating how to act. There was a hard curl at the corners of her mouth, and a contraction of the eyelids which showed me that tears were ready to start. Yes, there was no doubt whatever that she was in distress, and needed assistance.

She was speaking earnestly with one of the uniformed doorkeepers, an elderly attendant whom I knew quite well, a highly-respectable pensioner in whom the management reposed the greatest confidence.

Noticing me standing there, he came forward with a military salute, saying—

"Excuse me, sir. But I have a lady here who's in a rather curious difficulty. You know London well, sir?"

"I think so," I answered, smiling.

"Well, will you speak with her a moment, sir?"

"What's her trouble?" I inquired, somewhat surprised, nevertheless crossing with him to where she stood, and raising my hat. I confess that she was so eminently beautiful, her face so absolutely flawless in its contour and innocent in its expression, that she had fascinated me. I was beneath the spell of her marvellous beauty.

Many women had smiled upon me, women who were more than passing fair; but never had my eyes fallen upon one whose purity of soul was so mirrored in her eyes, or whose face was so childlike and so perfect. Those tendrils, soft as floss silk, were of that delicate gold which the majority of women lose with their teens; those eyes possessed the true clearness which innocence alone can impart.

"If I can render you any assistance I will do so with pleasure," I said, addressing her, adding, "I noticed a moment ago that you appeared to be in distress."

"You are extremely kind," she answered, raising her eyes to mine for an instant. Her glance was steady and searching, and I saw that she was undecided whether to trust me. "You were quite correct in thinking I am in distress, and if you really could help me I should be so much obliged."

"Then what troubles you?" I inquired, well satisfied with her answer, and anxious that she should make me her confidant.

"I have been separated from my friends, and am a stranger to London," she replied. "You will laugh," she added, "but I am really lost, for I don't know my way back to my friends' house."

"You know the address, I suppose?" I laughed, for to me the idea of one being thus lost in London was amusing.

"Yes: Ellerdale Street."

"Where?"

"I don't know," she answered, "except that it's a long way from here; somewhere on the other side of London. We came by train."

"Ellerdale Street," I repeated reflectively. "I've never heard of it." There are, of course, thousands of streets in the suburbs of which nobody ever hears, save when somebody commits a crime of more than ordinary violence, and papers give the unknown thoroughfare undue prominence.

"But the strange thing is that my friends, two ladies, should have disappeared so quickly," she went on, pausing on the pavement before the theatre as we went out and gazing blankly about her. "They must surely have missed me, and if so, one would think they would remain till everybody had gone, and then search for me."

"Yes," I said, "it is certainly rather remarkable," and together we walked to the corner of Leicester Street, where there is another exit of the theatre, but my pretty companion could discover neither of the ladies who had accompanied her.

Her voice was low and refined, her well-gloved hands small; yet her severe style of dress seemed to speak of poverty which she would fain conceal. She wore no jewellery, not even a brooch; and I fell to wondering whether she might be a governess, or perhaps a shop-assistant who had come from a provincial town to "better herself" in London.

For fully a quarter of an hour we strolled together, backwards and forwards before the railings of the Empire, which soon became dark and deserted, until we were practically the only loiterers. It certainly struck me as more than strange that her companions, knowing her to be a stranger to London, should thus leave her to her own devices in Leicester Square at midnight. Again, it was curious that she herself should only know the name of the road, and not the district.

"You said your friends live in Ellerdale Street," I exclaimed at last, after we had been chatting about the performance, and she had criticised the singers with an artlessness which betrayed that she was entirely unaccustomed to the music-hall. "The best course will be to ask a cabman."

A hansom was standing at the kerb.

"Do you know of any street named Ellerdale Street?" I asked the driver.

"No, sir, I don't," he answered, after a pause, during which time he thought deeply. "There's Ellerslie Road up in Shep'erd's Bush, and Ellesmere Road out at Bow, but I don't know of any others." Then, turning to another man on a cab behind him, he asked:

"I say, Sandy, do you know Ellerdale Street?"

"No, don't know it at all. Ask a policeman," was the other's gruff response.

"I'm giving you a lot of trouble," my companion said apologetically. "It is really too bad, and you must think me very foolish to get separated from my friends like this. How it occurred I really don't know. They went out in front of me, and the crowd kept me from coming out of my seat. Then, when I got into the promenade I found they had vanished, as if by magic."

"It's evident that the street is not well-known," I said, "for hansom-cab drivers are really encyclopaedias of London geography, having to pass an examination in it before being granted a driver's licence by the police. It must be somewhere far out in the suburbs."

Then a thought suddenly occurred to me.

"The only thing I can suggest," I continued, "is that you should walk round to my chambers in Charing Cross Road, for I have there a Directory which will no doubt give us some clue to the whereabouts of your friends."

She paused, and looked at me rather strangely I thought. I had expected her to be eager to act as I suggested, but found her somewhat loth to accompany me. Yet, was this not natural? I was an utter stranger. Perhaps, too, she had seen some drama in the provinces where the villain invariably wears a starched shirt-front and smokes cigarettes, for it seemed as though she held me in fear.

"You are very kind," she answered, "but I really think—"

"No," I said, divining her thoughts. "It is impossible for you to wander the streets until morning. You must allow me to help you. Come."

"I've been thinking it would be best, perhaps, for me to go to an hotel," she said.

"As you wish," I replied. "But you must find out this unknown street either now or tomorrow morning, and if you take my advice you will lose no time in ascertaining where your friends really live, for they will be anxious about you."

For a few moments she reflected, then exclaimed—

"Yes, you're right after all. I'm sure you are extremely kind."

And together we crossed the Square and continued along Cranbourne Street to the colossal block of redbrick flats wherein my chambers were situated.

Chapter Two.
This Crucifix.

ON ASCENDING TO THE third floor, Simes, my man, opened the door and she advanced timidly down the tiny passage to my sitting-room. It was not a very large apartment, but I had furnished it comfortably a couple of years before, and it presented a rather cosy appearance with the table-cover and velvet *portières* of sage green to match, a couple of big roomy saddlebag chairs of club dimensions, a high, carved-oak buffet, with its strip of white cloth spread as daintily as in the dining-room of any well-appointed house, for Simes was an excellent man, as natty as a chamber-maid. He took a pride in keeping my rooms spick and span. An ex-trooper of Hussars, he had seen service with me in Egypt before I left the Service, and was a model servant, obeying with military precision, and was eminently trustworthy, save where whiskey was concerned. He could not be expected to resist the temptation of taking a drop from my tantalus on odd occasions.

Upon the walls of my room were a few choice pictures which I had purchased from time to time, together with a pencil caricature of myself drawn by one of the *Punch* artists who was an old friend, and a couple of plaques which had been given me by the lady who painted them. In the middle of the room stood the square table with a bowl of flowers in the centre, on one side of the fireplace a revolving bookstand, and on the other nearest the window, which looked down upon Charing Cross Road, a small triangular table of rosewood, whereon stood some curios which I had picked up during my pleasure trip round the world.

I give this detailed description of my own quarters because it will be found necessary in order to properly understand the story.

"What a pretty room!" was my fair unknown's first exclamation.

"Do you think so? I'm glad you like it," I laughed, for most of my visitors were in the habit of making similar observations. "Do sit down," and I drew forward one of the big armchairs.

With a word of thanks she seated herself, and when I placed a hassock at her feet she stretched out one tiny foot upon it coquettishly, although with such natural grace that there was nothing fast about her.

I stood upon the hearthrug looking at her, and when our eyes met she laughed a bright, merry laugh, all the misgivings she had previously entertained having now vanished.

"First, you must be faint, for it is so late," and touching the bell Simes instantly answered, and I ordered port wine and glasses.

She protested instantly, but on being pressed sipped half a glass and left the remainder.

We chatted on as Simes, who had been waiting on us, with a glance of wonder, left and closed the door.

Then, rising, I took down the Directory from the bookcase and opened it at the "Streets." She rose from her chair, and gazed eagerly upon the great puzzling volume until I came to Ellerdale Street.

"Ellerdale Street, Lewisham," I read aloud. "From Porson Street to Ermine Road. Do those names bring back to you any recollection of the whereabouts of your friends' house?"

"No," she reflected, with a perplexed expression. "I've never heard of them."

"The street is apparently near Loampit Vale," I said. "That would be the principal thoroughfare. You no doubt came from Lewisham Road Station by the Chatham and Dover Railway to Victoria—or perhaps to Ludgate Hill?"

She shook her head. Apparently she had not the slightest idea of the geography of London. Upon this point her mind was an utter blank.

"How long have you been in London?" I inquired.

"Nearly a week; but I've not been out before. My aunt has been ill," she explained.

"Then you live in the country, I suppose?"

"Yes, I have lived in Warwickshire, but my home lately has been in France."

"In France!" I exclaimed, surprised. "Where?"

"At Montgeron, not far from Paris."

"And you have come to London on a visit?"

"No. I have come to live here," she replied; adding, "It is absurd that the first evening I go out I am so utterly lost. I know my way about Paris quite well."

"But Paris is not London," I said. "The suburbs of our metropolis are veritable Saharas, with their miles and miles of streets where the houses are exactly similar, as if the jerry-builders had not two ideas of architecture."

It certainly was extraordinary that none of the thoroughfares which I had named gave her any clue to this remote street in which was situated her temporary home. She read down the names of the occupiers of the houses, but could not find her aunt's name. True, there were some omissions, as there always are, and I began to fear that the Directory would not help us.

On turning over the page, however, I saw in italics: *"Ellerdale Road. See Hampstead."*

"Ah!" I cried, "there is another; but it's Ellerdale Road," and after a few moments' eager search I discovered it. "This road runs from Fitzjohn's Avenue to Arkwright Road in Frognal. Have you ever heard of them before?"

It was really remarkable that a young girl should thus be so utterly lost in London. I, a man-about-town, knew the West End as I knew the way around my own chambers; and I thought I knew London; but now, on reflection, saw how utterly ignorant I was of the great world which lies beyond those few thoroughfares wherein are situated the theatres, the clubs, and the houses of the wealthy. For the bachelor who lives the life of London the world revolves around Piccadilly Circus.

My pretty companion stood puzzled. It was apparent that she had never heard of any of the thoroughfares I had mentioned, yet it was equally extraordinary that any persons living in London should be entirely ignorant of the district in which they resided.

"The thoroughfare in Hampstead is Ellerdale Road, while that in Lewisham is Ellerdale Street. It must be either one or the other, for they are the only two in London?" I said.

"How far are they apart?" she inquired, looking up from the book, dismayed.

"I don't know the distance," I was compelled to admit. "But the one is on one side of London, and the other is in the opposite direction—perhaps nearly eight miles away."

"I believe it's Ellerdale Street. I've always called it that, and neither of my aunts has corrected me." Then suddenly, as she glanced round the room, she started as if in terror, and pointing to the little side-table, cried—

"Oh, look!"

I turned quickly, but saw nothing.

"Why, what is it?" I inquired in quick concern. But in an instant her face, a moment before suddenly blanched by some mysterious fear, relaxed into a smile, as she answered—

"Nothing! It was really nothing. I thought—I thought I saw something in that corner."

"Saw something!" I exclaimed, advancing to the table. "What do you mean?"

"Nothing," and she laughed a strange, forced laugh. "It was really nothing, I assure you."

"But surely your imagination did not cause you to start like that," I said dubiously. She was, I felt convinced, trying to conceal something from me. Could she, I wondered, be subject to hallucinations?

Then, as if to change the subject, she crossed to my side, and pointing to an antique ivory cross upon an ebony stand, much battered and yellow with age, which I had picked up in a shop on the Ponte Vecchio, in Florence, long ago, she exclaimed—

"What a quaint old crucifix!"

And she took it up and examined it closely, as a connoisseur might look at it.

"The figure, I see, is in silver," she observed. "And it is very old. Italian, I should say."

"Yes," I replied, rather surprised at her knowledge. "How did you know that?"

But she smiled, and declared that she only guessed it to be so, as I had half an hour ago spoken of a recent winter spent in Italy. Then, after admiring it, she placed it down, and again turned, sighed heavily, and bent over the Directory, which was still open upon the table.

As she did so, she suddenly burst forth—

"At last! I've found it. Look! there can be no mistake. It isn't Ellerdale Street, but Ellerdale Road!"

And bending beside her I read where she pointed with her slim finger the words, "16, Popejoy, Mrs"

"Is that your aunt's name?" I asked.

"Yes," she replied.

"And yours?" I asked.

But she pursed up her lips and did not seem inclined to impart this knowledge to me.

"My name is really of no account," she said. "We shall not meet again."

"Not meet again?" I cried, for the thought of losing a friend so beautiful and so charming was an exceedingly unhappy one. "Why shall we not meet? You are going to live in London now, you say," and taking a card from my cigarette-case I handed it to her.

With her clear, brilliant eyes fixed upon mine, she took the card almost mechanically, then glanced at it.

"I'm greatly indebted to you, Mr Cleeve," she said. "But I don't see there is any necessity for you to know my name. It is sufficient, surely, for you to reflect that you one night befriended one who was in distress."

"But I must know your name," I protested. "Come, do tell me."

She hesitated, then lifted her eyes again to mine and answered—

"My name is Aline."

"Aline," I repeated. "A name as charming as its owner."

"You want to pay me compliments," she laughed, blushing deeply.

"And your surname?" I went on.

"Cloud," she replied. "Aline Cloud."

"Then your aunt's name is Popejoy, and you are living at 16, Ellerdale Road, Hampstead," I said, laughing. "Well, we have discovered it all at last."

"Yes, thanks to you," she replied, with a sigh of relief. Then looking anxiously at the clock, she added, "It's late, therefore I must be going. I can get there in a cab, I suppose?"

"Certainly," I answered; "and if you'll wait a moment while I get a thick coat I'll see you safely there—if I may be allowed."

"No," she said, putting up her little hand as if to arrest me, "I couldn't think of taking you out all that way at this hour."

I laughed, for I was used to late hours at the club, and had on many a morning crossed Leicester Square on my way home when the sun was shining.

So disregarding her, I went into my room, exchanged my light overcoat for a heavier one, placed a silk muffler around my neck, and having fortified myself with a whiskey and soda, we both went out, and entering a cab started forth on our long drive up to Hampstead.

The cabman was ignorant of Ellerdale Road, but when I directed him to Fitzjohn's Avenue he at once asserted that he would quickly find it.

"I hope we may meet again. We must!" I exclaimed, when at last we grew near our journey's end. "This is certainly a very strange meeting, but if at any time I can render you another service, command me."

"You are extremely good," she answered, turning to me after looking out fixedly upon the dark, deserted street, for rain was falling, and it was muddy and cheerless. "We had, however, better not meet again."

"Why?" I inquired. Her beauty had cast a spell about me, and I was capable of any foolishness.

"Because it is unnecessary," she replied, with a strange vagueness, yet without hesitation.

We were passing at that moment the end of a winding thoroughfare, and at a word the cabman turned his horse and proceeded slowly in search of Number 16.

Without much difficulty we found it, a good-sized detached house, built in modern style, with gable ends and long windows; a house of a character far better than I had expected. I had believed the street to be a mean one, of those poor-looking houses which bear the stamp of weekly rents, but was surprised to find a quiet, eminently respectable suburban road at the very edge of London. At the back of the houses were open fields, and one or two of the residences had carriage-drives before them.

There was still a light over the door, which showed that the lost one was expected, and as she descended she allowed her little, well-gloved hand to linger for a moment in mine.

"Good night," she said, merrily, "and thank you ever so much. I shall never forget your kindness—never."

"Then you will repay me by meeting me again?" I urged.

"No," she answered, in an instant serious. "It is best not."

"Why? I trust I have not offended you?"

"Of course not. It is because you have been my friend tonight that I wish to keep apart from you."

"Is that the way you treat your friends?" I inquired.

"Yes," she replied, meaningly. Then, after a pause, added, "I have no desire to bring evil upon you."

"Evil!" I exclaimed, gazing in wonderment at her beauty. "What evil can you possibly bring upon me?"

"You will, perhaps, discover some day," she answered, with a hollow, artificial laugh. "But I'm so very late. Good night, and thank you again so much."

Then turning quickly, with a graceful bow she entered the gate leading to the house, and rang the bell.

I saw her admitted by a smart maid, and having lit a fresh cigarette settled myself in a corner, and told the cabman to drive back to Charing Cross Mansions.

The man opened the trap-door in the roof of the conveyance, and began to chat, as night-cabmen will do to while away the time, yet the outlook was very dismal—that broad, long, never-ending road glistening with wet, and lit by two straight rows of street-lamps as far as the eye could reach right down to Oxford Street.

I was thinking regretfully of Aline; of her grace, her beauty, and of the strange circumstances in which we had become acquainted. Her curious declaration that she might cause me some mysterious evil sorely puzzled me, and I felt impelled to seek some further explanation.

I entered my chambers with my latch-key, and the ever-watchful Simes came forward, took my hat and coat, drew forward my particular armchair, and placed the whiskey and syphon at my elbow.

I had mixed a final drink, and was raising my glass, when suddenly my eyes fell upon the little triangular side-table where the curios were displayed.

What I saw caused me to start and open my eyes in amazement. Then I walked across to inspect it more closely.

The ivory crucifix, the most treasured in my collection, had been entirely consumed by fire. Nothing remained of it but its ashes, a small white heap, the silver effigy fused to a mass.

"Simes!" I cried. "What's the meaning of this?"

"I don't know, sir," he answered, pale in alarm. "I noticed it almost the instant you had left the house. The ashes were quite warm then."

"Are you sure you haven't had an accident with it?" I queried, looking him straight in the face.

"No, sir; I swear I haven't," he replied. "Your cab had hardly driven away when I found it just as it is now. I haven't touched it."

I looked, and noted its position. It was in the exact spot where Aline had placed it after taking it in her hand.

I recollected, too, that it was there where she had seen the object which had so disturbed her.

That some deep and extraordinary mystery was connected with this sudden spontaneous destruction of the crucifix was plain. It was certainly an uncanny circumstance.

I stood before that little table, my eyes fixed upon the ashes, amazed, open-mouthed, petrified.

A vague, indefinite shadow of evil had fallen upon me.

Chapter Three.
Woman's World.

THE MORE I REFLECTED, the greater mystery appeared to surround my pretty acquaintance of that well-remembered evening.

Three days went by, and, truth to tell, I remained in an uncertain, undecided mood. For a year past I had been the closest friend and confidant of Muriel Moore, but not her lover. The words of love I had spoken had been merely in jest, although I could not disguise from myself that she regarded me as something more than a mere acquaintance. Yet the strange, half-tragic beauty of Aline Cloud was undeniable. Sometimes I felt half-inclined to write to her and endeavour to again see her, but each time I thought of her, visions of Muriel rose before me, and I recollected that I admired her with an admiration that was really akin to love.

On the third evening I looked in at the St. Stephen's Club, finding Roddy stretched in one of the morocco-covered chairs in the smoking-room, with a long whisky and soda on the table by his side.

"Hullo!" he cried gaily, as I advanced, "where did you get to the other night?"

"No, old fellow," I answered, sinking into a chair near him; "ask yourself that question. You slipped away so very quickly that I thought you'd met some creditor or other."

"Well," he answered, after a pause, "I did see somebody I didn't want to meet."

"A man?" I asked, for my old chum had but few secrets from me.

"No; a woman."

I nodded.

At that instant a thought occurred to me, and I wondered whether Roddy had encountered Aline, and whether she was the woman he did not wish to meet. "Was she young?" I asked, laughing.

"Not very," he replied vaguely, adding, "There are some persons who, being associated with the melancholy incidents in one's life, bring back bitter memories that one would fain forget."

"Yes, yes; I understand," I said.

Then presently, when I had got my cigar under way, I related to him what had afterwards occurred, omitting, however, to tell him of the remarkable fusion of my crucifix. The latter fact was so extraordinary that it appeared incredible.

He listened in silence until I had finished, and then I asked him—

"Now, you've had a good long experience of all kinds of adventure. What do you think of it?"

"Well, when you commenced to tell me of her loneliness I felt inclined to think that she was deceiving you. The alone-in-London dodge has too often been worked. But you say that she was evidently a lady—modest, timid, and apparently unused to London life. What name did she give you?"

"Cloud—Aline Cloud."

"Aline Cloud!"—he gasped, starting forward with a look of inexpressible fear.

"Yes. Do you know her?"

"No!" he answered promptly, instantly recovering himself.

But his manner was unconvincing. The hand holding his cigar trembled slightly, and it was apparent that the news I had imparted had created an impression upon him the reverse of favourable.

I did not continue the subject, yet as we chatted on, discussing other things, I pondered deeply.

"Things in the House are droning away as usual," Roddy said, in answer to a question. "I get sick of this never-ending talk. The debates seem to grow longer and longer. I'm heartily weary of it all." And he sighed heavily.

"Yet the papers report your speeches, and write leaders about them," I remarked. "That speech of yours regarding Korea the other night was splendid."

"Because I know the country," he replied. "I'm the only man in the House who has set foot in the place, I suppose. Therefore, I spoke from personal observation."

"But with the reputation you've gained you ought to be well satisfied," I urged. "You are among the youngest men in the House, yet you are hailed as a coming man."

"That's all very well," he answered. "Nevertheless I wish I'd never gone in for it," and he yawned and stretched himself.

Then, after a pause, he said reflectively—

"That was really a remarkable adventure of yours—very remarkable! Where did you say the girl lived?"

"In Ellerdale Road, Hampstead. She lives with an aunt named Popejoy."

"Ah!" he exclaimed, then lapsed into a sullen silence, his brow clouded by a heavy, thoughtful look, as though he were reflecting upon some strange circumstance of the past.

I remained about an hour, when suddenly the division-bell rang and we parted: he entering the House to record his vote, I to stroll along to my own club to write letters.

Whether Roddy was acquainted with my pretty companion I was unable to determine. It seemed very much as if he were, for I could not fail to notice his paleness and agitation when I had pronounced her name. Still I resolved to act with discretion, for I felt myself on the verge of some interesting discovery, the nature of which, however, I knew not.

Next evening, in response to a telegram, Muriel Moore met me, and we dined together on the balcony of Frascati's Restaurant, in Oxford Street.

First let me confess that our attachment was something of a secret, for there was considerable difference in our social positions; I had known her for years, indeed ever since her hoydenish days when she had worn short frocks. Her father, a respectable tradesman in Stamford, a few miles from Tixover, had failed, and within a year had died, with the result that at nineteen she had drifted into that channel wherein so many girls drift who are compelled to seek their own living, and had become an assistant at a well-known milliner's in Oxford Street. In the shop world milliners' assistants and show-room hands rank higher than the ordinary girl who serves her wealthier sisters with tapes, ribbons, or underclothing, therefore Muriel had been decidedly fortunate in obtaining, this berth. It was, no doubt, on account of her beauty that the shrewd manageress of the establishment had engaged her, for her chief duty seemed to be to try on hats and bonnets for customers to witness the effect, and as nearly everything suited her she was enabled to effect many advantageous sales. Dozens of women, ugly and a trifle *passé*, were cajoled into believing that a certain hat suited them when they saw it upon her handsome, well-poised head.

She was dark, with refined, well-cut, intelligent features; not the doll-like, dimpled face of the average shop-girl, but a countenance open and handsome, even though her hair was arranged a trifle coquettishly, a fact which she explained was due to the wishes of the manageress. Her mouth was small, and had the true arch of Cupid, her teeth even and well-matched, her chin pointed and showing considerable determination, and her eyes black as those of any woman of the South. Many men who went with their wives and sisters to choose hats glanced at her in admiration, for she was tall, with a figure well-rounded, a small waist and an easy, graceful carriage, enhanced perhaps by the well-fitting costume of black satin supplied her by the management.

My family had bought their smaller drapery goods of her father for years, and it was in my college days that I had first seen and admired her in the little old-fashioned shop in St. Martin's, in Stamford. Old Mr Moore, a steady-going man of antiquated ideas, had been overtaken and left behind in the race of life, for cheap "cash drapers" had of recent years sprung up all around him, his trade had dwindled down, until it left him unable to meet the invoices from Cook's, Pawson's, and other firms of whom he purchased goods, and he was compelled to file his petition.

I knew nothing of this, for I was abroad at the time. It must, however, have been a terrible blow to poor Muriel when she and her father were compelled to leave the old shop and take furnished rooms in a back street at the further end of the town, and a still more serious misfortune fell upon her when a few months later her father died, leaving her practically alone in the world. Through the influence of one of the commercial travellers from London, who had been in the habit of calling upon her father, she had obtained the berth at Madame Gabrielle's, and for the past year had proved herself invaluable at that establishment, one of the most noted in London as selling copies of "the latest models."

We did not very often meet, for she well understood that a union was entirely out of the question. We were excellent friends, purely Platonic, and it gave her pleasure and variety to dine sometimes with me at a restaurant. There was nothing loud about her; no taint of the London shop-girl, whose tastes invariably lie in the direction of the lower music-halls, Cinderella dances, and Sunday up-river excursions. She was a thoroughly honest, upright, and modest girl, who, compelled to earn her own living, had set out bravely to do so.

From where we sat dining we could listen to the music and look down upon the restaurant below. The tables were filled with diners and the light laughter and merry chatter general.

We had not met for nearly a month, as I had been down to Tixover, where we had had a house-party with its usual round of gaiety, shooting and cycling. Indeed, since June I had been very little in London, having spent the whole summer at Zermatt.

"It seems so long since we were last here," she exclaimed suddenly, casting her eyes around the well-lit restaurant. "I suppose you had quite a merry time at home?"

"Yes," I answered, and then began to tell her of all our doings, and relating little bits of gossip from her home—that quiet, old-fashioned market town with its many churches, its broad, brimming Welland winding through the meadows, and picturesque, old-world streets where the grass springs from between the pebbles, and where each Friday the farmers congregate at market. I told her of the new shops which had sprung up in the High Street, of the death of poor old Goltmann who kept the fancy shop where in my youth I had purchased mechanical toys, and of the latest alterations at Burleigh consequent upon the old Marquis's death. All this interested her, for like many a girl compelled to seek her living in London, the little town where she was born was always dearly cherished in her memory.

"And you?" I said at last. "How have you been going along?"

She placed both her elbows on the table and looked straight into my eyes.

"Fairly well," she answered, with a half-suppressed sigh. "When you are away I miss our meetings so much, and am often dull and miserable."

"Without me, eh?" I laughed.

"Life in London is terribly monotonous," she said as I pushed the dessert-plate aside, and lit a cigarette. "I often wish I were back in Stamford again. Here one can never make any friends."

"That's quite true," I replied, for only those who have come from the country to earn their bread know the utter loneliness of the great metropolis with its busy, hurrying millions. In London one may be a householder for ten years without knowing the name of one's next-door neighbour, and may live and work all one's life without making scarce a single friend. Thus the average shop-girl is usually friendless outside her own establishment unless she cares to mix with that crowd of clerks and others who are fond of "taking out" good-looking shop-assistants.

I often felt sorry for Muriel, knowing how dull and monotonous was her life, but while I sat chatting to her that evening a vision of another face rose before me—the pale face with the strange blue eyes, the beautiful countenance of the mysterious Aline.

It seemed very much as if Roddy knew my mysterious friend. If so, it also seemed more than likely that I had been deceived in her; because was not Roddy a well-known man about town, and what more likely than that he had met her in London? To me, however, she had declared that she had only arrived in London a week before, and had never been out. Whatever was the explanation, Roddy's concern at hearing her name was certainly extraordinary.

I therefore resolved to seek her again, and obtain some explanation.

Why, I wondered, had she made that vague prophecy of evil which would befall me if we continued our acquaintanceship? It was all very extraordinary. The more I thought of it, the more puzzling became the facts.

Chapter Four.
Not Counting the Cost.

THE AFTERNOON WAS DAMP, chilly, and cheerless as I stood at my window awaiting Aline. I had written to her, and after some days received a reply addressed from somewhere in South London declining to accept my invitation, but in response to a second and more pressing letter I had received a telegram, and now stood impatient for her coming.

Outside, it was growing gloomy. The *matinée* at the Garrick Theatre was over, and the afternoon playgoers had all gone their various ways, while the long string of light carts belonging to the *Pall Mall Gazette* stood opposite, ready to distribute the special edition of that journal in every part of London. The wind blew gustily, and the people passing were compelled to clutch their hats. Inside, however, a bright fire burned, and I had set my easiest chair ready for the reception of the dainty girl who held me beneath her spell.

Even at that moment I recollected Muriel, but cast her out of my thoughts when I reflected upon Aline's bewitching beauty.

Moments passed as hours. In the darkening day I stood watching for her, but saw no sign, until I began to fear she would disappoint me. Indeed, the clock on the mantel-shelf, the little timepiece which I had carried on all my travels, had already struck five, whereas the hour she had appointed was half-past four.

Suddenly, however, the door opening caused me to turn, and my pretty companion of that night was ushered in by Simes.

"I'm late," she said apologetically. "I trust you will forgive me."

"It is a lady's privilege to be late," I responded, taking her hand, and welcoming her gladly.

She took the chair at my invitation, and I saw that she was dressed extremely plainly, wearing no ornaments. The dress was not the same she had worn when we had met, but another of more funereal aspect. Yet she was dainty and chic from her large black hat, which well suited her pale, innocent type of beauty, down to her tiny, patent-leather shoe. As she placed her foot out upon the footstool I did not fail to notice how neat was the ankle encased in its black silk stocking, or how small was the little pointed shoe.

"Why did you ask me to come here?" she asked, with a slightly nervous laugh when, at my suggestion, she had drawn off her gloves.

"Because I did not intend that we should drift apart altogether," I answered. "If you had refused, I should have come to you."

"At Ellerdale Road?" she exclaimed in alarm.

"Yes; why not? Is your aunt such a terrible person?"

"No," she exclaimed in all seriousness. "Promise me you will not seek me—never."

"I can scarcely promise that," I laughed. "But why were you so reluctant to come here again?" I inquired.

"Because I had no desire to cause you any unnecessary worry," she replied.

"Unnecessary worry? What do you mean?" I asked, puzzled.

But she only laughed, without giving me any satisfactory answer.

"I'm extremely pleased to see you," I said, and in response to my summons Simes entered with the tea, which she poured out, gracefully handing me my cup.

"I'm of course very pleased to come and see you like this," she said when my man had gone; "but if my aunt knew, she wouldn't like it."

"I suppose she was concerned about you the other night, wasn't she?"

"Oh yes," she replied with a smile. "We've often laughed over my absurd ignorance of London."

"Do you intend to live always with your aunt?"

"Ah, I do not know. Unfortunately there are some in whose footsteps evil always follows; some upon whom the shadow of sin for ever falls," and she sighed as she added, "I am one of those."

I glanced across at her in surprise. She was holding her cup in her hand, and her face was pale and agitated, as though the confession had involuntarily escaped her.

"I don't understand?" I said, puzzled. "Are you a fatalist?"

"I'm not quite certain," she answered, in an undecided tone. "As I have already told you, I hesitated to visit you because of the evil which I bring upon those who are my friends."

"But explain to me," I exclaimed, interested. "Of what nature is this evil? It is surely not inevitable?"

"Yes," she responded, in a calm, low voice, "it is inevitable. You have been very kind to me, therefore I have no desire to cause you any unhappiness."

"I really can't help thinking that you view things rather gloomily," I said, in as irresponsible a tone as I could.

"I only tell you that which is the truth. Some persons have a faculty for working evil, even when they intend to do good. They are the accursed among their fellows."

Her observation was an extraordinary one, inasmuch as more than one great scientist has put forward a similar theory, although the cause of the evil influence which such persons are able to exercise has never been discovered.

About her face was nothing evil, nothing crafty, nothing to lead one to suspect that she was not what she seemed—pure, innocent, and womanly. Indeed, as she sat before me, I felt inclined to laugh at her assertion as some absurd fantasy of the imagination. Surely no evil could lurk behind such a face as hers?

"You are not one of the accursed," I protested, smiling.

"But I am!" she answered, looking me straight in the face. Then, starting forward, she exclaimed, "Oh! why did you press me to come here, to you?"

"Because I count you among my friends," I responded. "To see me and drink a cup of tea can surely do no harm, either to you or to me."

"But it will!" she cried in agitation. "Have I not told you that evil follows in my footsteps—that those who are my friends always suffer the penalty of my friendship?"

"You speak like a prophetess," I laughed.

"Ah! you don't believe me!" she exclaimed. "I see you don't. You will never believe until the hideous truth is forced upon you."

"No," I said, "I don't believe. Let us talk of something else, Aline—if I may be permitted to call you by your Christian name?"

"You have called me by that name already without permission," she laughed gaily, her manner instantly changing. "It would be ungenerous of me to object, would it not?"

"You are extremely philosophical," I observed, handing her my cup to be refilled.

"I'm afraid you must have formed a very curious opinion of me," she replied.

"You seem to have no inclination to tell me anything of yourself," I said. "I fancy I have told you all about myself worth knowing, but you will tell me nothing in exchange."

"Why should you desire to know? I cannot interest you more than a mere passing acquaintance, to be entertained today and forgotten tomorrow."

"No, not forgotten," I said reproachfully. "You may forget me, but I shall never forget our meeting the other night."

"It will be best if you do forget me," she declared.

"But I cannot!" I declared passionately, bending and looking straight into her beautiful countenance.

"I shall never forget."

"Because my face interests you, you are fascinated! Come, admit the truth," she said, with a plain straightforwardness that somewhat took me aback.

"Yes," I said. "That's the truth. I freely admit it."

She laughed a light, merry, tantalising laugh, as if ridiculing such an idea. Her face at that instant seemed more attractive than ever it appeared before; her smiling lips, half-parted, seemed pouted, inviting me to kiss them.

"Why should a man be attracted by a woman's face?" she argued, growing suddenly serious again. "He should judge her by her manner, her thoughts, her womanly feeling, and her absence of that masculine affectation which in these days so deforms the feminine character."

"But beauty is one of woman's most charming attributes," I ventured to remark.

"Are not things that are most beautiful the most deadly?"

"Certainly, some are," I admitted.

"Then for aught you know the influence I can exert upon you may be of the most evil kind," she suggested.

"No, no!" I hastened to protest. "I'll never believe that—never! I wish for no greater pleasure than that you should remain my friend."

She was silent for some time, gazing slowly around the room. Her breast heaved and fell, as if overcome by some flood of emotion which she strove to suppress. Then, turning again to me, she said—

"I have forewarned you."

"Of what?"

"That if we remain friends it can result in nothing but evil."

I was puzzled. She spoke so strangely, and I, sitting there fascinated by her marvellous beauty, gazed full at her in silence.

"You speak in enigmas," I exclaimed.

"You have only to choose for yourself."

"Your words are those of one who fears some terrible catastrophe," I said. "I don't really understand."

"Ah! you cannot. It's impossible!" she answered in a low, hollow voice, all life having left her face. She was sitting in the armchair, leaning forward slightly, with her face still beautiful, but white and haggard. "If I could explain, then you might find some means to escape, but I dare not tell you. Chance has thrown us together—an evil chance—and you admire me; you think perhaps that you could love me, you—"

"I do love you, Aline!" I burst forth with an impetuosity which was beyond my control, and springing to my feet I caught her hand and pressed it to my lips.

"Ah!" she sighed, allowing the hand to remain limp and inert in mine. "Yes, I dreaded this. I was convinced from your manner that my fascination had fallen upon you. No!" she cried, rising slowly and determinedly to her feet. "No! I tell you that you must not love me. Rather hate me—curse me for the evil I have already wrought—detest my name as that of one whose sin is unpardonable, whose contact is deadly, and at whose touch all that is good and honest and just withers and passes away. You do not know me, you cannot know me, or you would not kiss my hand," she cried, with a strange glint in her eyes as she held forth her small, white palm. "You love me!" she added, panting, with a hoarse, harsh laugh. "Say rather that you hold me in eternal loathing."

"All this puzzles me," I cried, standing stone still. "You revile yourself, but if you have sinned surely there is atonement? Your past cannot have been so ugly as you would make me believe."

"My past concerns none but myself," she said quickly, as if indignant that I should have mentioned an unwelcome subject. "It is the future that I antici-pate with dread, a future in which you appear determined to sacrifice yourself as victim."

"I cannot be a victim if you love me in return, Aline," I said calmly.

"I—love you?" She laughed in a strange, half-amused way. "What would you have? Would you have me caress you and yet wreck your future; kiss you, and yet at the same moment exert upon you that baneful power which must inevitably sap your life and render you as capable as myself of doing evil to your fellow-men? Ah! you do not know what you say, or you would never suggest that I, of all women, should love you."

I gazed at her open-mouthed in amazement. Such a speech from the lips of one so young, so beautiful, so altogether ingenuous, was absolutely without parallel.

"I cannot help myself. I love you all the same, Aline," I faltered.

"Yes, I know," she replied quickly, with that same strange light in her eyes which I had only noticed once before. At that instant they seemed to flash with a vengeful fire, but in a second the strange glance she gave me had been succeeded by that calm, wistful look which when we had first met had so impressed me.

The idea that she was not quite responsible for her strange speeches I scouted. She was as sane as myself, thoughtful, quick of perception, yet pos-sessing a mysteriousness of manner which was intensely puzzling. This extraordinary declaration of hers seemed as though she anticipated that some terrible catastrophe would befall me, and that now the influence of her beauty was upon me, and I loved her, the spell would drag me to the depths of despair.

"A woman knows in an instant by her natural intuition when she is loved," she continued, speaking slowly and with emphasis. "Well, if you choose to throw all your happiness to the winds, then you are, of course, at liberty to do so. Yet, if you think that I can ever reciprocate your love you have formed an entirely wrong estimate of my character. One whose mission it is to work evil cannot love. I can hate—and hate well—but affection knows no place in my heart."

"That's a terrible self-denunciation," I said. "Have you never loved, then?"

"Love comes always once to a woman, as it does to a man," she replied. "Yes, I loved once."

"And it was an unfortunate attachment?"

She nodded.

"As unfortunate as yours is," she said, hoarsely.

"But cannot I take your lover's place?" I bent and whispered passionately. "Will you not let me love you? I will do so with all my heart, with all my soul."

She raised her fine eyes to mine, and after a moment's pause, added—

"I am entirely in your hands. You say you love me now—you love me because you consider my beauty greater than that of other women; because I have fascinated you." And sighing she slowly sank into her chair again. Then she added, "You wish me to be yours, but that I can never be. I can be your friend, but recollect I can never love you—never!" Then, putting forth her white hand she took mine, and looking into my face with a sweet, imploring expression, she went on—

"Think well of what I have said. Reflect upon my words. Surely it is best to end our friendship when you know how impossible it is for me to love you in return."

"Then you will not allow me to take the place in your heart that your lost lover once occupied?" I said, with deep disappointment.

"It is impossible!" she answered, shaking her head gravely. "The love which comes to each of us once in a lifetime is like no other. If doomed to misfortune, it can never be replaced. None can fill the breach in a wounded heart."

"That is only too true," I was compelled to admit. "Yet I cannot relinquish you, Aline, because I love you."

"You are infatuated—like other men have been," she said, with a faint, pitying smile. "Holding you in esteem as I do, I regret it."

"Why?"

"This is but the second time we have met, and you know nothing of my character," she pointed out. "Your love is, therefore, mere admiration."

I shook my head. Her argument was unconvincing.

"Well," she went on, "I only desire that you should release me from this bond of friendship formed by your kindness to me the other night. It would be better for you, better for me, if we parted this evening never to again meet."

"That's impossible. I must see you from time to time, even though you may endeavour to put me from you. I do not fear this mysterious evil which you prophesy, because loving you as firmly as I do, no harm can befall me."

"Ah, no!" she cried. "Do not say that. Think that the evil in the world is far stronger than the good; that sin is in the ascendency, and that the honest and upright are in the minority. Remember that no man is infallible, and that ill-fortune always strikes those who are least prepared to withstand the shock."

I remained silent. She spoke so earnestly, and with such heartfelt concern for my welfare, that I was half-convinced of her sincerity of purpose. The calmness of her words and her dignity of bearing was utterly mystifying. Outwardly she was a mere girl, timid, unused to the world and its ways, honest-eyed and open-faced; yet her words were those of a woman who had had a long and bitter experience of loves and hatreds, and to whom a lover was no new experience. Beneath these strange declarations there was, I felt certain, some hidden meaning, but its nature I utterly failed to grasp.

I was young, impetuous, madly in love with this mysterious, beautiful woman who had come so suddenly into my otherwise happy, irresponsible life, and I had made my declaration of affection without counting the cost.

"I care not what evil may fall upon me," I said boldly, holding her hand in tightening grip. "I have heard you, and have decided that I will love you, Aline."

Again I raised her hand, and in silence she allowed me to kiss her fingers, without seeking to withdraw them.

She only sighed. I thought there was a passing look of pity in her eyes for a single moment, but could not decide whether it had really been there or whether it was merely imaginary.

"Then, if that is your decision, so let it be!" she murmured hoarsely.

And we were silent for a long time.

I looked into her beautiful eyes in admiration, for was I not now her lover? Was not Aline Cloud my beloved?

The dying day darkened into night, and Simes entering to draw down the blinds compelled us to converse on topics far from our inmost thoughts.

She allowed me to smoke, but when I invited her to dine, she firmly declined.

"No," she answered. "For today this is sufficient. I regret that I called to visit you—I shall regret it all my life through."

"Why?" I demanded, dismayed. "Ah, don't say that, Aline! Remember that you've permitted me to love you."

"I have only permitted what I cannot obviate," she answered, in a hard, strained voice. I saw that tears were in her eyes, and that she was now filled with regret.

Yet I loved her, and felt that my true, honest affection must sooner or later be reciprocated.

Without further word she rose, drew on her gloves, placed her warm cape around her shoulders and pulled down her veil. Then she stretched forth her hand.

"You will not remain and dine? Do!" I urged.

"Not tonight," she answered, in a voice quite different from her usual tone. "I will accept your invitation on another occasion."

"When shall I see you?" I asked. "May I hope tomorrow?"

"I will call when it is possible," she replied. "You say you love me. Then promise me one thing."

"Anything you wish I am ready to grant," I answered.

"Then do not write to me, or seek me. I will call and see you whenever my time admits."

"But may I not write?" I asked.

"No," she answered firmly. "No letters must pass between us."

I saw that she meant to enforce this condition, therefore did not argue, but reluctantly took leave of her after her refusal to allow me to accompany her back to Hampstead.

Again she allowed me to kiss her hand, then turning slowly she sighed and passed out, preceded by Simes, who opened the door for her.

I sank back into my chair when the door closed upon her, puzzled yet ecstatic. This woman, the most beautiful I had ever seen, had allowed me to love her.

I had at last an object in life. Aline Cloud was my well-beloved, and I would live only for her. In those moments, as I sat alone gazing into the fire, I became filled with a great content, for infatuation had overwhelmed me.

The clock striking seven at last aroused me to a sense of hunger, and I rose to dross before going along to the club to dine. As I did so, however, my eyes suddenly fell upon the mantel-shelf, and I stood amazed, dumbfounded, rooted to the spot.

Upon the shelf there had been a small wooden medallion, a specimen of the Russian peasants' carving, representing the head of a Madonna—I had bought it in Moscow a year before—but an utterly astounding thing had occurred.

I could scarce believe my own eyes.

It had been consumed by an unseen fire, just as the crucifix had been, and nothing but a little white ash now remained!

"Good heavens!" I gasped; and with my finger touched the ashes.

They were still warm!

I stood wondering, my gaze fixed upon the consumed Madonna, reflecting that upon the occasion of Aline's last visit my crucifix was destroyed in the same manner by some unseen agency, and now, strangely enough, this second sacred emblem in my possession had with her presence disappeared, falling into ashes beneath my very eyes.

The mysterious influence of evil she confessed to possessing was here illustrated in a manner that was unmistakable.

In an instant all the strange words she had uttered swept through my bewildered brain as I stood there terrified, aghast.

The mystery surrounding her was as inexplicable as it was startling.

Chapter Five.
Not Counting the Cost.

THE BONY-FACED MAN.

Daily the problem grew more puzzling.

The fusing of the crucifix and the carved medallion of the Madonna were clearly due to the presence of the mysterious Aline, the beautiful woman who had warned me against the strange evil she exerted over those with whom she came in contact. Such occurrences seemed supernatural; yet so curious were her words and actions, and so peculiar and impressive her beauty, that I could not help doubting whether she actually existed in flesh and blood, or only in some bright vision that had come to hold me in fascination. Yet Simes had seen her, and had spoken with her. There was therefore no doubt that she was a living person, even though she might be a sorceress.

Nevertheless, they were something more than mere conjuring feats which caused the sacred objects in my room to spontaneously consume in her presence. Had she not told me plainly that evil followed in her footsteps? Did not these two inexplicable events fully bear out her words?

I called Simes, and when I showed him the Madonna he stood glaring at it as one terrified.

"I don't like that lady, sir," he exclaimed, glancing at me.

"Why not?"

"Well, sir, pardon me for saying so, but I believe she can work the evil of the very Devil himself."

That was exactly my own opinion; therefore I preserved silence.

As lover of a woman possessed of a mysterious influence, the like of which I had never before heard, my position was certainly an unique one. In the days which followed I tried to argue with myself that I did not love her; to convince myself that what she had alleged was true, namely, that I admired but did not love her. Yet all was in vain. I was fascinated by her large blue eyes, which looked out upon me with that calm, childlike innocence, and remaining beneath their spell, believed that I loved her.

The mystery with which she had surrounded herself was remarkable. Her refusal to allow me to call upon her, or even to write, was strange, yet her excuse that her aunt would be annoyed was plausible enough.

Compelled, therefore, to await her visit, I remained from day to day anxious to meet her because I loved her.

On entering the club one afternoon I found Roddy alone in the smoking-room, writing a letter.

"Well!" he cried, merrily, gripping my hand. "How goes it—and how's your little mystery going on?"

I sank into a chair close to him and told him of Aline's visit.

"And you're clean gone on her—eh?" he queried.

I shrugged my shoulders and gave him a vague reply.

"Well, take care," he said in a serious tone. "If I were you I'd find out who and what she is. She might be some adventuress or other."

"Do you suspect her to be an adventuress?" I inquired quickly.

"My dear fellow, how can I tell? There seems to me something rather shady about her, that's all."

I pondered. Yes, he spoke the truth. There was something shady about her. She would tell me absolutely nothing of herself.

We smoked together for half an hour, then parted, for he was compelled to go down to the House, as a dutiful legislator should.

A week passed yet I saw not Aline, nor had any word from her. From day to day I existed in all anxiety to once again look upon that face so angelic in its beauty and so pure in expression. Indeed, more than once I felt inclined to break the promise I had made her and call at Ellerdale Road, but I refrained, fearing lest such a course might annoy her.

One evening, a fortnight after she had visited me, I was walking along the Bayswater Road towards Oxford Street, skirting the railings of Hyde Park, when suddenly I noticed before me two figures, a man and a woman. They were walking slowly, deep in conversation.

In an instant I recognised the slim, perfect figure in the black jacket and black hat as that of Aline, and drew back to escape observation.

Her companion was tall, thin, and rather ill-dressed. As they passed beneath a street-lamp I discerned that he was about forty, with lank black hair, a long black moustache, and a sallow, bony face—a countenance the reverse of prepossessing. His silk hat had seen better days, his frock-coat was tightly buttoned for warmth, as he had no overcoat, and his boots were sadly run down at heel. As this seedy individual walked beside her she was speaking rapidly, while he, bonding to her, was listening intently.

The meeting was such an unexpected one that at first I was at a loss what to do. Next moment, however, with the fire of jealousy aroused within me, I resolved to follow them and watch. They strolled slowly along until they came to Victoria Gate, and then turned into the Park, at that hour dark and deserted. I noticed that as they entered she took his arm, and it appeared as if they were going in the direction of Grosvenor Gate, which leads out into Park Lane; for they crossed the Ring, and continued straight ahead along the tree-lined avenue. But few lights were there, so following at a respectable distance, I managed to keep them in sight.

Soon, however, they rested upon a seat at foot of a great old beech, and continued their conversation. I had, of course, a keen desire to learn the nature of this exchange of confidences, but the problem was how to approach sufficiently near and yet escape observation. At first I was inclined to relinquish my endeavours, but suddenly it occurred to me that I might get over the railing on to the grass, and in the darkness approach noiselessly behind the tree where they were seated.

Therefore, turning back some distance to a bend in the path, where they could not detect me, I sprang over the iron fencing, and treading softly, cautiously made my way up behind them, until I actually stood behind the tree within three yards of them, but with the railing between us.

Then, scarce daring to breathe, I waited to catch their words. Of this shabby-genteel fellow, evidently her lover, I was madly jealous; but my anger was instantly changed to surprise when I heard the nature of their conversation.

"But you must!" he was saying earnestly.

"I tell you, I won't!" she answered decisively. "The risk is too great—far too great."

"But as I've already told you, it's absolutely imperative."

He spoke roughly, but with a refinement which showed him to be educated. He bore outward evidence of having come down in the world.

"I wouldn't act like that if I were offered a thousand pounds," she declared.

"But it must be done," he urged.

"Not by me."

"Do you intend to back out, then?" he inquired roughly.

"I merely tell you plainly that you and your ruffianly associates have gone quite far enough. That's all," she answered calmly. Her words were not those which a woman usually uses towards her lover.

He gave vent to a short, brutal laugh, as if enjoying her indignation.

"It's all very well to talk like this, Aline," he said; "but you know quite well that argument is useless. You must do it."

"I will not, I tell you!" she cried fiercely.

"Well, we shall see," he answered. "Recollect that you are one of us, and as such, to break away is impossible."

"I know that, only too well," she answered bitterly. "But it is terrible—horrible! As each day passes I am more and more convinced that the truth must soon be discovered."

"And if it is?"

"I will never live to bear the exposure," she said, in the hoarse, low voice of one desperate.

"My dear girl," he exclaimed, "you who have beauty and a plausible tongue have the world before you; yet you always refuse to seize your opportunity. You who possess the power of the King of Evil, whose touch is deadly and whose caress is venomous, could rule an empire if you wished; yet you are inert, lethargic, and refuse to assist us, even in this."

"I will not sin deeper than I have already sinned," she answered. "I will have no hand in it."

"Why not?"

"It is horrible!" she protested. "And I tell you, once and for all, that I will have nothing to do with the affair."

"You're a fool!" he cried roughly.

"True! I am, or I would never have fallen thus into the trap you and your friends baited so cunningly."

"You are beautiful!" he answered, with a harsh laugh. "A beautiful woman is always a safe trap for fools."

"If men admire me I cannot help it; if they love me then it is against my wish, for since that day long ago, when the Spirit of Evil entered into me, love has known no place in my heart."

"Well spoken!" he exclaimed. "If you have no love for him the rest is quite easy."

"Though all love within me is dead, I yet have a woman's heart, and womanly feeling," she said. "I know that my beauty is only a curse; I am well aware that men who have admired me have been drawn irresistibly to their doom. Ah!" and she shuddered in shame, "it is terrible—terrible!"

"Yet why should you regret?" he queried. "You are not of their world; you have nothing in common with them. You have been given beauty, the most marvellous, perhaps, in all the world; diabolic beauty, which causes you to be remarked wherever you go; which has caused the downfall of the upright, and has wrecked the lives of those who trust in the guardian Spirit of Good."

"Yes, I know," she answered quickly. "Yet I am tired of it all. I am aware that my power for the working of evil among my fellow-creatures is greater than that of any other person of flesh and blood; that at my touch objects held sacred are defiled and consumed, that sight of my face may cause a veritable saint to turn from his asceticism and become an evil-doer. All this I know, alas! All this is due to the influence of evil, which once I might have striven against, had I wished."

"You possess the *beauté du Diable*," he said. "Are you not the daughter of Satan?"

"If I am I decline to commit any further crime at your bidding," she answered, with indignation. "You have held me enthralled until now, but I tell you that you have strained the bond until it will ere long break. Then I shall be free."

"I'm pleased that you have such pleasant anticipations," he replied. "A woman who once gives herself over to the Evil One can never regain her freedom."

"But she can refuse to increase the enormity of her sin by committing crime at the bidding of the man who holds her beneath his thrall," she answered.

"You know what such refusal means?" he said in a threatening tone.

"Yes—death. Well, I do not fear it. Within me a new love has been awakened. I now love for the first time in all my life."

"Yet you have already said that in your heart love knows no place."

"I tell you I love him!" she cried. "He shall not suffer!"

She was evidently referring to me. I held my breath, eager to catch every syllable. Perhaps this man was urging her to kill me!

"The power you possess to work evil is irresistible," he said briefly.

"Alas! I know it," she answered. "Those with whom I am in daily contact little dream of who or what I really am, or they would shun me as they would shun a leper."

"Why should they?" her bony-faced companion asked. "Evil has been dominant in the world for all ages, and the Prince of Darkness has still the ascendency!"

"But is not mine the blackest—the foulest of all crimes?" she shuddered.

"Only one touch," he urged. "Your hand is fatal."

"Ah! why do you taunt me thus?" she cried. "Is it not enough that I should be degraded and outcast, overburdened by sin for which I cannot hope for forgiveness, and that my position should be irretrievably lost? Is it not enough that in me all the evils of the world are concentrated, and that I am shut out from happiness for ever?"

"You had your choice," the man answered. "It is true that you are one unique among the millions of your fellow-creatures. The blackness of your heart is concealed by the purity of your face, and your real being so disguised that none suspect. If your real identity were discovered some prophets would declare that the end of the world was near." And he laughed coarsely.

"Yes, yes," she cried quickly. "But do not taunt me. I know too well the far-reaching influence which emanates from me, and the fatal effect of my touch upon all that is held sacred by those who believe in the Supreme. I have striven to do good, and have only wrought evil; I have been charitable, and my efforts have only resulted in bringing disaster upon the needy. Those whom I thought to benefit have rewarded me by curses, because all that I do is the work of the wicked. I have struggled to lead a double life, and have failed. I have tried to counterbalance the evil I am compelled to achieve by doing good works such as might endear me in the eyes of those who believe in the Supreme; but all, alas, has been in vain—all futile. I am now convinced that in my heart there can remain no good feeling, no womanly love, no charitableness towards my fellows."

"It is only what might be expected," he said in a dry tone. "Your great beauty is given you to cover your heart. You are soulless."

"Yes," she cried. "That is true—only too true. I have no soul, no conscience, no regret!"

She spoke in a hard tone, as though utterly wearied of life. Her voice had lost its music, and her speech was of one in blank despair.

"If you are without regret, then what I have suggested is the more easy of accomplishment," he said, in a low intense voice. "Remember that no power on earth can withstand your influence."

"I will not!" she cried, starting up in fierce determination. "Through your evil counsel I have already wrought that which I shall ever regret," she went on. "I have placed myself beneath the thraldom irrevocably, and have brought upon those who admired me a doom which has destroyed their happiness and wrecked their lives. I have now a lover—a man who, because of my good looks, is infatuated, as others have been."

"It has been decided!" her companion said, with a calmness that was appalling.

"But I love him!" she declared. "I myself will be his protector!"

"You intend to defy the resolution which has been arrived at?"

"I have no intention of committing further sin," she said. "I may be an evil-doer and one of the accursed, but none shall say that I deliberately acted in such manner towards one who became fascinated by my beauty. Rather would I disfigure my face by burns or acid in order to render myself ugly and unattractive."

"No woman would do that of her own free will," he laughed.

"No ordinary woman could," she said. "But recollect who I am. Reflect upon my far-reaching influence for evil—an influence which is felt throughout this kingdom. I tell you that rather than continue I would kill myself."

The man laughed aloud.

"I admit all that," he said. "If the people of London knew the truth they would, I believe, tear you limb from limb. But they are ignorant; therefore you are but an ordinary girl of more than extraordinary beauty."

"Which means that my beauty will always ruin those upon whom I may bestow a glance. As my touch is fatal to certain objects of adoration, so is my love-look fatal to those who admire me. No," she added, after a brief pause, "I have determined to act as this man's protector, instead of his destroyer."

"You are relenting," he observed with sarcasm. "Soon you will proclaim your repentance."

"No!" she cried fiercely. "I shall never repent, because of you. To you I owe the major part of this evil of which I am possessed, and to you—"

"It was your choice," he interrupted, with a brutal laugh. "You accepted the challenge, and gave your soul to the Evil One. Why blame me?"

"At your instigation," she went on in fierce anger. "To the world I am a pure, ingenuous girl; yet beneath this veil of virtue and purity I work these veritable miracles of evil, possessing a power which ofttimes appals me, an irresistible influence that nothing can withstand. I am unique in the world as possessing this superhuman faculty of being able to impart evil to those with whom I come into contact, be they pure as angels. You taunt me," she added. "But some day you will crave mercy of me, and then I will show you none—none! I will be hard-hearted as flint—as relentless as you are tonight!"

"You wish to break away from the compact, but you shall not," the man said firmly, between his teeth. "If you prefer defiance, well and good. But I merely point out that obedience is best."

She paused. She was, I surmised, deep in reflection.

"Very well," at last she answered, in a hoarse, unnatural voice. "Now that I have sunk so low I suppose it is impossible to sink further. But recollect that this same influence that I will exert over this, my latest victim, I will one day exert over you. I warn you. One day ere long you will crave pity at my feet."

"Never from you," the man said, with a short defiant laugh.

"I have only prophesied once before," she answered meaningly. "Whether or no that came true you are well aware. In this world of London I am, as yet, unknown, but when the true facts are known this great metropolis will stand aghast in terror. Our positions will then be reversed. You will be the victim, and I triumphant."

"Proceed," he laughed. "All this is intensely interesting."

There was a pause, longer than before.

"Then you declare that I must do this thing?" she asked, in a strange, hollow voice, the voice of one dismayed.

"Yes," her companion answered; "you must—swiftly and secretly. It is imperative."

Without further word she rose slowly to her feet, and staggered away down the gravelled path, while her companion, hesitating for a few seconds, rose with a muttered imprecation and strode along after her. A moment later they were out of hearing.

The remainder of their extraordinary conversation was lost to me.

One suspicion alone possessed me. That thin, shabby man had sentenced me to death.

Chapter Six.
Two Mysteries.

THE DISCOVERY I HAD accidentally made was the reverse of reassuring.

Aline had admitted herself possessed of some mysterious power which caused sacred objects to consume, the power of evil which she feared would also fall upon me. I recollected how when she had visited me she had urged me to hate her rather than love her, and I now discerned the reason. She had feared lest her subtle influence upon me should be fatal.

Through the days which passed her strange words rang ever through my ears. She was a woman unique in all the world; a woman who, living in teeming London, was endowed with faculties of abnormal proportions, and possessed an unearthly power utterly unknown to modern science. I thought of the fusing of my crucifix and my Madonna, and shuddered. Her beauty was amazing, but she was a veritable temptress, a deistical daughter of Apollyon.

My first feeling after leaving the Park was one of repugnance; yet on reflection I found myself overcome by fascination, still bewitched by her beautiful face, and eager to meet her once again. Surely nothing maleficent could remain hidden beneath such outward innocence?

Thus I waited long and wearily for her coming, remaining in from day to day, or whenever I went out leaving word with Simes as to where I could be found if she called. In my turbulent state of mind I imagined many strange things.

The more I reflected, the more complicated became the enigma.

At length one morning Simes opened my door suddenly and ushered her in. I flung down my newspaper and rose to meet her, but next instant drew back in surprise and alarm.

She was dressed in an elegant costume of pale grey trimmed with white lace and heavy embroidery of pearls, a dress which could only have been turned out by a first-class house, for it bore a Parisian chic, being modelled in latest style. Her tiny shoes and gloves were of grey suede to match the dress, and beneath her big black hat with ostrich feathers her face looked sweet and winning as a child's.

But the flush of health had faded. Her cheeks were just as beautiful as they had ever been, but the bloom of youth had died from them, and her complexion was a yellowish brown, like that of a woman of sixty. The light in her blue eyes had faded; they were now dull and leaden.

"At last!" I cried happily. "I am so glad you've come, for I've waited so long, Aline."

She allowed her hand to rest in mine, then sank wearily into my armchair without a word.

"You are not well," I cried, in concern. "What ails you?"

"Nothing!" she gasped. "It is nothing. In a few minutes it will pass." Then she added, as if on second thought, "Perhaps it was your stairs. The lift is out of order." And she rested her head upon the back of the chair and looked up at me with pitying eyes.

All life had apparently gone out of her beautiful face. That vivacity that had attracted me had given place to a deep, thoughtful look, as though she were in momentary fear. Her face seemed blanched to the lips.

"May I get you something?" I asked. "Let me give you some brandy," and taking the bottle from the tantalus I gave her a liqueur-glass full of cognac, which she swallowed at one gulp.

"Why have you not called before?" I inquired, when, at length, she grew less agitated. "I have expected you daily for so long."

"I've been away in the country," she answered. "But do not think that I have not remembered you."

"Nearly three weeks have gone by since you were last here," I said. "It is too cruel of you not to allow me to write to you."

"No," she said decisively, "you must not write. You have already promised me, and I know you will not break any compact you make."

"But I love you, Aline," I whispered, bending forward to her.

"Yes, alas! I know that," she responded, rousing herself. "Yet, why carry this folly further?"

"Folly you call it?" I exclaimed regretfully. "Because you cannot love me in return you tell me I am foolish. Since you have been absent I have examined my own heart, and I swear that my love is more than mere admiration. I think of no one in the world besides yourself."

"No, no," she said uneasily. "There is some other woman whom you could love far better, a woman who would make you a true and faithful wife."

"But I can love no one else."

"Try," she answered, looking me straight in the face. "Before we met you loved one who reciprocated your affection."

"Who?"

"You wish me to tell you?" she replied in a hard, bitter tone. "Surely you cannot affect ignorance that you are loved by Muriel Moore?"

"Muriel!" I gasped in amazement. "How did you know?"

She smiled.

"There is but little that escapes me," she answered. "You loved each other before our romantic meeting, and I, the woman who must necessarily bring evil upon you, have come to separate you. Yet you calmly stand by and invite me to wreck your life! Ah! you cannot know who I am, or you would cast me from your thoughts for over."

"Then who are you?" I blurted forth, in blank amazement.

"I have already told you. You have, of your own free will, united yourself with me by a declaration of love, and the consequences are therefore upon your own head."

"Cannot you love like other women?" I demanded. "Have you no heart, no feeling, no soul?"

"No," she sighed. "Love is forbidden me. Hatred takes its place; a fierce, deadly hatred, in which vengeance is untempered by justice, and fatality is always inevitable. Now that I confess, will you not cast me aside? I have come here to you to urge you to do this ere it is too late."

"You speak so strangely that I'm bewildered," I declared. "I have told you of my love, and will not relinquish you."

"But for the sake of the woman who loves you. She will break her heart."

"Muriel does not love me," I answered. "I have spoken no word of affection to her. We were friends—that is all."

"Reflect! Is it possible for a girl in such a position as Muriel Moore to be your friend without loving you! You are wealthy, she is poor. You give her dinners with champagne at the gayest restaurants; you take her to stalls at theatres, or to a box at the Alhambra; you invite her to these rooms, where she drinks tea, and plays your piano; and it is all so different from her humdrum life at Madame Gabrielle's. Place yourself for one moment in her position, with a salary of ten shillings a-week and dresses provided by the establishment, leading a life of wearying monotony from nine in the morning till seven at night, trying on bonnets, and persuading ignorant, inartistic women to buy your wares. Would you not be flattered, nay, dazzled, by all these attentions which you show her? Would you not become convinced that your admirer loved you if he troubled himself so much about you?"

Her argument was plain and forcible. I had never regarded the matter in that light.

"Really, Aline," I said, "I'm beginning to think that you are possessed of some power that is supernatural."

She laughed—a laugh that sounded strangely hollow.

"I tell you this—I argue with you for your own sake, to save you from the danger which now encompasses you. I would be your protector because you trust me so implicitly, only that is impossible."

In an instant I recollected her declaration to her bony-faced companion in the Park. Had she actually resolved to kill me?

"Why should I relinquish you in favour of one for whom I have no affection?" I argued.

"Why should you kiss the hand that must smite you?" she asked.

Her lips were bloodless; her face of ashen pallor.

"You are not yourself today," I said. "It is not usual for a woman who is loved to speak as you speak. The love of a man is usually flattering to a woman."

"I have come to save you, and have spoken plainly."

"What, then, have I done that I deserve punishment?" I inquired in breathless eagerness.

"You love me."

"Surely the simple offence of being your lover is not punishable by death?"

"Alas! it is," she answered hoarsely. "Compelled as I am to preserve my secret, I cannot explain to you. Yet, if I could, the facts would prove so astounding that you would refuse to believe them. Only the graves of those who have loved me—some of them nameless—are sufficient proof of the fatality I bring upon those whom my beauty entrances."

She raised her head, and her eyes encountered a photograph standing on a table in the window. It was Roddy's.

"See there!" she said, starting, raising her hand and pointing to it. "Like yourself, that man loved me, and has paid the penalty. He died abroad."

"No," I replied quickly. "You are mistaken. That picture is the portrait of a friend; and he's certainly not dead, for he was here smoking with me last night."

"Not dead!" she cried, starting up and crossing to it. "Why, he died at Monte Carlo. He committed suicide after losing all he had."

"No," I replied, rather amused. "That is the Honourable Roderick Morgan, member of Parliament."

"Yes, that was the name," she said aloud to herself. "Roddy Morgan they called him. He lost seven thousand pounds in one day at roulette."

"He has never to my knowledge been to Monte Carlo," I observed, standing beside her.

"You've not always accompanied him everywhere he has been, I presume?" she said.

"No, but had he been to Monte Carlo he would certainly have told me."

"Men do not care to speak of losses when they are as absurdly reckless as he was."

The idea that Roddy had committed suicide at Monte Carlo seemed utterly absurd, nevertheless in order to convince her that he was still very much alive I picked up the paper and pointed to his name in the Parliamentary debate of the previous night.

"It is strange, very strange!" she said, reflecting. "I was in the Rooms when he shot himself. While sitting at one of the tables I saw them carry him away dead."

"You must have made some mistake," I suggested.

"I was playing at the same table, and he continued to love me, although I had warned him of the consequences, as I have now warned you. He lost and lost. Each time he played he lost, till every farthing he possessed had gone. Then I turned away, but ere I had left the room there was the sound of a pistol-shot, and he fell across the table dead."

She had the photograph in her hand, and bent to the light, examining it closely.

"It cannot be the same man," I said.

"Yes, it is," she responded. "There can be no mistake, for the ring which secures his cravat is mine. I gave it to him."

I looked, and there sure enough was an antique ring of curious pattern, through which his soft scarf was threaded.

"It is Etruscan," she said. "I picked it up in a shop in Bologna."

I glanced quickly at her. Her face was that of a girl of twenty; yet her speech was that of a woman of the world who had travelled and become utterly weary. The more I saw of her the more puzzled I became.

"Then if the man you knew was the original of that photograph he certainly is not dead. If you wish, I will send my man for him."

"Ah, no!" she cried, putting up her hand in quick alarm. "He has suffered enough—I have suffered enough. No, no; we must not meet—we cannot. I tell you he is dead—and his body lies unmarked in the suicides' cemetery at Monte Carlo."

I shrugged my shoulders, declaring that my statement should be sufficient to convince her.

Quickly, however, she turned to me, and with her gloved hand upon my arm, besought me to release her.

"Hate me!" she implored. "Go to your friend, if he really is alive as you declare, and ask of him my character—who and what I am."

"I shall never hate you—I cannot!" I declared, bending again towards her and seeking her hand, but she instantly withdrew it, looking into my face with an expression of annoyance.

"You disbelieve me!" she said.

"All that you say is so bewildering that I know not what to believe," I answered.

"In this room you have, I suppose, discovered certain objects reduced to ashes?" she asked in a hoarse tone.

"Yes, I have," I answered breathlessly.

"Then let them be sufficient to illustrate the influence of evil which lies within me," she answered, and after a pause suddenly added: "I came here to fulfil that which the irresistible power has decreed; but I will leave you to reflect. If you have regard for me, then hate me. Transfer your affections to Muriel Moore, the woman who really loves you; the woman who weeps because you refrain from caressing her; the woman who is wearing out her life because of you."

She held her breath, her lips trembled and her hands quivered, as though the effort of speaking had been too great.

"I love you!" I cried. "I cannot forget you, Aline. I adore you!"

"No, no!" she said, holding up both her hands. "Enough! I only pray that the evil I dread may not befall you. Farewell!" and bowing low she turned, and swept out of the room, leaving me alone, bewildered, dumbfounded.

The words she had uttered were completely confounding. She was apparently possessed of attainments which were supernatural; indeed, she seemed to me as a visitant from the Unknown, so strangely had she spoken; so mysterious had been her allegations regarding Roddy.

For nearly an hour I remained deep in thought, plunged in abject despair. Aline the beautiful had left me, urging me to transfer my affections. The situation was extraordinary. She had, it seemed, gone out of my life for ever.

Suddenly I roused myself. Her extraordinary statement that Roddy had committed suicide at Monte Carlo oppressed me. If she really knew Muriel's innermost thoughts, then it was quite feasible that she knew more of my friend than I had imagined. Besides, had he not left the theatre hurriedly on catching sight of her? There was a mystery which should be elucidated. Therefore I assumed my hat and coat and went round to Roddy's chambers in Dover Street, Piccadilly, to endeavour to obtain some explanation of her amazing statement.

He lived in one of those smoke-blackened, old-fashioned houses with deep areas, residences which were occupied by families fifty years ago, but now mostly let out as suites of chambers. The front door with its inner swing-door was, as usual, open, and I passed through and up the stairs to the second floor, where upon the door was a small brass plate bearing my friend's name.

The door was ajar, and pushing it open I walked in, exclaiming cheerily as was my habit—

"Anybody at home?"

There was no response. Roddy was out, and his man had evidently gone downstairs to obtain something. I walked straight on into the sitting-room, a good-sized, comfortable apartment, which smelt eternally of cigars, for its owner was an inveterate smoker; but as I entered I was surprised to discover Roddy in his old velvet lounge-coat, sitting alone in his chair beside the fire.

"Morning, old chap!" I cried. But he was asleep and did not move.

I crossed the room and shook him by the shoulder to awaken him, at the same moment looking into his face.

It was unusually pale.

In an instant a terrible thought flashed across my mind, and I bent eagerly towards him. He was not asleep, for his eyes were still wide-open, although his chin had sunk upon his breast.

I placed my hand quickly upon his heart, but could detect no movement. I touched his cheek. It was still warm. But his eyes told the appalling truth. They were bloodshot, stony, discoloured, and already glazing. The hideous, astounding fact could not be disguised.

Roddy Morgan was dead!

Chapter Seven.
What Ash Knew.

THE SHOCK CAUSED ME by this discovery was indescribable.

My first action on recovering was to alarm those in the house, but it was found that Ash, Roddy's man, was absent.

The three occupants of the other chambers, men I knew, entered, and endeavoured to restore their friend to consciousness. But all efforts were in vain. A doctor from Burlington Street was quickly fetched, and after a brief examination pronounced that life had been extinct about half an hour, but there being no sign of violence he could make no surmise as to the cause of death without a post-mortem.

Roddy had evidently been sitting beside the fire reading the newspaper and smoking when he expired, for at his side his cigar had dropped and burned a hole in the carpet, while the newspaper was still between his stiffening fingers.

A detective and a constable were very soon on the scene, but as the doctor expressed an opinion that it was a case of sudden death, most probably from syncope, the appearance of the body leading to that conclusion, the plain-clothes officer merely made a few notes, and awaited with me the return of the man Ash, in order to question him.

In the meantime the others left the presence of the dead, and I had an opportunity of glancing round the place. I was well acquainted with Roddy's chambers, for I often smoked with him of an evening, therefore I knew their arrangement almost as well as I knew that of my own. But this discovery was to me a staggering blow. Over the mantel-shelf was a mirror, and stuck in its frame were a truly miscellaneous collection of cards of invitation for all sorts and descriptions of festivities. One card, however, attracted my attention as being unusual, and I took it down to examine it. It was not a card of invitation, but a small, oblong piece of pasteboard ruled in parallel squares, each column being headed by the letter "N," alternate with the letter "R." In the squares were hurriedly scribbled a curious collection of numbers.

At first I could not recollect where I had seen a similar card before, but it suddenly dawned upon me that it was one of those used by professional gamblers at Monte Carlo, to record the numbers which come up at the roulette-table, the "R" standing for Rouge, and the "N" for Noir. The discovery was interesting. I carefully examined the pencilled figures, and saw they were in Roddy's own hand.

Did not this bear out Aline's allegation that he had been to Monte Carlo?

I said nothing to the detective, but replaced the card in the frame of the mirror.

The detective strolled around the other rooms in an aimless sort of way, and when he returned I asked—

"What is your opinion of this affair?"

"I really don't know, sir," he answered in a puzzled tone. "It may be suicide."

"Suicide!" I gasped, recollecting Aline's declaration. "What causes you to surmise that?"

"From the fact that the valet is absent," he answered. "The gentleman, if he desired to take his own life, would naturally send his servant out on an errand."

"But the cigar on the carpet? How do you account for that?" I inquired. "If he meant to deliberately take his life he would instinctively cast his lighted cigar into the fire."

The officer was silent. He was a keen, shrewd, clean-shaven man of about forty, whose name I afterwards learnt was Priestly.

"Your argument is a sound one," he answered after a long pause. "But when a man is suffering from temporary insanity, there is no accounting for his actions. Of course, it's by no means evident that your friend has committed suicide, because there is absolutely no trace of such a thing. Nevertheless, I merely tell you my suspicion. We shall know the truth tomorrow, when the doctor has made his post-mortem. At the station, when I go back, I'll give orders for the removal of the body to the mortuary. I presume that you will communicate the news to his friends. You said, I think, that his uncle was the Duke of Chester, and that he was a Member of Parliament. Are his parents alive?"

"No. Both are dead," I answered, glancing again around the room, bewildered because of Aline's strange statements only an hour before.

Could she, I wondered, have known of this? Yet when I remembered the doctor's assertion that poor Roddy had not been dead half an hour, it seemed plain that at the time she had alleged he had committed suicide at Monte Carlo he was still alive and well.

The room was undisturbed. Nothing appeared out of place. In the window looking down into Duke Street, that quiet thoroughfare so near the noisy bustle of Piccadilly, and yet so secluded and eminently respectable, stood the writing-table, which he set up after his election, in order to attend to his correspondence. "I must send some letters to my constituents and to the local papers now and then," he laughingly explained when I chaffed him about it. "Scarcely a day goes past but what I have to write, excusing myself from being present at some local tea-fight or distribution of school-prizes. To every sixpenny muffin-tussle I'm expected to give my patronage, so that they can stick my name in red letters on the bill announcing the event. Politics are a hollow farce."

His words all came back to me now as I glanced at that table. I recollected how merry and light-hearted he had been then, careless of everybody, without a single thought of the morrow. Yet of late a change had certainly come upon him. In my ignorance I had attributed it to the weight of his Parliamentary honours, knowing that he cared nothing about politics, and had been forced into them by his uncle. Yet there might have been an ulterior cause, I reflected. Aline herself might have been the cause of his recent melancholy and despair.

She had evidently known him better than I had imagined.

Upon the table I noticed lying a large blue envelope, somewhat soiled, as if it had been carried in his pocket for a long time. It was linen-lined, and had therefore resisted friction, and instead of wearing out had become almost black.

I took it up and drew out the contents, a cabinet photograph and a sheet of blank paper.

I turned the picture over and glanced at it. It was a portrait of Aline!

She had been taken in a *décolleté* dress, a handsome evening costume, which gave her an entirely different character from the plain dress she had worn when we had first met. It was a handsome bodice, beautifully trimmed; and her face, still childlike in its innocence, peered out upon me with a tantalising smile. Around her slim throat was a necklet consisting of half a dozen rows of seed-pearls, from which some thirty amethysts of graduated sizes were suspended, a delicate necklet probably of Indian workmanship. The photograph was beautifully taken by the first of the Paris photographers.

There was no address on the envelope; the sheet of note-paper was quite plain. Without doubt this picture had been in his possession some considerable time.

The detective, who had covered the dead man's face with a handkerchief, had passed into the bedroom and was searching the chest of drawers, merely out of curiosity, I suppose, when my eyes caught sight of a scrap of paper in the fireplace, and I picked it up. It was half-charred, but I smoothed it out, and then found it to be a portion of a torn letter. Three words only remained;

but they were words which were exceedingly curious. They were "*expose her true...*" The letter had been torn in fragments and carefully burned even to this fragment, but it had only half consumed, and probably fallen from the bars.

At first I was prompted to hand it to the detective; but on reflection resolved to retain it. I alone held a key to the mystery, and was resolved to act independently with care and caution in an endeavour to elucidate the extraordinary affair.

In a few moments the officer made his re-appearance, saying—

"It's strange, very strange, that the valet doesn't come back. If he's not here very soon, I shall commence to suspect him of having some hand in the affair." Then, after a pause, during which his eyes were fixed upon the man whose face was hidden, he added, "I wonder whether, after all, a crime has been committed?"

"That remains for you to discover," I replied. "There seems no outward sign of such a thing. The doctor has found no mark of violence."

"True," he said shrewdly. Then, with his eyes fixed upon the carpet, he suddenly exclaimed, "Ah! what's this?" and bending, picked up something which he placed in the hollow of his hand, exposing it to my view.

It was a purely feminine object. A tiny pearl button from a woman's glove.

"A lady's been here recently, that's very evident. We must find out who she was."

"A lady!" I gasped, wondering in an instant whether Aline had called upon him.

"The outer door is open all day, I think you said," he went on.

"Yes."

"In that case it is probable that if she came during this man Ash's absence, nobody would see her."

"Very probably," I said. "We can only wait until Ash returns."

"But it's already half an hour since you made the discovery, and nearly an hour since the gentleman died; yet the man has not returned," the detective observed dubiously.

At that moment we heard a footstep on the stair, but instead of the dead man's valet, an inspector in uniform entered. The detective briefly explained the circumstances in a dry, business-like tone, the inspector walked through the rooms with his hands behind his back, and after a survey of the place, and a promise to send some men to remove the body to the mortuary, left again.

So startling had been the discovery, and so curious the whole of the events of that morning, that I had scarcely felt any grief at the loss of my friend. It did not seem really true that Roddy Morgan, my very best chum, was actually dead; cut off in a moment in the prime of his manhood by some mysterious, but fatal, cause, which even the doctor had not yet decided.

As the minutes passed, slowly ticked out by the clock upon the mantel-shelf, I could not help sharing with the detective some doubts regarding Ash. Had he absconded?

If murder had actually been committed, then robbery was not the object of the crime, for on the writing-table were lying a couple of five-pound notes open, without any attempt at concealment. Roddy was always a careless fellow over money matters.

At last, at nearly half-past two, we heard the click of a key in the latch, and there entered the man whom we had been awaiting so long.

He walked straight into the sitting-room, but when he saw us, drew back quickly in surprise, muttering—

"I beg pardon, gentlemen."

"No, come in," the detective said, and as he obeyed his eyes fell upon his master, reclining there with his face covered with the silk handkerchief.

"Good heavens, sir, what's happened?" he gasped, pale in alarm.

"A very serious catastrophe," the officer answered. "Your master is dead!"

"Dead!" he gasped, his clean-shaven face pallid in fright. "Dead! He can't be!"

"Look for yourself," the detective said. "He expired about noon."

Ash moved forward, and raising the handkerchief with trembling fingers, gazed upon the cold, set face of the man whom he had for years served so faithfully and well.

"What can you tell us regarding the affair?" asked the detective, with his dark eyes set full upon the agitated man.

"Nothing, sir. I know nothing," he answered.

"Explain what your master was doing when you left, and why you went out."

"About eleven o'clock, when I was polishing his boots in the kitchen, he called me," answered the man, without hesitation. "He gave me a note, and told me to go to the departure platform of King's Cross Station, and wait under the clock there for a youngish lady, who would wear a bunch of white flowers in her breast. I was to ask her if she expected him, and if so, to give her the letter. I took a cab there, waited at the spot he indicated for two whole hours, but saw no one answering the description; therefore I returned."

"And the note?" asked the officer.

"Here it is," answered Ash, placing his hand in his coat-pocket, and producing a letter.

The detective took it eagerly.

"It is not addressed," he remarked in surprise. Then, tearing it open, he took out the single sheet of note-paper.

There was no writing upon it. The paper was perfectly blank.

"This complicates matters," he said, turning to me. "The unknown lady who had made the appointment at King's Cross evidently wished for an answer in the affirmative or negative. This was the latter. A blank sheet of paper, denoting that there was nothing to add."

"Extraordinary!" I ejaculated. Then addressing Ash, I asked: "When you left your master what was he doing?"

"Sitting at the table, sir. He had his cheque-book open, for just before I went out he gave me a cheque for my month's wages. They were overdue a week, and I was hard up; so I asked for them."

"Did he hesitate to give you them, or did he make any remarks to lead you to think he was financially embarrassed?" I inquired.

"Not at all, sir. He had forgotten, and added an extra sovereign because he had kept me waiting. My master always had plenty of money, sir."

"Do you remember him going to Monte Carlo?" I asked.

"No, sir. Once I heard him tell Captain Hamilton that he'd been there, but it isn't since I've been employed by him."

"How long is that?"

"Nine years next May, sir."

"And have you had no holiday?"

"Of course I have, sir. Sometimes a week, sometimes a fortnight; and last year he gave me a month."

"What time of the year was it?"

"In February. He went up to Aberdeen, and told me there was no need for me to go, and that I could shut up the chambers and have a holiday. I did, and went down to Norfolk to visit the friends of the girl I'm engaged to."

"And he was gone a month?"

"Yes. A few days over a month."

"You had letters from him, I suppose?" I suggested.

"Only one, about four or five days after he had left."

"Then for aught you know he may have left Aberdeen and gone to Monte Carlo?" I said.

"Of course he may have done, sir. But he told me nothing about it."

"Did you notice anything unusual about his manner when he came back to town?"

"He seemed nervous; especially when I've gone in to him to announce a lady visitor. He seemed to fear that some lady would call whom he didn't want to see."

"But he often took ladies to the Gallery down at the House," I remarked, for Roddy was never so happy as when escorting two or three ladies over the House, or giving them tea on the long terrace beside the Thames. He was essentially a lady's man.

"Yes, sir. But there was one he used to describe to me, and he told me often that if she ever came I was to tell her that he had left London."

"What was she like?" asked the officer, pricking up his ears.

"Well," replied Ash, after some reflection, "as far as I could make out, she was about twenty or so; very good-looking, and generally dressed in black. Of course, I never saw her, for she never called."

The description he had given answered exactly to that of Aline. The mystery had become more complicated than I had anticipated. The next fact to ascertain was the cause of death.

"Why have you made these inquiries regarding Monte Carlo?" the detective asked me. "Did he go there?"

"I believe so," I replied. "Of course, it is not proved, but I suspect that when he went to Aberdeen he afterwards went secretly to the Riviera."

"Why secretly?"

"Ah! that I'm unable to tell," I answered, resolved to keep the knowledge I possessed to myself. But pointing to the card in the frame of the mirror I explained that that was a gambling-card used only at Monte Carlo, and that the figures were in my friend's handwriting.

The officer took it down interestedly, carefully scrutinised it, asked several questions regarding it, and then replaced it in the position it had occupied.

All three of us went to the writing-table, and the officer quickly discovered the cheque-book. Opening it he found by the counterfoil that what Ash had said about his cheque for wages was correct, but, further, that another cheque had been torn out after his, and that the counterfoil remained blank.

"This is suspicious," the detective observed quickly. "It looks very much as if there's been a robbery. We must stop the cheque at the bank," and he scribbled down the number of the counterfoil.

"If a robbery has been committed, then my friend has been murdered," I said.

"That's more than likely," replied the officer. "The story Ash tells us is certainly remarkable, and increases the mystery. If we can find this lady who made the appointment at King's Cross, we should no doubt learn something which might throw some light on the affair. Personally, I am inclined to disbelieve the theory that death has been due to natural causes. In view of the facts before us, either suicide or murder seem much more feasible theories.

Yet we must remember that a man who would deliberately send his man out before committing suicide would also fasten the door. You found it open."

This circumstance had not before occurred to me. Yes, a man who intended to take his own life would not have left the door open.

Ash, hearing our argument, at once declared that he had closed the door when he had gone out. Therefore, it seemed proved that Roddy had received a visitor during the absence of his valet.

Chapter Eight.
Within Grasp.

SCARCELY HAD WE CONCLUDED our conversation when the police arrived, and removed the body to the mortuary, in order that the doctor might make his examination; then, there being nothing to detain me further in the dead man's chambers, I left in company with the detective, the latter having given Ash orders not to disturb a single thing in the rooms. If it were proved that the member for South-West Sussex had actually been murdered, then another examination of the place would have to be made.

The more I reflected upon the puzzling circumstances, the more bewildering they became.

I called upon two men, close friends of Roddy's, and told them of the sad circumstances of his death; how he had died quite suddenly during his man's absence on a commission.

But I had no need to carry the distressing news, for as I passed the corner of the Haymarket the men selling the evening papers were holding the contents bills, whereon were displayed the words in big type, "Mysterious Death of an M.P." Newspapers are ingenious enough not to give away their information by putting the name of the deceased, thereby compelling the public to pay their pennies in order to learn where the vacancy has been caused by the Avenger. Nowadays the breath is scarcely out of the body of a Parliamentary representative than the papers publish the figures of the previous elections and comment on the political prospects of the division.

I bought a paper, and there saw beneath the brief announcement of Roddy's death quite a long account of the political position in his constituency, the name of the opposition candidate, and the majority by which my friend had been elected. Poor Roddy's death did not appear so important to that journal as the necessity of wresting the seat from the Government.

Next afternoon the inquest was held at the St. James's Vestry Hall, and was attended by more newspaper reporters than members of the public. I arrived early and had a chat with the detective Priestly, who had questioned Ash, but he told me that nothing further had been discovered.

The usual evidence of identification having been taken, I was called and described the finding of the body. Then the valet Ash was called in and related the story which he had already told the detective.

"You have no idea who this lady was whom your master desired to avoid?" the Coroner asked him.

"No," answered the man.

"And as far as you are aware there was no reason for Mr Morgan taking his life?"

"None. He was exceedingly merry all the morning, whistling to himself, and once or twice joking with me when I waited on him at breakfast."

The doctor was then called, and having given his name and stated his professional qualifications, said—

"When I saw the deceased he was dead. I should think about half an hour had elapsed since respiration ceased. The room appeared in perfect order, and there was no sign whatever of foul play. On making a cursory examination I found one of the hands contracted, the fingers bent in towards the palm. This morning I made a post-mortem at the mortuary, and on opening the hand I discovered this within it," and from his vest pocket he took a piece of white tissue paper, which he opened.

Every neck was craned in Court to catch sight of what had been discovered, and I standing near him saw as he handed it to the Coroner that it was a tiny piece of soft black chiffon about half an inch square, evidently torn from a woman's dress.

The Coroner took it, and then remarked—

"This would appear to prove that the deceased had a visitor immediately before his death, and that his visitor was a lady."

"That is what I surmise," observed the doctor. "My examination has proved one or two things." There was a stir in Court, followed by a dead and eager silence.

"I found no external mark of violence whatsoever," the doctor continued in a clear tone, "and the clenched hand with the piece of muslin within did not point to death from any unnatural cause. The only external marks were two very curious ones which are entirely unaccountable. On each elbow I found a strange white scar, the remains of some injury inflicted perhaps a year ago. The eyes, too, were discoloured in a manner altogether unaccountable. On further examination, I found no trace whatever of any organic disease. The deceased was a strong athletic man, and was suffering from no known malady which could have resulted fatally."

"Did you make an examination of the stomach?" inquired the Coroner.

"I did. Suspecting suicide by poison, I made a most careful analysis, assisted by Dr Leverton, of King's College Hospital, but we failed to discover any trace of poison whatsoever."

"Then you cannot assign any cause for death in this instance?" observed the Coroner, looking up sharply in surprise.

"No," answered the doctor. "I cannot."

"Have you a theory that deceased died from the effects of poison?"

"Certain appearances pointed to such a conclusion," the doctor responded. "Personally, before making the post-mortem, I suspected prussic acid; but all tests failed to detect any trace of such deleterious matter."

"Of course," said the Coroner, who was also a medical man of wide experience, clearing his throat, as he turned to the jury, "the presence of poison can be very easily discovered, and the fact that the analyses have failed must necessarily add mystery to this case."

"Having failed to find poison," continued the doctor, "we naturally turned our attention to other causes which might result fatally."

"And what did you find?" inquired the Coroner eagerly, his pen poised in his hand.

"Nothing!" the witness answered. "Absolutely nothing."

"Then you are quite unable to account for death?"

"Utterly. Several of the circumstances are suspicious of foul play, but we have found not the slightest trace of it. The marks upon the elbows are very curious indeed—circular white scars—but they have, of course, nothing to do with Mr Morgan's sudden death," I recollected the portion of charred paper which I had picked up, the discovery of the glove-button, and its connection with the tiny scrap of black chiffon. Yes, there was no doubt that he had had a visitor between the time that Ash went out to meet the mysterious woman at King's Cross and the moment of his death.

"The affair seems enveloped in a certain amount of mystery," observed the Coroner to the jury after the doctor had signed his depositions. "You have the whole of the evidence before you—that of the valet, the friend of deceased who discovered him, the police who have searched the chambers, and the doctor who made the post-mortem. In summing up the whole we find that the unfortunate gentleman died mysteriously—very mysteriously—but to nothing the medical men have discovered could they assign the cause of death. It would certainly appear, from the fact that a portion of a woman's dress-trimming was discovered in the dead man's clenched hand, that he had a secret visitor, and that she desired to escape while he wished her to remain. Yet there was no sign of a struggle in the rooms, and no one saw any person enter or leave. Again, we have it in evidence that deceased, at the hour of his death, sent a message to some unknown lady whom his valet had instructions to meet on the railway platform at King's Cross. This meeting had undoubtedly been pre-arranged, and the lady expected the unfortunate gentleman to keep it. Perhaps watching from a distance, and not seeing Mr Morgan, she did not approach the clock, and hence the valet did not give her the mysterious blank and unaddressed letter. After this, the suggestion naturally occurs whether or not this same lady visited Mr Morgan in the absence of his valet. She may have done, or may not. But in this Court we have nothing to do with theories. It is your duty, gentlemen of the jury, to say whether this gentleman actually died from natural causes, or whether by suicide or foul means. We must recollect that the police have discovered what may eventually throw some light on the affair, namely, the fact that a cheque is missing from deceased's cheque-book, leaving the counterfoil blank. By means of that cheque it is just possible that the identity of the unknown person who visited Mr Morgan may be established. I think, gentlemen," continued the Coroner, after a pause, "I think you will agree with me that in these strange circumstances it would be unwise to go further into the matter. By exposing all the evidence the police have in their possession we might possibly defeat our inquiry; therefore I ask you whether you will return a verdict that the death of this gentleman has resulted from natural causes, or whether you think it wiser to return an open verdict of 'Found dead,' and leave all further inquiries in the hands of the police."

Those in Court stirred again uneasily. There had been breathless silence while the Coroner had been speaking save for the rustling of the paper and "flimsies" used by the reporters, and the departure of one or two uniformed messenger-lads carrying "copy" to the evening journals for use in their special editions.

The foreman of the jury turned to his fellow-jurymen and inquired whether they desired to consult in private. But all were of one opinion, and without leaving the room returned a verdict of "Found dead." At the club that night everybody read the evening papers, and in the smoking-room everybody propounded his own view of the mystery. Some were of opinion that their friend had fallen a victim of foul play, while others who, like myself, had noticed his recent depressed spirits and inert attitude, were inclined to think that he had taken his own life in a fit of despondency. They declared that he had sent Ash out on a fool's errand in order to be alone, and that the blank note was really nothing at all. The only argument against that theory was the fact that I had found the door leading to his chambers open. This was incompatible with the idea that he had deliberately taken his own life.

As the person who had made the startling discovery, I was, of course, questioned on every hand regarding all the minor details of the terrible scene. The men who held the opinion that he had been murdered desired to make out that the furniture had been disturbed, but having very carefully noted everything, I was able to flatly contradict them. Thus the evening passed with that one single subject under discussion—the murder of the man who had been so popular amongst us, and whom we had all held in such high esteem.

Next morning, near noon, while reading the paper beside my own fire, Simes entered, saying—

"There's Ash, sir, would like to see you."

"Show him in," I exclaimed at once, casting the paper aside, and an instant later the dead man's valet made his appearance, pale and agitated.

"Well, Ash," I said, "what's the matter?"

"I'm a bit upset, sir; that's all." And he panted from the effort of ascending the stairs. Therefore, I motioned him to a seat.

"Well, have the police visited your master's rooms again?"

"No, sir. They haven't been again," he replied. "But I made a thorough examination last night, and I wish you'd come round with me, if you'd be so kind, sir. I know you were my master's best friend, and I'm sure you won't let this affair rest, will you?"

"Certainly not," I answered in surprise. "But why do you wish me to go with you?"

"I want to ask your opinion on something."

"What have you discovered?"

"Well, sir, I don't know whether it is a discovery, or not. But I'd like you to see it," he said, full of nervous impatience.

Therefore, I called Simes to bring my hat and coat, and we went out together, taking a cab along to poor Roddy's chambers. They seemed strangely silent and deserted now, as we let ourselves in with the latch-key. No cheery voice welcomed me from the sitting-room within, and there was no odour of Egyptian cigarettes or overnight cigars; no fire in the grate, for all was cheerless and rendered the more funereal because of the darkness of the rainy day.

"This morning," explained Ash, "when I thought I had made a thorough examination of the whole place last night, I chanced to be taking a turn around this room and made a discovery which seems to me very remarkable." Then, pointing, he went on: "You see in that cabinet there's some old china."

"Yes," I answered, for some of the pieces were very choice, and I had often envied them.

"From where we stand here we can see a small casket of chased brass—Indian work, I think he called it."

"Certainly."

"Well, now, I chanced to pass this, and a thought occurred to me that I'd look what was in that box. I did so, and when I saw, I closed it up again and came to you to get your opinion."

With that he opened the glass doors of the cabinet, took forth the little casket and opened it.

Inside there was nothing but ashes. They were white ashes, similar to those I had found in my own rooms after Aline had departed!

"Good God!" I gasped, scarcely believing my own eyes. "What was in this box before?"

"When I opened it last week, sir, there was a rosary, such as the Roman Catholics use. It belonged to my master's grandmother, he once told me. She was a Catholic."

I turned the ashes over in my hand. Yes, there was no doubt whatever that it had been a rosary, for although the beads were consumed yet the tiny lengths of wire which had run through them remained unmelted, but had been blackened and twisted by the heat. There was one small lump of metal about the size of a bean, apparently silver, and that I judged to have been the little crucifix appended.

"It's extraordinary!" I said, bewildered, when I reflected that this fact lent additional colour to my vague theory that Aline might have visited Roddy before his death. "It's most extraordinary!"

"Yes, sir, it is," Ash replied. "But what makes it the more peculiar is the fact that about a year ago I found a little pile of ashes very similar to these when I went one morning to dust the master's dressing-table. He always kept a little pocket Testament there, but it had gone, and only the ashes remained in its place. I called him, and when he saw them he seemed very upset, and said—'Take them out of my sight, Ash! Take them away! It's the Devil's work!'"

"Yes," I observed. "This is indeed the Devil's work."

The mystery surrounding the tragic affair increased hourly.

I examined the brass box, and upon the lid saw a strange discolouration. It was the mark of a finger—perhaps the mark of that mysterious hand, the touch of which had the potency to consume the object with which it came in contact. I placed the box back upon the table, and could not resist the strange chill which crept over me. The mystery was a more uncanny one than I had ever heard of.

"Now tell me, Ash," I said at last. "Did your master ever entertain any lady visitors here?"

"Very seldom, sir," the man answered. "His married sister, Lady Hilgay, used to come sometimes, and once or twice his aunt, the Duchess, called, but beyond those I don't recollect any lady here for certainly twelve months past."

"Some might have called when you were absent, of course," I remarked.

"They might," he said; "but I don't think they did."

"Have you ever seen any letters that you've posted addressed to a lady named Cloud?"

He reflected, then answered—

"No, sir. The name is an unusual one, and if I'd ever seen it before I certainly should have remembered it."

"Well," I said, after some minutes of silence, "I want you to come with me and try and find a lady. If we do meet her you'll see whether you can identify her as a person you've seen before. You understand?"

"Yes," he replied, with a puzzled look. "But are we going to see the woman whom the police suspect visited my master while I was absent?"

"Be patient," I said, and together we went out, and re-entering the cab drove up to Hampstead.

The mystery of my friend's death was becoming more inexplicable. Therefore I had resolved to seek Aline, and at all costs demand some explanation of the extraordinary phenomena which had taken place in Roddy's rooms as well as in my own.

Chapter Nine.
Mrs Popejoy's Statement.

"Is Miss Cloud at home?" I inquired of the maid, as Ash stood behind in wonder.

"She doesn't live here, sir," replied the girl.

"Doesn't live here?" I echoed dubiously. "Why, only a short time ago I saw her enter here!"

"Well, sir, I don't know her. I've never heard the name."

"Is Mrs Popejoy in?" I inquired.

"Yes, sir. If you wish to see her, please step inside."

We both entered the hall, the usual broad passage of a suburban house, with its cheap hall-stand, couple of straight-backed wooden chairs, and a long chest in imitation carved oak. The girl disappeared for a few moments, and on returning ushered us into the dining-room, where we found a rather sour-looking old lady standing ready to greet us. She was about sixty, grey-haired, thin-faced, and wore a cap with faded cherry-coloured ribbons.

"Mrs Popejoy, I believe?" I exclaimed politely, receiving in return a bow, the stiffness of which was intended to show breeding. Then continuing, I said: "I have called on a rather urgent matter concerning your niece, Miss Aline Cloud; but the servant tells me she is not at home, and I thought you would perhaps tell me where I can find her without delay."

"My niece!" she exclaimed in surprise. "My poor niece died ten years ago."

"Ten years ago!" I gasped. "And is not Miss Cloud your niece?"

"I have no niece of that name, sir," she answered. "The name indeed is quite strange to me. There must be some mistake."

"But your name is Popejoy," I exclaimed, "and this is Number sixteen, Ellerdale Road?"

"Certainly."

"Truth to tell, madam," I said, "I have called on you in order to assure myself of a certain very extraordinary fact."

"What is it?"

"Well, late on a certain night some weeks ago I accompanied Miss Cloud, the lady I am now in search of, to this house. I sat in the cab while she got out, and with my own eyes saw her admitted by your maid. This strikes me as most extraordinary, in lace of your statement that you know nothing of her." The old lady reflected.

"What cock-and-bull story did she tell you?" she inquired quickly. "Explain it all to me, then perhaps I can help you."

There was something about Mrs Popejoy's manner that I did not like. I could have sworn that she was concealing the truth.

"Well," I said, "I met Miss Cloud at a theatre, and she told me that you and another lady had accompanied her; that you had got separated, and being a stranger in London she did not know her way home. Therefore I brought her back, and saw her enter here."

The old lady smiled cynically.

"My dear sir," she said, "you've been very neatly imposed upon. In the first place, I have no niece; secondly, I've never entered a theatre for years; thirdly, I've never heard of any girl named Cloud; and fourthly, she certainly does not live here."

"But with my own eyes I saw her enter your door," I said. "I surely can believe what I have seen!"

"It must have been another house," she answered. "There are several in this road similar in appearance to mine."

"No. Number sixteen," I said. "I looked it up previously in the Directory and saw your name. There can be no mistake."

"Well, sir," snapped the old lady, "I am mistress of this house, and surely I ought to know whether I have a niece or not! What kind of lady was she?"

"She was young, fair-haired, blue-eyed, and very good-looking. She had lived in France previously, at Montgeron, near Paris."

"Ah!" the old lady cried suddenly. "Why, of course, the hussy! Now I remember. It is quite plain that she duped you."

"Tell me," I exclaimed eagerly. "Where is she now?"

"How should I know? She wasn't my niece at all. A few weeks ago I advertised in the *Christian World* for a companion, and engaged her. She came one afternoon, and said that coming from France she had left all her luggage at Victoria. She was exceedingly pleasant, took tea with me, and afterwards at her request I allowed her to go down to Victoria to see about her boxes. That was about six o'clock, but she did not return until nearly two o'clock in the morning, and when I questioned her she said that she had been unable to find the office where her luggage had been placed, and had been wandering about, having lost her way. I didn't believe such a lame story, and the consequence was that she left after a week, and I haven't seen her since."

I stood dumbfounded.

"That's a strange story, sir," observed Ash, who was standing near.

"It's amazing!" I said. "And it complicates matters very considerably."

Turning to Mrs Popejoy, I inquired—

"When you corresponded with her, to what address did you write?"

"To a village post-office somewhere in the Midlands. It was a funny name, which I can't remember."

"Do you recollect the county?"

"No. I didn't put the county. The first letter I wrote was to initials at the office of the newspaper; and in reply I received a letter from Paris, with a request that further letters might be addressed to Miss—what was her name?—Cloud, at this post-office."

"Then to you she gave her name as Cloud?" I said quickly.

"Yes. At first when you mentioned it I did not recollect. Now I remember."

"Then you have no idea where she is now!" I said.

"Not the slightest," the old lady snapped. "I was very glad to see the back of the hussy, for I believe she was no better than she should be, staying out till that hour of the morning. I told Ann to turn out the gas and go to bed, but it seems that she didn't, and waited up till that unearthly hour. And do you know what," continued old Mrs Popejoy in a confidential tone, "I believe that there was something very mysterious about her. I have a very shrewd suspicion that she meant to rob me, or do me some evil or other."

"Why?" I asked eagerly. "What mystery was there surrounding her?"

"Well," she responded after some little hesitation, "I was very glad indeed when she went off in a flounce, and I hope she'll never darken my door again. You may think me very timid, but if you had seen what I discovered after she had gone you'd have been of my way of thinking."

"What did you discover?" I asked, surprised.

"Well, in her bedroom there was, in a small silver box, an old ring that my late husband had prized very much. It had belonged to one of the Popes, and had been blessed by him. The relic was no doubt an extremely valuable one."

"And when she went?" I asked.

"When she went I had a look round her room to see that nothing had been taken, but to my surprise I found the ring and the box actually burnt up. Only the ashes remained! There was a picture of the Virgin also in the room, an old panel-painting which my husband had picked up in Holland, and what was most extraordinary was that although this picture had also been wholly consumed, the little easel had been left quite intact. Some Devil's work was effected there, but how, I can't imagine."

This was certainly a most startling statement, and the old lady was evidently still nervous regarding it. Did it not fully bear out what had already occurred in my own rooms and in those of the man whose life had so suddenly gone out?

"Do you think, then, that the picture was deliberately burned?" I inquired.

"I examined the ashes very closely," she replied, "and found that by whatever means the picture was destroyed, the table-cloth had not even been singed. Now, if the picture had been deliberately lighted, a hole must have been burned in the cloth; but as it was, it seemed as though the picture, which the Roman Catholics hold in such reverence, had been destroyed by something little short of a miracle."

"Have you preserved the ashes?"

"No," responded the old lady; "Ann threw them into the dustbin at once. I didn't like to keep them about."

"And what is your private opinion?" I asked, now that we had grown confidential.

"I believe," she answered decisively, "I believe that the hussy must have been in league with the very Evil One himself."

Such was exactly my own opinion, but I had no desire to expose all my feelings, or confess the fascination which she had held over me by reason of her wondrous beauty. It was strange, I thought, how, evil though her heart, she had uttered those ominous warnings. True, I had loved her; I had adored her with all the strength of my being; but she in return had only urged me to love my Platonic little friend Muriel. She who held me powerless beneath her thrall had, with self-denial, released me in order that I might transfer my affections to the bright-eyed woman who was wearing out her heart at Madame Gabrielle's; she had implored me to cast her aside, and thus escape the mysterious unknown fate which she predicted must inevitably fall upon me.

The reason why she had forbidden me to call at Mrs Popejoy's, or to address a letter there, was now quite plain. She had deceived me, and I could trust her no further.

Yet had she actually deceived me? Had she not plainly told me that she was an evil-doer, a malefactor, one whose mission was to bring ill-fortune to her fellow-creatures. Yes, Aline Cloud was a mystery. More than ever I now felt that she was the possessor of some unknown subtle influence, some unseen supernatural power by which she could effect evil at will.

"I suppose," I said, in an endeavour to allay the nervous old lady's fears, "I suppose there is some quite ordinary explanation for the strange occurrence. Many things which at first appear inexplicable are, when the truth is made plain, quite ordinary events. So it was, I suppose, with the picture and the ring which were consumed by what appears like spontaneous combustion."

"I don't know," she replied. "I've thought over it a great deal, but the more I think of it, the more extraordinary it seems."

"I regret to have troubled you," I said. "I must try and find her at whatever cost, for the matter is a most important one. If you should by any chance come across her again, or if she visits you, I should be obliged if you would at once communicate with me," and I handed her a card.

"Certainly, sir," she replied. "The hussy entirely misled you, and I should like to be able to fathom the mystery how my picture and ring were reduced to ashes. If I ever do see her again, depend upon it that I'll let you know." Then, with woman's curiosity, pardonable in the circumstances, she asked, "Is the matter on which you wish to speak to her a personal one?"

"It is, and yet it is not," I responded vaguely. "It concerns another person—a friend."

With that I shook her hand, and accompanied by Ash, walked out and left the house.

As we drove back down the Hampstead Road I turned to the valet and said—

"Do you remember whether a tall, dark, shabby-genteel man in a frock-coat and tall hat—a man with a thin, consumptive-looking face—ever called upon your master?"

I was thinking of Aline's companion, and of their remarkable conversation. At that moment it occurred to me that it might be of Roddy they had spoken, and not of myself. Did he urge her to kill my friend? Ash reflected deeply.

"I don't remember any man answering that description," he responded. "After he became a Member of Parliament one or two strange people from his constituency called to see him, but I don't recollect anybody like the man you describe. How old was he?"

"About forty; or perhaps a trifle over."

The man shook his head. "No," he declared, "I don't think he ever called."

"When your master sent you out with the note that morning had you any suspicion that he meant to receive a secret visitor? Now, don't conceal anything from me. Together we must fathom this mystery." He hesitated, then turning to me, answered—

"Well, to tell the truth, sir, I did."

"What caused you to suspect?"

"First, the letter being unaddressed was a rather curious fact," he responded slowly. "Then, I was to meet a lady whom he did not describe further than that she was youngish, and would wear a bunch of flowers. All this appeared strange, but my curiosity was further aroused because he had dressed more carefully than he usually did in a morning, as though visitors were coming."

"Was he down at the House on the previous night?"

"Yes, sir; I took a telegram down there, and delivered it to him in the Lobby. He opened it, read it, and uttered a bad word, as if its contents annoyed him very much. Then I returned, and he arrived home about half an hour after midnight. I gave him some whiskey and soda, and left him smoking and studying a big blue-book he had brought home with him."

"Have you any suspicion that the telegram had any connection with the mysterious lady whom you were sent to meet?"

"I've several times thought that it had. Of course I can't tell."

A silence fell between us. At last I spoke again, saying—

"Remember that all you have heard today must be kept secret. Nobody must know that we have been to Mrs Popejoy's. There is a mystery surrounding this lady named Cloud, and when we get to the bottom of it we shall, I feel certain, obtain a clue to the cause of your poor master's death. You, his faithful servant, were, I feel assured, devoted to him, therefore it behoves us both to work in unison with a view to discovering the truth."

"Certainly, sir; I shall not utter a single word of what I have heard today. But," he added, "do you believe that my poor master was murdered?"

"It's an open question," I replied. "There are one or two facts which, puzzling the doctors, may be taken as suspicious, yet there are others which seem quite plain, and point to death from natural causes."

Then, having given him certain instructions how to act if he discovered anything further regarding the mysterious Aline, he alighted at the corner of Cranbourne Street, while I drove on to my own rooms, full of saddest memories of the man who had for years been one of my closest friends.

Chapter Ten.
In Duddington.

WHEN THE WINTER RAINS made London dreary, rendering the Strand a veritable quagmire, and when the shops began to display Christmas cards and Christmas numbers, I went South, as I did each year, accompanied by my married sister and her husband, in search of sunshine. I knew the Riviera well. I had enjoyed the rather dull exclusiveness of Cannes; I had stayed one season at the Grand at Nice and capered through Carnival in a clown's dress of mauve and green; I had spent a fortnight once in Mentone, that paradise of the consumptive; and I had paid some lengthy bills at the Hotel de Paris at Monte Carlo. My brother-in-law, however, had taken a little white villa on the olive-clad hillside at Beaulieu, which we found was on the verge of everything.

But to me life on the Riviera soon becomes tiresome. A couple or three visits to "the Rooms;" a "five o'clock" or two at La Reserve; tea in a wicker chair in the entrance-hall of that colossal hotel, the Excelsior, at Cimiez, which is patronised by Her Majesty; a dinner at the London House at Nice, and one at the Hermitage at "Monty," and I become tired of the ever-azure sea, of the Noah's Ark gardens, of the artificiality and of the constant brightness of the Riviera "season." I long for my old English home in the country where, in the springtime, all the beauties of the outdoor world come to one with a sense of novelty after the winter's cold and frost.

Therefore at the end of March I returned, passing through London, and travelling down to my father's place at Tixover, which was, as always, my pleasant home.

What though the trees were still leafless, and the flowers few; every day, almost every hour, fresh green buds were swelling and opening in the balmy air; the delicate pink of the almond blossom was flushing the bare twigs in the kitchen-garden, primroses were coyly showing themselves in the coppices and hedgerows, as I drove along from Stamford, while in the sheltered places in the woods as I passed I saw sheets of wild hyacinths, "like strips of the sky fallen," delicate snowdrops, and a wealth of daffodils.

As I drove along that morning through Worthorpe and Colly Weston to Duddington, the quaint little old Northamptonshire village within a mile of which lies Tixover Hall, it was, though a trifle chilly after the Riviera, one of those bright days which make even the elderly feel young and sprightly again; days on which even the saddest among us are influenced by the infectious brightness of the atmosphere. At no other season of the year is there that delicious sensation of life, of resurrection in the very air, as the grey old earth awakens from her winter sleep and renews her youth again.

As the old bay mare trotted down the short, steep hill from the cross-roads, and Banks was telling me all the gossip of the countryside—how my old friend Doctor Lewis, of Cliffe, had taken to cycling, how an entertainment had been held at the schools, and how somebody in the Parish Council had been making himself obnoxious—we suddenly entered Duddington, the queer old village with its rows of comfortable, old-fashioned cottages, with their attics peeping from beneath the thatch. In the air was that sweet smell of burnt wood peculiar to those peaceful Midland villages, and as we passed the inn, and turning, crossed the bridge which led out to the right to Tixover, a couple of villagers pulled their forelocks as a token of respect, I felt tired after two days of incessant travelling, nevertheless there was about that old-world place a home-like feeling, for I had known it ever since I had known myself. Those elderly people who peered out of their cottage doors as we passed, and who gave me a merry, laughing greeting, had known me ever since the days when my nurse used to take me for drives in the donkey-cart, while those broad, green meadows on either side of the wandering river had belonged to my family for generations.

A mile away, along a straight road with gradual ascent, a belt of firs came into view, and away through the trees I could distinguish the old, red chimneys of the Hall, the house which for three centuries past had been the residence of my ancestors. Then a few moments later, as we turned into the drive, our approach was heralded by the loud barking of Bruce and Nero, whose ferocity was instantly calmed when I alighted at the door and met my mother at the foot of the great oak staircase.

The old place, with its wide, panelled hall, its long, big rooms, its antiquated furniture—rather the worse for wear perhaps—and its wide hearths where wood fires were still burning, had an air of solidity and comfort after the stuccoed and painted villa at Beaulieu, where the salon with its gilt furniture was only large enough to hold four people comfortably, and the so-called terrace was not much wider than the overhanging eaves.

Yes, Tixover was a fine old place, perhaps not architecturally so handsome as many residences in the vicinity, yet my father, like his father and grandfather before him, did not believe in modernising its interior, hence it was entirely antique with genuine old oak of the time of the first Charles,—queer old high-backed chairs, covered with time-dimmed tapestry that had been worked by hands that had fallen to dust in the days before the Plague devastated London. The old diamond-panes set in lead were the same as in the turbulent days when the Roundheads assembled about Stamford and Cromwell camped outside Cliffe. There was everything one could desire at Tixover—fishing in the river which ran through the grounds, shooting in those extensive woods on the Stamford Road, hunting with the Fitzwilliam pack, who several times in the season met at the cross-roads, a mile and a half away, while the roads, although a trifle hilly, were nevertheless almost perfect for cycling.

But when a man has broken his home ties and lives in London, to return to the home of his youth is only pleasant for a limited period. Tixover was a quiet, restful place, but after a month it generally became dreary and dull, and I usually left it with a sigh of relief, and returned to London eager to get back to my own chambers, my club, and the men I knew. Why it was I could never tell. I suppose it is the same with all other men. To those who like town life the country is only tolerable for a time, just as those who set out with a determination to live abroad generally return after a year or so, wearied and homesick.

I found life at home just as even and undisturbed as it had been since my sister Mary had married and I had left to live in London. My parents aged but slowly, and were both still active, therefore I was warmly welcomed, and as that evening I sat in the old familiar drawing-room, with its dingy paintings, its crackling wood fire, and its rather uncomfortable chairs in comparison with my own soft saddlebag ones, I related how we had spent the season on the Riviera; of our excursions to Grasse and Aspremont, of my brother-in-law's luck in winning two zeros in succession, and of my own good fortune in being invited on a week's yachting trip around Corsica and back to Cannes. My parents were interested in all this, for they once used to go to Nice regularly to escape the winter, in the days before the Paillon was covered in or the public gardens were made. Now, however, they no longer went South, preferring, as they put it, the warmth of their own fireside.

It was not surprising. To elderly people who are not in robust health the long journey is fatiguing, while to the invalid "ordered abroad" by irresponsible doctors, the shaking up on the P.L.M. proves often the cause of sudden and fatal collapse.

Of Muriel I had heard but little. I had written to her twice from Beaulieu, and sent her an occasional box of flowers from one of the well-known florists in Nice, yet her letters in return were merely brief notes of thanks, and I feared that perhaps I had annoyed her by too long neglect. There seemed in her letters a tone of complaint which was unusual; therefore, I began to reflect whether it would not be as well to take a trip to town shortly, to see how Simes was keeping my rooms, and entertain her to the usual little dinner at Frascati's.

In the days immediately succeeding my return to Tixover, I drove about a good deal, visiting various friends in the vicinity and making dutiful calls upon my mother's friends. It was always my custom, too, to call upon some of my father's older tenants; the people who had been kind to me when I was a mischievous lad. I found that such informal visits, where I could drink a glass of fresh milk or homemade wine, were always appreciated, and, truth to tell, I found in them some very pleasant reminiscences of my youth.

One afternoon, when I came in from driving to Oundle, I found my mother taking tea with a stranger, in the pleasant, old-fashioned drawing-room, the mullioned windows of which looked out upon a broad sweep of well-kept lawn, bounded by the river and the meadows beyond.

"Ah! Here's Clifton!" my mother exclaimed as I entered, and at that moment the man who was sitting with her taking tea turned and faced me.

"Let me introduce you. Mr Yelverton, our new curate—my son Clifton."

"Why, Jack!" I cried, wringing his hand, "and it's actually you—a clergyman!" And I gazed at his clerical garb in blank amazement.

"Yes, it's me," he answered cheerily. "I certainly didn't think that I should ever get an appointment in your country."

"But how is it?" I cried, after I had explained to my mother how we had been chums at Wadham.

"I never thought you'd go in for the Church."

"Nor did I," he admitted, laughing. "But I'm curate of Duddington, and this is my first visit to your mother. I had no idea that this was your home. There are many Cleeves, you know."

He was a merry, easy-going fellow, this old college companion of mine, a veritable giant in stature, fair, with a long, drooping moustache that a cavalry officer might have envied, broad shouldered, burly, a magnificent type of an Englishman. As he stood there towering above me, he looked strangely out of place in his long, black coat and clerical collar. An officer's uniform would have suited him better.

I had left Oxford a couple of terms before he had, and on going abroad lost sight of him. He had been accredited by all as a coming man on account of his depth of learning. When I had last seen him, some six years before, he was living in Lincoln's Inn, and reading for the Bar.

I referred to that occasion when we had met in the Strand, and he replied—
"Yes, but I preferred the Church. My uncle, you know, is Bishop of Galway."
Then I recollected that such was the case. He had no doubt been induced
to go in for a clerical life by this relative. Maternal uncles are responsible for
a good deal in shaping a man's career.

"Well, you're always welcome to Tixover, my dear old fellow," I said, "and
I'm sure my mother will always be very pleased to see you."

"Of course," she said, smiling sweetly. "Any friend of Clifton's is always
welcome here. I hope you won't treat us formally, Mr Yelverton, but look in
and see us whenever you can spare time."

Yelverton thanked her warmly, and as I took my tea I began to chat about
the parish, about the shortcomings of his predecessor, an abominable young
prig who lisped, flirted outrageously, thought of nothing but tennis, and
whose sermons were distinct specimens of oratorical rubbish. To all the
countryside he was known as "Mother's darling," an appellation earned by
the fact that his mother, a fussy old person, used to live with him and refer to
him as her "dear boy."

But Jack Yelverton was of an entirely different stamp—a manly, good-hu-
moured, even-tempered fellow who had no "side," and whose face and figure
showed him to be designed as a leader among men. At college he had been
noted for his careful judgment, his close and diligent studies of abstruse sub-
jects, and his remarkable grasp of things which even the Dons found difficult.
Yet he was an inveterate practical joker, and more than once got into an ugly
scrape, from which, however, he always managed to ingeniously wriggle out.

I was extremely glad to find my old friend installed in Duddington, for
during the years that had passed I had often wondered what had become of
him. More than once poor Roddy, who had been one of us at Wadham, had
expressed a wish that we could find him, for we had all three been closest
friends in the old days. And yet he had actually been appointed our curate
and spiritual adviser, and had come to visit Tixover without knowing it was
my home.

We laughed heartily over the situation.

He told me how he had taken lodgings with Mrs Walker, a cheerful old soul
who lived at a pleasant cottage halfway up the village street, an old-fashioned
place with a flower-garden in front and a little paved walk leading up to the
rustic porch. Assisted by her daughter, old Mrs Walker had lodged curates in
Duddington for many years, knew all their wants, and was well versed in the
diplomatic treatment of callers, and the means by which her lodger could be
prevented from being disturbed when working at his sermon.

We chatted on for half an hour, and when he rose to leave he invited me to walk up to the village after dinner, and have a smoke with him.

"My rooms are not palatial, you know, my dear fellow," he said, "but I can give you a good cigar, if you'll come."

"Certainly; I shall be delighted," I answered, and we parted.

Soon after eight that evening I knocked at Mrs Walker's door, and was ushered by her daughter into the small, clean, but rather shabbily-furnished best room. It smelt strongly of the geraniums, which grew high in a row before the window, and as I entered Jack Yelverton rose and greeted me cheerily, giving me his easy chair, taking down a box of cigars from the shelf, and producing a surreptitious bottle of whiskey, a syphon, and a couple of glasses from a little cupboard in the wall.

"I'm jolly glad you've come," he said, when he had reseated himself, and I had got my weed under way. "The surprise today has indeed been a pleasant one. Lots of times I have thought of you, and wondered where and how you were. But in the world men drift apart, and even the best resolutions of correspondence made at college are mostly broken. However, it is a very pleasant meeting this, for I feel already that I'm among friends."

"Of course you are, old chap," I answered. "My people will always be pleased to see you. Like yourself, I'm awfully glad we've met. But you're the very last man I should have imagined would have gone in for the Church. It isn't your first appointment, I suppose?"

"No," he answered reflectively, gazing at the end of his cigar. "It came about in this way. I studied for a couple of years at Lincoln's Inn, but somehow I didn't care much for the law, and one day it occurred to me that with my knowledge of theology I might have a chance of doing good among my fellow-men. I don't know what put it into my head, I'm sure, but straight away I saw my uncle the Bishop, and the result was that very soon afterwards I was appointed curate at Framlingham, in Suffolk. This disappointed me. I felt that I ought to work in one of the overcrowded cities; that I might, with the income my father had left me, alleviate the sufferings of some of the deserving poor; that I might be the means of effecting some good in the world. At last I was successful in obtaining an appointment under the Vicar of Christ Church, Commercial Street, Spitalfields, where I can tell you I had plenty of opportunity for doing that which I had set my mind upon. A curate's life in the East End isn't very pleasant if he does his duty, and mine was not a very salubrious locality. The air of the slums is poisonous. For three years I worked there," he went on after a slight pause. "Then I exchanged to St. Peter's, Walworth, and then, owing to ill-health, I was compelled to come here, into the country again. That's briefly been my life since we parted."

"Well," I said, convinced of his earnestness of purpose in the life he had adopted, for a man does not seek an appointment in a London slum unless he feels a strong incentive to work in the interests of his fellow-men, "you'll get all right very soon here, I hope. The air is fresh, your parish isn't very large, and old Layton, the rector, is an easy-going old chap—one of the old school."

"Yes, I know," he said; "I've been here already ten days, and I've seen that the work is mere child's play. The rector has got into a groove, like all rural rectors. But, to tell the truth, I only accepted the appointment because the doctor ordered me a change. When I'm quite strong again I shall go back, I hope, to London. When I entered the Church it wasn't with any thought of gain. I've enough to keep me comfortably. I had, and have still, in view work which I must achieve."

Jack Yelverton was an enthusiast. I was rather surprised, I confess, at finding him so energetic in religious work, for when at Wadham he had been quite the reverse. Still, there was an air of deep sincerity in his words. His face, too, was pale and lined, as if he had worked until his constitution had become jaded and worn. On his mantel-shelf was a marble clock, with the neat inscription on a silver plate stating that it had been subscribed for by the parishioners of the poor East End parish as a token of their esteem.

He rose to turn down the lamp, which was smoking, and as he did so sighed. Then casting himself in his chair again, he remarked—

"I don't know how long I shall be able to stand this rusticating. You know, Clifton, I wasn't born to rusticate."

"No, I know that," I said. "Like myself, you prefer town."

"Ah, you have your clubs, your friends, theatres, concerts, river-parties, merry little dinners, all that makes life worth living," he said. "But if you worked with me for a week your heart would bleed to see the appalling poverty and distress; how the poor strive and struggle to live; how their landlords, with hearts like stone, sell them up and drive them to the last extremity; how the keepers of the low-class public-houses sell them intoxicants which drive them mad, and how at last the police lay hands upon them as drunkards and thieves. You don't know, my dear fellow—you can't know—how lower London lives. When I reflect upon some of the painful scenes of poverty and distress to which I have been witness, and remember the heartfelt gratitude with which any slight assistance I have given has been accepted, I feel somehow angry with the wealthy—those who spend their money recklessly within that small area around Charing Cross, and will contribute to any Mansion House fund to aid foreigners because their names will be printed as donors in the daily papers, but, alas! who begrudge a single sixpence to the starving poor in the giant city which brings them their wealth. They are fond of talking of missions to the East End and all that, but it isn't religion half these people want, it's bread for their starving wives and children, or some little necessities for the sick."

"Yes," I observed, "I suppose all sorts of absurd bunkum is talked about religious work among the London poor. Poor Roddy Morgan used to hold a similar opinion to yourself. He was an ardent supporter of a philanthropic movement which had its headquarters somewhere in the Mile End Road."

"Ah! poor Roddy!" he sighed. "His was, indeed, a sad end. That such a good, honest, upright fellow should have been murdered like that was truly a most melancholy circumstance."

"Murdered!" I exclaimed. "How do you know he was murdered?"

There had been no suggestion in the papers of foul play, therefore my friend's declaration was extremely remarkable.

"I know the truth!" he answered, very gravely.

"What do you mean?" I exclaimed, starting forward quickly. "Are you actually aware of the cause of poor Roddy's death? Tell me."

"No, Clifton," he responded, shaking his head, as rising he stood determinedly before me, his brows knit in a thoughtful attitude. "A confession made to me by one who seeks the forgiveness of God I may not divulge. Remember," he added in a firm voice, "remember that I am a clergyman; and confidences reposed in me I must not abuse. Therefore do not seek the truth from me. My lips are sealed."

Chapter Eleven.
Purely Confidential.

JACK YELVERTON'S DECLARATION HELD me dumb. He knew the truth, yet could not divulge, because any confession made to him by one who sought spiritual guidance was sacred.

I pressed him to tell me something which might give me a clue to the truth, but he only grew additionally grave, and answered—

"Roddy was my friend, as well as yours, Clifton. If it were possible, don't you think that I would bring the guilty to punishment? Ah! don't speak of it," he sighed. "In this affair I've suffered enough. If you knew how the possession of this secret oppresses me, you would be silent on that sad topic always."

I said nothing. His face had grown haggard and drawn, and I could see that his conscience was torn by a tumult of emotions.

It was certainly extraordinary, I reflected, as I smoked on in silence, while he stood leaning against the mantel-shelf with his eyes fixed upon the opposite wall. That day I had again met after years of separation this man who had once been among my best friends, and he was actually in possession of the secret which I had been longing through those winter months to learn—the secret of the tragic death of poor Roddy Morgan.

But he was a clergyman. Had he been a member of any other profession he might, in the interests of justice, betray the murderer—for there was no doubt now that Roddy had been murdered—but he was a servant of his Master, and words spoken in confidence into his ear by the penitent were as the secrets of the Roman Catholic confessional. From him I could hope for no word of the truth.

At last he spoke again, telling me that the real reason he had accepted a country curacy was because of this terrible secret ever oppressing him.

"But," he added quite resignedly, "it is, I suppose, a burden placed upon me as a test. Now I know the truth I feel as an accessory to the crime; but to divulge would be to break faith with both God and man."

His words admitted of no argument. I sat silent, oppressed, smoking and thinking. Then at length I rose to go.

"We are friends still, Clifton," he said, as he gripped my hand warmly. "But you understand my position, don't you?"

"Yes," I answered. "That you cannot speak is plain. Good night," and I went forth into the quiet village street where the only light came from the cottage windows here and there. The good people of Duddington go to bed early and rise with the dawn, therefore there was little light to guide my steps down the hill and up the road to the Hall. Nothing stirred, and the only sound was the dismal howl of a distant sheep-dog.

During the fortnight that followed I saw plenty of the new curate. His manner had, however, changed, and he had grown the same merry, buoyant companion as he had been in our college days.

Into Duddington Jack Yelverton had come as a perfect revelation of the ways and manners of the Church. For the past twenty years the estimable rector had preached regularly once each Sunday, and been usually assisted by a puny, consumptive-looking youth, fresh from college; but the smart, clever, witty sermon from this ecclesiastical giant was electrifying. People talked of it for days afterwards, discussed the arguments he had put forward so boldly, and were compelled to admit that he was an earnest, righteous, and upright man.

He dined with us once or twice, afterwards taking a hand at whist; we cycled together over to Oundle by way of Newton and Fotheringhay; on another occasion we rode to Uppingham to visit a man who had been with us at Wadham and was now one of the masters at Uppingham School; and several times I drove him to Peterborough and to Stamford. Thus we were together a good deal, and the more I saw of him the more convinced I became that he was thoroughly earnest in his purpose, and that he had not adopted the Church from motives of gain, like so many men whose relatives are ecclesiastical dignitaries.

A letter I received one morning from Muriel caused me to decide upon a visit to town, and I left the same evening, returning once more to my chambers in Charing Cross Mansions. Next day being Sunday, I sent Simes, on my arrival, round to Madame Gabrielle's with a note inviting Muriel to call at eleven and go with me to spend the day at Hampton Court. I knew that she always liked a ramble in Bushey Park, for town-stifled as she was, it reminded her of Burleigh, the great demesne of the Cecils outside Stamford.

She accepted, and at eleven next morning Simes ushered her in. She was quietly dressed in black, the dash of bright cerise in her hat well suiting her complexion.

"Well," she said, putting forth her hand as she entered. "I really thought you had quite forgotten me. Your note last night gave me a great surprise."

"I suppose if the truth were known you were engaged for today, eh?" I asked mischievously, for I took a keen delight in chaffing her about her admirers.

"Well, you've pretty well guessed the truth," she laughed, blushing slightly as she took the chair I offered her.

"What is he this time—dark or fair?" I asked.

"Dark. A rather nice fellow-cashier in a bank in the City."

"And he takes you out often, I suppose?"

"Two or three times a week," she answered, quite frankly. "We go to a music-hall sometimes, or, if not, down to the Monico."

"The Monico!" I laughed, remembering how popular that restaurant was with shop-assistants and clerks. "Why always the Monico?"

"Ah!" she smiled. "We can't afford Frascati's, the Café Royal, or Yerrey's. We get a little life at the Monico at small cost, and it doesn't matter to us whether our neighbours wear tweeds or not. A man not in evening dress in the Café Royal, Verrey's, or Jimmy's is looked upon as an outsider; so we avoid those places."

"And you like him, eh?" I inquired, amused.

"As much as I like all the others," she responded with a light, irresponsible air, toying with the handle of her umbrella. "Life in London is frightfully dull if a girl has nobody to take her out. She can't go about alone as she can in the country, and girls in business are not very friendly towards each other. You've no idea how many jealousies exist among girls in shops."

"I suppose if a man goes to Madame Gabrielle's to buy a bonnet for a present, or something, you all think he ought to take notice of you?" I laughed.

"Of course," she replied. "But it's the travellers from the wholesale houses who are most sought after by the girls; first, because they are generally pretty well to do, and secondly, they often know of good 'cribs' of which they tell the girls who are their favourites, and give them a recommendation into the bargain."

"I always used to think that the shop-walker in the drapery places had a pretty lively time of it. Is that so?"

"They're always jealous of the travellers," she said. "The shop-walker fancies himself a lady-killer because he's trained to do the amiable to the customers, and he can get the girls in his department into awful hot water if he likes; therefore he doesn't care much for the good-looking town traveller, who comes in his brougham and has such a very gay and easy life of it. Girls in drapers' shops are compelled to keep in with the shop-walker, but they hate him because he's usually such a tyrant."

"Then you may thank your stars that you haven't a shop-walker," I laughed.

"But we've got old Mrs Rayne and the manager, who are both quite as nasty to us as any shop-walker could be," she protested quickly. "Rayne is constantly nagging at one or other of us if we don't effect a sale. And that's too bad, for, as you know, many ladies come in merely to look round and price the hats. They have no intention whatever of buying, and make lame excuses that the shape doesn't suit them, or that the colour is too gaudy. It isn't fair to us."

"Of course not," I said. "But forget all your business worries for today, and let's have a pleasant hour or two out in the country. There's a train from Waterloo at twelve; so we'll go to Teddington and walk across Bushey Park. Do you care for that?"

"Of course," she cried, delighted. "Why, it's fully ten or even eleven months since we were there last time. Do you remember, we went down last Chestnut Sunday? Weren't the trees in the avenue beautiful then?"

"Yes," I said, remembering the pleasant afternoon we had afterwards spent on the river. But it was now too early in the season for boating in comfort, therefore to wander about would, I knew, be far more enjoyable.

Therefore, we took a cab over to Waterloo, and travelling down to Teddington, lunched at the Clarence, and afterwards, in the bright spring sunshine, strolled up the avenue, where already the trees were bursting into leaf. There were but few people, for as yet the season was considered too early. On summer Sundays, when London is dusty and the streets of closed shops palpitate with heat, then crowds of workers come there by all sorts of conveyances to get fresh air and obtain sight of the cooling scenery. But in early spring it is too far afield. Yet there is no more beautiful spot within easy reach of London, and in the quietness of a bright spring day, when the grass is green, when everything is bursting into bud, and the birds are singing merrily as if thankful that winter has passed, I had always found it far more pleasant than in the hot days, when omnibuses tear wildly along the avenue, raising clouds of dust, when carts full of coarse-voiced gentlemen from the East shout loudly, and chaff those who are seated on the tops of the four-horsed 'buses, and when the public-houses are filled to overflowing by crowds of ever-thirsty *bona-fide* travellers.

In the warm sunshine, which reminded me of those perfect March days we had had on the Riviera, we wandered together across the Park, chatting merrily, she relating to me all the principal events of her toilsome life during the past six months, which comprised that period when the metropolis is at its worst, and when wet Sundays render the life of London's workers additionally dismal. In winter the life of the shop-assistant is truly a dreary, monotonous existence, working nearly half the day by artificial light in an atmosphere unhealthily warmed by one of those suffocating abominations called gas-stoves; and if Sunday happens to be inclement there is absolutely nothing to do save to wait for the opening of the big restaurants at six o'clock in the evening. To sit idle in a café and be choked with tobacco-smoke is all the recreation which shop-assistants in London can obtain if the Day of Rest be wet.

Truly the shop-assistant's life is an intensely dismal one. Knowing all this, I felt sorry for Muriel.

"Then the winter has been very dull," I observed, after she had been telling me of the miserable weather and her consequent inability to get out on Sundays.

"Yes," she answered. "I used to be envious when you wrote telling me of the sunshine and flowers you had on the Riviera. It must be a perfect Paradise. I should so like to go there and spend a winter."

"As far as natural beauties are concerned, the coast is almost as near Paradise as you can get on this earth," I said, laughing. "But Monte Carlo, although delightful, is far nearer an approach to the other place—the place which isn't often mentioned in polite society—in fact, somebody once said, and with a good deal of truth, that the door of the Casino was the entrance-gate to hell."

"I'd like to see the gambling-rooms just once," she said.

"You are best away from them," I answered. "The moral influence of the tables cannot fail to prove baneful."

"I was disappointed," she said, "when I heard you had left London without wishing me good-bye. You had never done so before. I called at your chambers, and Simes told me you had gone abroad. Surely you could have spared ten minutes to wish me farewell," she added reproachfully.

I glanced at her and saw a look of regret and disappointment upon her face. Yes, she was undeniably beautiful.

I told myself that I had always loved Muriel, that I loved her still.

Her eyes met mine, and I saw in their dark depths a deep and trusting love. Yet I was socially her superior, and had foolishly imagined that we could always remain friends without becoming lovers. When I reflected how years ago I used to chat with her in her father's shop, in the days when she was a hoydenish schoolgirl, and compared her then with what she was now, I saw her as a graceful, modest, and extremely beautiful woman, who possessed the refinement of speech and grace of carriage which many women in higher standings in life would have envied, and whom I knew was honest and upright, although practically alone and unprotected in that great world of London.

"You must forgive me," I said. "I ought to have seen you before I went away, but I left hurriedly with my sister and her husband. You know what a restless pair they are."

"Of course," she answered. "But you've been back in England several weeks. Mary Daffern wrote to me and said she had seen you driving in Stamford nearly three weeks ago."

"Yes," I replied. "I was sick of the eternal rounds of Nice and Monte Carlo, so travelled straight to Tixover without breaking my journey in town. But surely," I added, "it doesn't matter much if I don't see you for a month or two. It never has mattered."

Her eyes were fixed upon the ground, and I thought her lips trembled.

"Of course it does," she responded. "I like to know how and where you are. We are friends—indeed, you are the oldest friend I have in London."

"But you have your other admirers," I said. "Men who take you about, entertain you, flatter you, and all that sort of thing."

"Yes, yes," she answered hurriedly. "But you know I hate them all. I merely accept their invitations because it takes me out of the dreary groove in which my work lies. It's impossible for a woman to go about alone, and the attentions of men amuse me rather than gratify my natural woman's vanity."

She spoke sensibly, as few of her age would speak. Her parents had been honest, upright, God-fearing folk, and she had been taught to view life philosophically.

"But you have loved," I suggested. "You can't really tell me with truth that of all these men who have escorted you about of an evening and on Sundays there is not one for whom you have developed some feeling of affection."

She blushed and glanced up at me shyly.

"It really isn't fair to ask me that," she protested, flicking at the last year's leaves with the point of her umbrella. "A woman must have a heart like stone if she never experiences any feeling of love. If I replied in the negative I should only lie to you. That you know quite well."

"Then you have a lover, eh?" I exclaimed quickly, perhaps in a tone of ill-concealed regret.

"No," she responded, in a low, firm voice, "I have no lover." Then after a few moments' pause she inquired, "Why do you ask me that?"

"Because, Muriel," I said seriously, taking her hand, "because I desire to know the truth."

"Why?" she asked, looking at me in mingled amazement and alarm. "We are friends, it is true; but your friendship gives you no right to endeavour to learn the secret of my heart," and she gently withdrew her hand from my grasp.

I was silent, unable to reply to such an argument.

"And you love this man?" I said, in a rather hard voice.

But she merely shrugged her shoulders, and with a forced laugh answered—

"Oh, let's talk of something else. We are out to enjoy ourselves today, not to discuss each other's love affairs."

We had approached the Diana fountain, and she stood pensively beside it for a moment watching the shoal of lazy carp, some of which have lived in that pond for over a century.

"I do not wish to discuss my own affairs of the heart, Muriel," I burst forth passionately, as I stood beside her. "Yet, as one who holds you in esteem, who has ever striven for your welfare, I feel somehow that I ought to be still your confidant."

"You only wish to wring my secret from me because it amuses you," she protested, her eyes flashing resentfully. "You know that's the truth. When you have nothing better to do you bring me out, just because I'm company. If you had held me in esteem, as you declare you do, you would have at least wished me farewell before you went abroad for the winter."

This neglect had annoyed her, and in sudden pique she was reproaching me in a manner quite unusual to her. I had never before seen her assume so resentful an air.

"No," I responded, pained that she should thus charge me with amusing myself at leisure with her society, although when I reflected I was compelled to admit within myself that her words were the absolute truth. For several years I had merely treated her as a friend to be sought when I had no other person to dine with or accompany me out. Yes, of late, I had neglected Muriel sadly.

"I don't think you are quite fair," I said. "That I hold you in esteem you must have seen long, long ago, and the reason why I did not wish you farewell was because—well, because I was just then very much upset."

"You had met a woman whom you believed you loved," she said harshly. "It is useless to try and conceal the truth from me."

"I have not attempted to conceal anything," I responded, nevertheless starting at her mention of that woman who had been enveloped in such mystery, and who, after a few days' madness, had now so completely gone out of my life. How could she have known?

In answer she looked me straight in the face with her dark, fathomless eyes.

"You have told me nothing of your love," she exclaimed in a hoarse tone. "If you cannot trust me with your confidences as once you used to do, then we can no longer remain the fast friends we have been. We must drift apart. You have already shown that you fear to tell me of your fascination—a fascination that was so near to becoming fatal. You know nothing of Aline Cloud—of who or what she is—yet you love her blindly!" Her well-arched brows knit themselves, her face became at that instant pale and hard set, and she held her breath, as if a sudden determination had swept upon her.

She knew my secret, and I stood confused, unable to reply to those quick, impetuous words which had involuntarily escaped her.

Did she love me? I wondered. Had jealousy alone prompted that speech? Or was she really aware of the truth concerning the blue-eyed woman whom I had adored for those few fleeting days, and whom I was now seeking to hunt down as a criminal?

Chapter Twelve.
"You! Of All Men!"

"No," I ADMITTED, "I was not aware who Aline Cloud was, nor did I know that you were acquainted with her."

She started. She had unwittingly betrayed herself.

"I—acquainted with her!" she cried in a voice of indignation. "You are mistaken."

"But you know her by repute," I said. "Tell me the truth about her."

She laughed, a light, nervous laugh, her eyes still fixed upon the water.

"You love her!" she exclaimed. "It is useless for me to say anything."

"No, no, Muriel," I cried. "I do not love her. How could I love her when I know nothing whatsoever of her? Why, I only saw her twice."

"But you were with her a sufficient length of time to declare your love."

How could she know? I wondered. Aline herself must have told her. She uttered a falsehood when she declared that she did not know the mysterious fair-faced woman whose power was so mysterious and unnatural.

I was puzzled.

"Well," I said at length, "I admit it. I admit that in a moment of mad ecstasy I made a foolish declaration of affection—an avowal which I have ever since regretted."

She gave me a pitying, scornful look, a glance which proved to me how fierce was her hatred of Aline.

"If you had told me of your fascination I might have been able to have explained the truth concerning her. But as you have thought fit to preserve your secret, no end can now be gained by the exposure of anything I know," she said, quite calmly.

"What do you know about her, Muriel?" I inquired, laying my hand upon her arm in all seriousness. "Tell me."

But she shook her head, rather sadly perhaps. The bright expression of happiness which had illuminated her countenance until that moment had died away and been replaced by a look of dull despair. The sun shone down upon her brightly, the birds were singing in the trees and all around was gladness, but she seemed troubled and oppressed as one heartbroken.

"No!" she answered in a low tone, her breast slowly heaving and falling. "If you have really escaped the enthralment it is enough. You may congratulate yourself."

"Why?"

"Merely because you have avoided the pitfall set in your path," she answered. "She was beautiful. It was because of her loveliness that you became entranced, was it not?"

"There is no necessity to conceal anything," I said.

"You speak the truth."

"And you had some illustrations of the evil influence which lay within her?" Muriel asked.

I recollected how my crucifix had been mysteriously reduced to ashes, and nodded in the affirmative, wondering whether I should ever succeed in obtaining knowledge of the truth which she evidently possessed.

"Yet you had the audacity to love her!" she laughed. "You thought that she—this woman whom all the world would hound down if they knew the true facts—could love you in return! It is amazing how a pretty face can lead the strongest-willed man to ruin."

I rather resented her attitude in thus interfering in my private affairs. That I admired her was true; yet I was not her lover, and she had no right to object to any of my actions.

"I cannot see that I have been so near ruin as you would make out," I exclaimed, philosophically. "An unrequited love is an incident in most men's lives."

"Ah! she spared you!" she cried. "If she had smitten you, you would have perished as swiftly as objects dissolve into ashes when she is present. At least she pitied you. And you were doubly fortunate."

"Yes," I said, reflecting upon her words, at the same time recollecting her mysterious connection with poor Roddy Morgan. "She was without doubt endowed with a power that was inexplicable."

"Inexplicable!" she echoed. "It was supernatural. Things withered at her touch."

"If I, your friend, am fortunate in my escape, would it not be but an act of friendship to explain to me all you know concerning her?"

Her dark, luminous eyes met mine in a long, earnest glance.

"No!" she answered, after a moment's reflection. "I have already explained. You have escaped; the incident is ended." And she added with a laugh, "Your neglect of me was, of course, fully justified in such circumstances."

"Now, that's unfair, Muriel," I exclaimed. "I had no intention of neglecting you, neither had I the slightest suspicion that you desired me to say farewell to you. Have you not told me that you have an admirer whom you could love? Surely that is sufficient. Love him, and we may always remain friends, as we now are."

"No!" she responded, with a dark look of foreboding. "We cannot remain friends longer. Our mutual confidence is shattered. We may be acquaintances, but nothing more."

I had not mentioned poor Roddy's death, for it was a subject so painful that I discussed it as little as possible. Was it not, however, likely that if I explained all the circumstances and told her my suspicions, her hatred might lead her to disclose some clue whereby I might trace Aline Cloud?

Her words had caused me considerable misgiving, for it was now entirely plain that, contrary to what I had confidently believed, namely, that she loved me, she in reality held me in contempt as weak and fickle, influenced by every pretty face or wayward glance.

I looked at her again. Yes, my eyes were not love-blinded now. She was absolutely bewitching in her beauty. For the first time I became aware that there was but one woman I really loved, and that it was Muriel.

"I regret that you should not consider me to be still worthy your confidence," I said, bending towards her seriously. "I have admitted everything, and have expressed regret. What more can I do?"

"Forget her!" she answered, with a quick petulance. "It is best to forget."

"Ah!" I sighed. "That is unfortunately impossible."

"Then you love her still!" she cried, turning upon me. "You love her!"

"No," I answered. "I do not love her, because—"

"Because she treated you shabbily, and left without giving you her address, eh? You see, I know all the circumstances."

"You are mistaken," I protested. "I do not love her because I entertain a well-founded if perhaps absurd suspicion."

"Suspicion! What do you suspect?" she asked quickly.

Then, linking my arm in hers, I walked on, and commencing at the beginning told her of that fateful day when I discovered the tragic death of poor Roddy, and the circumstances which, combined with Aline's own confession, seemed to point to her being his visitor, immediately prior to his death.

As she listened her face grew ashen, and she perceptibly trembled. A violent emotion shook her slight frame, and as I continued to relate my dismal story and piece together the evidence which I felt certain must some day connect Aline with the tragedy, I was dumbfounded to discern that which, in a single instant, changed the whole aspect of the situation.

Muriel was speechless. She was trembling with fear.

"And you really suspect that your friend was murdered?" she exclaimed at last in the voice of one preoccupied. "If that had been really so, wouldn't the doctors have known?"

"Medical evidence is not always reliable," I answered. "From what I have already explained it is proved conclusively that some one visited him in his valet's absence."

"Who called there, do you think?"

"Ah! I don't know," I answered. "That is what I am endeavouring to discover."

She gave a slight, almost imperceptible sigh. It was a sigh of relief!

Could it be true that my little friend held locked within her breast the secret of Roddy's tragic end? I glanced again at her face as she strolled by my side. Yes, her countenance was now pale and agitated, its aspect entirely changed from what it had been half an hour before.

"Why cannot you tell me something of Aline?" I asked quietly, after a long silence.

"Because I am as entirely ignorant of her as you are," she answered without hesitation. "All I know is that she is a strange person—a woman possessed of powers so marvellous as to appear almost supernatural. Indeed, she seems the very incarnation of the Evil One himself. It was because of that I was angry when I knew that her beauty had entranced you."

"But you are acquainted with her," I declared. "Your words prove that."

"No, I have had no dealings with her," she answered. "I should fear to have, lest I should fall beneath her evil influence."

"Then how did you know of my acquaintance with her?" I asked, noting how charming she was, and wondering within myself why during all the years that I had known her I had not discovered the true estimate of her beauty until that afternoon.

"The information was conveyed to me," she responded vaguely.

"And you believed that I had forgotten you, Muriel?" I said tenderly, in a voice of reproach.

"It is certain that you were held powerless under that spell which she can cast over men at will. You reposed in contentment beneath her fascination, and called it love."

"But it was not love," I hastened to assure her. "I admired her, it is true, but surely you do not think that I could love a woman who is thus under suspicion?"

"Had your friend ever spoken of her?" she inquired after a brief silence.

"No," I said. "Aline, however, admitted that she knew him, but strangely enough declared that he had committed suicide at Monte Carlo months before."

"Then what she said could not be correct," Muriel observed thoughtfully.

"I really don't know what to believe," I answered, bewildered. "Her words were so strange and her influence so subtle and extraordinary that sometimes I feel inclined to think that she was some supernatural and eminently beautiful being who, having wrought in the world the evil which was allotted as her work, has vanished, leaving no more trace than a ray of light in space."

"Others who have known her have held similar opinions," my pretty companion said. "Yet she was apparently of flesh and blood like all of us. At any rate, she ate and drank and slept and spoke like every other human being, and certainly her loves and her hatreds were just as intense as those of any one of us."

"But her touch was deadly," I said. "As a magician is able to change things, so at her will certain objects dissolved in air, leaving only a handful of ashes behind. In her soft, white hand was a power for the working of evil which was irresistible, an influence which was nothing short of demoniacal."

Muriel held her breath, her eyes cast upon the ground. There was a mysteriousness in her manner, such as I had never before noticed.

"You are right—quite right," she answered. "She was a woman of mystery."

"Cannot you, now that I have made explanation and told you the reason of my apparent neglect, tell me what you know of her?" I asked earnestly.

"I have no further knowledge," she assured me. "I know nothing of her personally."

But her words did not convince me when I remembered how, on explaining my suspicions regarding Aline's complicity in the crime, she had betrayed an abject fear.

"No," I said dubiously. "You are concealing something from me, Muriel."

"Concealing something!" she echoed, with a strange, hollow laugh. "I'm certain I'm not."

"Well," I exclaimed, rather impatiently, "to-day you have treated me, your oldest friend, very unfairly. You tell me that I merely consider you a convenient companion to be patronised when I have no other more congenial acquaintance at hand. That I deny. I may have neglected you," I went on in deep earnestness, as we halted for a moment beneath the great old trees, "but this neglect of late has been owing to the tragedy which has so filled my mind. I have set myself to trace out its author, and nothing shall deter me in my investigations."

She was blanched to the lips. I noticed how the returning colour died from her face again at my words, but continuing, said—

"We have been friends. Those who know of our friendship would refuse to believe the truth if it were told to them, so eager is the world to ridicule the idea of a purely platonic friendship between man and woman. Yet ours has, until now, been a firm friendship, without a thought of love, without a single affectionate word."

"That is the reason why I regret that it must now end," she answered, faltering, her voice half-choked with emotion.

"End! What do you mean?" I cried, dismayed.

"Ah, no!" she exclaimed, putting up both her hands, as if to shut me out from her gaze. "Don't let us discuss it further. It is sufficient that we can exchange no further confidences. It is best now that this friendship of ours should cease."

"You are annoyed that I should have preferred the society of that strange, mysterious woman to yours," I said. "Well, I regret—I shall always regret that we met—for she has only brought me grief, anxiety, and despair. Cannot you forgive me?"

"I have nothing to forgive," she answered blankly. "To have admired this woman was surely no offence against me?"

"But it was," I declared, grasping her hand against her will.

"Why?"

I held my breath and looked straight into her dark, luminous eyes. Then, in as firm a voice as I could summon, I said—

"Because—because, Muriel, I love you?"

"Love me!" she gasped, with a look of bewilderment. "No! No!"

"Yes," I went on, in mad impetuousness, "for years I have loved you, but feared to tell you, because you might regard my declaration as a mere foolish fancy on account of our positions, and impossible of realisation because of the probable opposition of my family. But I have now told you the truth, Muriel. I love you!"

And with my hands holding hers, I bent for the first time to kiss her lips. But in an instant she avoided me, and twisted her gloved fingers from my grasp.

"You must be mad!" she cried, with a glint of indignation in her eyes. "You must be mad to think that I could love you—of all men!"

Chapter Thirteen.
The Old Love and the New.

I DREW BACK CRUSHED and humiliated.

Her tone of withering scorn showed that she no longer looked upon me with favour.

"For years I have loved you, Muriel," I said in as calm a tone as I could, "but I have feared to speak until today. Now that I have declared the truth cannot you trust me?"

"No," she replied, shaking her head determinedly. "It is useless. I cannot love you."

"Then you have tried and failed?" I gasped in dismay, looking into her white, agitated face.

"Yes, I have tried," she answered after a pause.

"And do you doubt me?" I demanded quickly.

"Without mutual confidence there can be no love between us," she responded in a dismal tone.

"But why can you not trust me? Surely I have given you no great offence?" I said, bewildered at her strange attitude.

"I regret that you should have declared love to me, that's all," she answered, quite philosophically.

"Why? Is it such a very extraordinary proceeding?"

"Yes," she replied petulantly. "You know well that marriage is entirely out of the question. What would your friends say if you hinted at such a thing?"

"The opinion of my friends is nothing to me," I replied. "I am fortunately not dependent upon them. No. I feel sure that is not the reason of your answer. You have some secret reason. What is it, Muriel?"

"Have I not already told you that I am loved?"

"And you reciprocate this man's love?" I said harshly.

She made no response, but I saw in this silence an affirmative.

"Who is he?" I inquired quickly.

"A stranger."

"And you have confidence in him?"

Her eyes filled with tears, and her breast heaved and fell quickly.

"No, no," she cried at last. "Say no more. This subject is painful to both of us. Do not let us discuss it."

"But I love you," I again repeated. "I love you, Muriel!"

"Then forget me," she answered, in a low, hoarse voice. "Forget me; for we can in future be only acquaintances—not even friends."

"Then you have promised your lover to end your friendship with me. He is jealous of me!" I cried. "Come, speak the truth," I added harshly.

"I have spoken the truth," she responded, in a voice rather calmer than before.

"And you discard my love?" I said, in tones of bitter reproach.

"Yes," she said, "it is true. I discard your love. You have spoken, and I give you my answer straightforwardly, much as it pains me."

"But will you not reconsider?" I urged. "When you reflect that I love you, Muriel, better than all the world besides, that I will do all in my power to secure your happiness, that you shall be my sole thought night and day, will your heart not soften towards me? Will you never reflect that you treated me, your oldest friend, a little unfairly?"

"If in the future I reproach myself, I alone shall bear the pricks of conscience," she answered, with surprising calmness.

"And this, then, is your decision?"

"Yes," she replied, in a blank, monotonous voice. "I am honoured by your offer, but am compelled to decline it."

Her words fell as a blow upon me. I had been confident, from the many little services she had rendered me, the interest she had taken in the arrangement of my bachelor's quarters, and her eagerness always to please me, that she loved me. Yet her sudden, inexplicable desire to end our friendship shattered all my hopes. She loved another. It was my own fault, I told myself. I had neglected her too long, and it was but what I might have expected.

In silence we walked on, emerging at length into the high road, and turning into that well-known hostelry the Greyhound, where we had tea in that great room so well patronised by excursionists on Sundays. We talked but little, both our hearts being too full for words. Our utterances were mere trivialities, spoken in order that those around us should not remark upon our silence. It was a dismal meal, and I was glad when we emerged again and entered the well-kept gardens of Hampton Court, bright with their beds of old-world flowers.

I was never tired of wandering through that historic, time-mellowed, old pile, where the sparrows twitter in the quiet court-yards, the peacocks strut across the ancient gardens, and the crumbling sundials mark the time, as they have done daily through three centuries.

In my gloomy mood, however, I fear I answered her chatter abruptly in monosyllables. It struck me as strange that she could so quickly forget and become suddenly light-hearted. Indeed, it seemed as though she were glad that the ordeal she had feared had passed, and was delighted with her freedom.

The bright air of the riverside was fresh and exhilarating, but the sun soon went down, and when it grew chill we took train back to Waterloo, and drove to Frascati's, where we dined.

"And is this actually to be our last dinner together?" I asked, as the soup was brought, for I recollected the many snug little meals we had eaten together in times gone by, and how she had enjoyed them as a change after the eternal joints of beef or mutton as supplied to the assistants at Madame Gabrielle's.

"It must be," she sighed.

"And you do not regret?"

Her lips quivered, and she glanced at me without replying.

"There is some mystery in all this, Muriel," I said, bending across to her earnestly. "Why do you refuse to explain to me?"

"Because I cannot. If I could, I would."

"Then if after tonight we are to part," I went on bitterly, "mine will be a dismal future."

"You have your own world," she said. "You will quickly forget me among your gay friends, as you have already forgotten me times without number."

I could not bear her reproaches; her words cut me to the quick.

"No. I have never forgotten you," I protested quickly. "I shall never forget."

"Did you not utter those same words to that woman who fascinated you a few months ago?" she suggested with a slight curl of the lip.

"If I did, it was because I was beneath the spell of her beauty—a beauty so mysterious as to be almost supernatural," I answered. "I love you nevertheless," I added in a low tone, so that none should overhear. "I swear I do."

"It is useless," she exclaimed, with a frown of displeasure. "Further discussion of the subject will lead to no alteration of my decision. You know me well enough to be aware that if I am determined no argument will turn me from my purpose."

"But my future depends upon you, Muriel," I cried in despair. "Through years—ever since the old days in Stamford—I have admired you, and as time has progressed, and you have become more beautiful and more refined, my admiration has developed into a true and honest love. Will you never believe me?"

"No," she answered. "I can never believe you. Besides, we could never be happy, for our paths in life will lie in very different directions."

"That's all foolish sentiment," I exclaimed. "I have to ask permission of no one as to whom I may marry. Why will you not reconsider this decision of yours? You know well—you must have seen long, long ago—that I love you."

"I have already told you my intention," she responded with a frigidity of manner that again crushed all hope from my heart. "To-night must be our last night together. Afterwards we must remember one another only as acquaintances."

"No, no!" I protested. "Don't say that."

"It must be," she responded decisively. All argument appeared useless, so I remained silent.

It was nine o'clock before we left the restaurant, too early for her to return to Madame Gabrielle's, therefore at my invitation she accompanied me to my chambers, and sat with me in my sitting-room for a long time. So long had we been platonic friends that I could not bring myself to believe that that was really her farewell visit. She sat in the same chair in which Aline had sat on the first night when she had so strangely come into my life, and now again she chatted on merrily, as in the old days, inquiring after mutual friends in Stamford, and what changes had been effected in sleepy, lethargic Duddington. I had told her all the latest gossip of the place, when suddenly I observed—

"Just now everybody in the village is taken up with the new curate."

"No curate gets on well for very long with old Layton," she remarked. "Mr Farrar was a splendid preacher, and they said it was because the rector was jealous of his talents that he got rid of him."

"Yes, Farrar was a clever fellow, but Yelverton, the new man, is an awfully good chap. He was at college with me, and you may judge my astonishment when I met him, after years of separation, in my mother's drawing-room."

"What did you say his name was?" she inquired, with knit brows.

"Yelverton—Jack Yelverton," I answered.

"Yelverton!" She uttered the name in a strange voice, and seemed to shrink at its pronouncement.

"Yes. He's a thoroughly good fellow. He was in London—believes in social reform among the poor, and all that sort of thing. Do you know him?"

"I—well, yes. If it is the same man, I've heard of him. He did a lot of good down in the East End somewhere," she answered evasively.

"I suppose all the girls will be running after him," I laughed. "It's really extraordinary what effect a clerical collar has upon some girls; and mothers, too, for the matter of that."

"They think the Church a respectable profession, perhaps," she said, joining in my laughter.

"Well, if you're a clergyman you are not compelled to swindle people; a proceeding which nowadays is the essence of good business," I said. "The successful commercial man is the fellow who is able to screw the largest amount of profits out of his customers; the rich stockbroker is merely a lucky gambler; and the company promoter is but a liar whose ingenuity is such that by exaggeration he obtains money out of the public's pockets to float his bubble concerns. It is difficult indeed nowadays to find an honest man in trade, and the professions are not much better off. Medicine is but too often quackery; the law has long been synonymous with swindling; parliamentary Honours are too often the satisfying of unbounded egotism; and the profession of the Church is more often than not followed by men to whom a genteel profession is a necessity, whose capabilities are not sufficient to enable them to enter journalism or literature, and who profess in the pulpit what they don't practise in private life."

She laughed again.

"That's a sweeping condemnation," she declared. "But there's a great deal of truth in it. Trade is mostly dishonest, and the more clever the rogue the larger the fortune he amasses."

"Yes," I argued; "the man who has for years gained huge profits from the public—succeeded in hoodwinking them with some patent medicine, scented soap, or other commodity out of which he has made eighty per cent, profit—is put forward as the type of the successful business man. There is really no morality in trade in these days."

"And this Mr Yelverton is actually curate of Duddington," she said pensively. "Strange that he should go and bury himself down there, isn't it?"

"He hasn't been well," I said. "Work in the slums has upset his health. He's a good fellow. Not one of those who go in for the Church as an easy means of obtaining five or six hundred a year and a snug parsonage, but an earnest, devout man whose sole object is to do good among his fellow-creatures. Would that there were more of his sort about."

Thus we chatted on. It seemed as though she knew more of Yelverton than she would admit, and that she had learned with surprise of his whereabouts.

Only once again, when she rose to go, I spoke to her of the great sorrow at my heart, and then alone with her in the silence of my room I implored her to reciprocate my love.

She stood motionless, allowing her hand to rest in mine, while I reiterated my declaration of affection. But when I had finished she withdrew her hand firmly, and with a negative gesture burst into tears.

I saw how agitated she was, how she trembled when her white hands came into contact with mine.

She tried to escape me, but I would not release her. Loving her as I did, I was determined that she should not slip away from me. Surely, I urged, I, her oldest friend, had a right to her rather than a stranger whom she had only known a few brief weeks. She was unjust to me.

Suddenly, while I was imploring earnestly that she would hesitate before thus casting my love aside, the clock of St. Martin's struck the half-hour.

She glanced at the clock upon the mantelpiece, exclaiming—

"See! It is half-past eleven! I must go at once. I shall be locked out now, as it is. I've been late so often recently. You know how strict our rules are."

"But tell me that I may hope, Muriel. Only tell me that I may hope."

"It is useless," she answered hastily, twisting free her hand, and re-arranging her veil at the mirror. "I have told you. Let me go."

"No, no! You shall not, unless you promise me. I love you, Muriel. You shall not pass out of my life like this."

"It will be midnight before I get back," she cried distressed. "I had no idea it was so late as this!"

"Your business matters not. To me your love is all—everything."

She stood erect before me, statuesque, queenly, looking upon me with her dark-brown eyes, in which I thought I detected a glance of pity. But it was only for an instant. Her face suddenly grew hard and set. There was a look of firm determination, which told me that my hope could never be realised; that she had spoken the truth; that she loved another.

"Good-bye," she said, in a voice half-choked with emotion, and as she put forth her hand I grasped it and pressed it to my lips.

"Good-bye, Muriel," I murmured, with a bitterness felt in the depths of my soul. "But may I not go with you to your door?"

"No," she responded, "I shall take a cab. Good-bye."

And as the tears again rose in her eyes she turned and went out.

I heard Simes saluting her a moment later, then the outer door closed, and I sat motionless, staring before me fixedly. I had, during that afternoon, awakened to the fact that I loved her; but it was, alas! too late. Another had supplanted me in her affections.

She had left me hopeless, crushed, grief-stricken, and desolate.

Next day passed drearily, but on the next I sent Simes along to Madame Gabrielle's with a note in which I asked Muriel to see me again, making an appointment to meet her at Frascati's that evening. "Let me see you once more," I wrote, "if for the last time. Do not refuse me, for I think always of you."

In half an hour my man returned, and by his face I knew that something unusual had occurred.

He had my note still in his hand.

"Well," I said inquiringly, "have you brought an answer?"

"Miss Moore is no longer there, sir," he answered, handing me back the note.

"Not there?" I exclaimed, surprised.

"No, sir. I saw the head saleswoman, and she told me that the young lady was not now in their employ."

"Not in their employ?" I echoed, starting up. "Has she left?"

"It appears, sir, that on Sunday night she broke one of the rules, which says that no assistant may be out after eleven o'clock. She arrived at midnight, and was yesterday morning instantly dismissed. They told me that she took her belongings and went away without scarcely uttering a word except to complain of the extremely harsh treatment she had received. The manager of the firm was, however, inexorable, for it appears that other assistants had constantly been breaking the rule, and only a week ago a serious warning was posted up in the dining-room. Miss Moore was therefore dismissed as an example to the others."

"It's infamous!" I cried. "Then no one knows where she now is?"

"No, sir. I made inquiries, but no one could tell me where I might probably find her. She was, they say, heartbroken at this treatment."

I said nothing, but taking the note, slowly tore it into tiny fragments.

The woman I loved so well was now cast upon the pitiless world of London, without employment, without friends, and probably without money. Yet where to look for her I knew not.

By her manner when we had parted, I felt confident that her natural pride would not allow her to seek my assistance. She would, I knew, suffer in silence alone rather than allow me to help her.

When I thought of the harshness of this firm she had served so diligently and well, I grew furious. It was unjust to discharge a girl instantly and cast her on the world in that manner. It was infamous.

Chapter Fourteen.
Jack Yelverton's Confession.

I WENT MYSELF NEXT morning and saw the manager of Madame Gabrielle, Limited, to demand an explanation. He was one of those frock-coated diviners of the depths of woman's mind—a person of polite deportment and address, who, although expressing extreme regret at having "to part with the young lady," nevertheless declared that it was impossible to carry on business if the rules were daily broken. The rules, he said, were framed in order that the establishment should be well conducted, and it was considered that eleven o'clock was quite late enough for any young female to be out in that neighbourhood.

I explained that it was entirely my fault, and that if I had known I would have called and apologised for her; but he merely raised his eyebrows and observed that the young lady had left, and the others had taken her summary dismissal as a salutary lesson. Inwardly I denounced him as a tyrannical taskmaster of the superior shop-walker class, and left with, I confess, very little good-feeling towards him. Muriel had long ago told me how on one occasion this man had attempted to kiss her, and she had smacked his face. He had now driven her out into the world at an instant's notice, merely because of the vengeful dislike which still rankled within him.

Several weeks passed. The June sun shone brightly in the London streets, giving promise of near holidays to those toiling millions who twice each day hurry across the Thames bridges to and from their labours, and whose only relaxation is a week at Margate or at Southend. But from me all desire for life and gaiety had departed.

Though evening after evening I sought Muriel, and also wrote to her relatives at Stamford in an endeavour to discover her whereabouts, yet all was in vain. She had disappeared entirely.

The thought struck me that on leaving Madame Gabrielle's she had perhaps immediately found another situation; but as the frock-coated manager had received no letter of inquiry about her that theory seemed scarcely feasible. More and more the circumstances puzzled me. When I reflected upon our conversation that Sunday afternoon in Bushey Park I was inclined to doubt her declaration that she knew nothing of the mysterious Aline. Again, her apparent fear and anxiety when I chanced to mention the death of poor Roddy was more than passing strange. That she had a minute knowledge of Aline's visits to me was quite plain, therefore what more natural than that she should be aware of the extraordinary acquaintance between Roddy and that woman whose touch consumed. Sometimes I was inclined to believe that she was in possession of the true circumstances of my friend's death; and at such moments the thought occurred to me that she, Muriel Moore, had been Roddy's female visitor, who had called in his valet's absence.

The thought was truly a startling one. Had she thus cast me aside because she feared me—because there was a terrible guilt upon her?

There was some inexplicable association between the fair-faced worker of evil, whom I knew as Aline Cloud, and this pure and honest woman whom I was ready to make my wife. Its nature was an enigma which drove me to despair in my constant efforts to solve it.

One morning, when in the depths of despair, I was sitting after breakfast idling over the newspaper, and wondering whether I could find Muriel by means of advertisement, Simes brought in a telegram, which summoned me at once to Tixover.

An hour later I left, and that afternoon arrived home to find that my father had been thrown from his horse, while riding towards Deene by a bridlepath, and was lying in a dangerous condition, with my old friend Dr Lewis, of Cliffe, and Dr Richardson, of Stamford, in attendance upon him. As may be imagined, my mother was in a state of terrible anxiety, and I at once telegraphed to my sister, who had left Beaulieu long before, and was now at Bournemouth. Next morning she arrived, but by that time my father had taken a turn for the better, and Dr Lewis, who was untiring in his attention, declared that the turning point was past and that he would recover. A good fellow was Lewis; a hardworking, careful, good-natured bachelor, who was known and respected throughout the whole countryside, because of his merry demeanour, the great pains he took with even the poorest, and the skill with which he treated one and all of his patients, from Countess to farm-labourer. Besides which, he was a remarkable whist player.

On the day of my arrival I feared the worst, but when I had been at Tixover for a day or two it was apparent that my father would recover, therefore all our spirits rose again, and one evening after dinner I went up to Mrs Walker's to have a smoke with Yelverton.

He greeted me with the cordiality of the old days at Wadham as I was ushered in, produced the inevitable whiskey from the cupboard, and we settled down to chat.

He related to me the principal local events of the past month, but with the air of one who was already tired of rusticating.

I remarked upon his apparent apathy, and in reply he said—

"I regret that I left London. All my interests were centred there. It was only my health which compelled me to give it up. But I suppose I shall go back some day," and he sighed and resumed the briar pipe he had been smoking when I entered.

On the table was a blotting-pad and some manuscript. He had tried that day to write his sermon, but was unable. He had been smoking and meditating instead.

"And as soon as you have got strong again you mean to leave us and go back to a London parish!" I exclaimed. "That's too bad. I hear you are getting on famously here."

"Getting on!" he repeated wearily. "Yes, and that's about all. My work lies in London. I'm not fitted for a country parson, because I can't be idle. I feel as if I must be always energetic; and too much energy on the part of a country curate generally causes his vicar annoyance. Many vicars think energy undignified."

"But, my dear fellow," I exclaimed, "if you're not well—and I see you're not well by your face and manner—why don't you take things easily? You need not kill yourself, surely! London seems to have a remarkable attraction for you. Surely life is much healthier here."

"Yes, you're right," he answered in a clear voice. "There is an attraction for me in London," and he looked into my face with a curious expression.

"An attraction outside your work?" I suggested. He hesitated. Then, suddenly, he answered—

"Yes. Why need I conceal it from you, Clifton? It is a woman."

"And you are in love?" I exclaimed.

"Yes," he responded, in a low tone. "But, hush! Not so loud. No one must know it here."

"Of course not. If you wish, it shall remain a secret with me," I said. "Are you engaged?"

"Oh no!" he exclaimed. "I love her, but have not yet spoken. I will tell you the truth; then you can advise me," and he paused. At last, continuing, he said: "When I joined the Church I made a solemn vow to God of celibacy; not because I hated women, but because I considered that my work, if done conscientiously, as I intended to do it, should be my sole thought. Mine is perhaps a rather extreme view, but I cannot think that a man can work for his Master with that thoroughness if he has a woman to love and cherish as when he is a bachelor and alone. Some may say that woman's influence upon man is softening and humanising; but I hold that the man who is single can apply himself more devoutly to his fellow-creatures than he who has home ties and family affairs. Well, I took Holy Orders and set myself to work. I know I am not a brilliant preacher, nor have I that gift of self-advertisement which some men cultivate by lecturing with limelight views; but I do know that I strove to act as servant to the Master I had elected to serve, and the thanks of the grateful poor and the knowledge that more than one person had been brought to repentance by my words, were more than sufficient repayment for my efforts. Time went on, and I became deeply absorbed in my work in those foetid slums, until one day I chanced to meet a woman who in an instant entranced me by her beauty. She gave me but a passing glance, but her eyes kindled in my soul the fire of love. We men are, indeed, frail creatures, for in a moment all my good resolutions fell to the ground, and I felt myself devoted to her. We met again, and again. I admired her. I saw how beautiful she was, and then found myself thinking more of her than of the Master whom I was serving. True it is, as it is written, 'No man can serve two masters,'" and he sighed heavily, and sat dejected, his chin upon his breast.

"And then?" I inquired.

"Some months went by," he said. "She was aware how deeply I had the welfare of the poor in my parish at heart, and in order, I suppose, to please me, she enrolled herself as a helper. Instead of pleasing me, however, this action of hers caused me loathing. I saw that she had only done this in order to be nearer me; that her pretence of religious fervour was feigned, in order that her actions might not appear irregular to the outside world. Ours was a mutual love, yet no word of affection had ever passed our lips. But I could not bear to be a party to this masquerade. A woman who took up arduous duties like she did, merely because 'slumming,' as it was called, happened to be the fashionable craze of the moment, was in no way fitted to become the wife of one whose duty lay ever in the homes of the suffering and needy. I tried to shake off her acquaintance, to discourage her, to frighten her by exaggerated stories of infectious disease, but she would not listen. She was determined, she declared, 'to work for the Church,' and encouraged by the vicar, continued to do so. I strove to live down my increasing admiration for her, but could not. Time after time I treated her with unpardonable rudeness, but she merely smiled, and was more tenacious than ever, until at last, in sheer desperation, I resigned, and came here. Now you know all the truth, Clifton," he added, in a lower tone. "I came down here to escape her!"

"And yet you are ready to again return to London—you want to get back again," I observed.

"Ah! yes!" he sighed, the dark look still upon his face. "It is my test. I have to choose between love and duty."

"And you choose the latter?"

"I am trying to do so. With God's help I hope to succeed," he answered, in a hoarse voice. "If love proves too strong, then I fall back to the level from which I have striven to rise—the level of the ordinary man."

"But are you certain you were not mistaken in the object of the lady in joining the work in which you were engaged? May not she have been determined to become self-sacrificing in the holy cause, just as you were?"

"No," he answered very decisively, "I cannot believe it. There were facts which were suspicious."

"What kind of facts?"

"In various ways she betrayed her insincerity of purpose," he answered. "Her friends were wealthy, and the vicar was acute enough to see that if she were encouraged she would bring additional funds to the church. But the poor themselves, always quick to recognise true sincerity, very soon discerned that she visited them without having their welfare at heart, and consequently imposed upon her."

There was nothing sanctimonious or puritanical about Jack Yelverton. The words he uttered came direct from his faithful, honest heart.

"And yet you love her!" I remarked, amazed. "That's just it. My admiration of her grace and beauty ripened into love before I was aware of it. I struggled against it, but became overwhelmed. Had she not feigned sincerity and taken up the work that I was doing, I should, I believe, have proposed marriage to her. But her action in trying to appear solicitous after the welfare of the sick, when I knew that her thoughts were all of the world, caused me a revulsion of feeling which ended in my resignation and escape."

"Escape!" I echoed. "One would think that you had fled from some feared catastrophe."

"I did fear a catastrophe," he declared. "I feared that I should marry and become devoted to my wife, instead of to my Master. Ah! Clifton, mine is a strange, a very strange position. You may think my words extremely foolish, but you cannot understand the circumstances aright. If you did, you would see why I acted as I have done."

"You acted quite wisely, I think," said I. "None could blame you for seeking a country curacy in such circumstances. To be thus run after by a woman is positively sickening."

"Ah, there you are mistaken!" he exclaimed quickly. "She didn't run after me. It was I who, attracted by her beauty, showed her by my actions that I loved her. From the first it was my own fault entirely. I have only myself to reproach."

"But you cannot actually reproach yourself, if you are still fond of her."

"Fond of her? I adore her!" he cried. "I only wish I did not. Have I not told you how I've fought against this feeling? Yet what's the use of striving against the deepest and most overwhelming passion in the world?"

"Could you not be happy with her, and yet live as upright, honest, and holy a life as you now do?" I suggested. "Does not the holy proverb say that a man who takes a wife obtains favour with the Lord?"

"Yes," he answered. "But as I have explained, it is easier for the man to devote himself to religious work when he is single than when he has a wife to occupy his thoughts. He must neglect the one or the other. Of that I am convinced. Besides, I have vowed to God to serve Him alone, and with His assistance I will do so. I will!" and his hands clenched themselves in the fierceness of his words.

Next day I drove my sister into Stamford, and having put up at that well-known old hostelry, the George, she went to do some shopping while I sauntered forth determined to make what inquiries I could of Muriel's whereabouts. All her relatives were in ignorance. One of them, an aunt, had received a brief note saying that she had left Madame Gabrielle's, and would send her new address. But she had not done so. From place to place I went, ever with the same question upon my lips, but ever receiving a similar reply. Muriel was utterly lost to all, as to me.

About six o'clock we set out to drive home, but the dull day had culminated in wet, and our journey was in the teeth of a tempestuous wind which drove the rain full into our faces, and made us both very uncomfortable. We had passed Worthorpe, and were halfway towards Colly Weston, on the high road to Duddington, when we approached a female figure in a black mackintosh cape, with difficulty holding her umbrella in the boisterous wind. She was walking towards Stamford, and my sister catching sight of her as we rapidly approached, said—

"I hope that woman is enjoying it."

It was already half dark, and the road was ankle-deep in mud, yet she strode on determinedly, heedless of the rough weather, and bent upon reaching the town before night fell entirely. At that part of the road it is flat and open—straight across a highway cut years ago through the Rockingham forest, which covered that part of the country, but the land is now divested of trees and cultivated.

Her face was set straight in the direction of Stamford, and with her umbrella held down firmly she did not notice our approach until just as we passed and our high wheels spattered her with mud. She drew her umbrella aside in surprise and looked up.

In an instant we had left her behind, but in that brief space of time I recognised her.

There could be no mistaking that face. It was a countenance which, once seen, rivetted itself upon the memory for ever because of its wondrous loveliness.

It was Aline Cloud.

Quickly I glanced back, but it was evident that with my hat drawn down over my eyes, and my collar turned up I was sufficiently disguised to escape recognition. She did not turn, but trudged on through the mud towards the town far across the valley, where the distant lights were already beginning to glimmer.

I was utterly mystified; and the more so when, a quarter of an hour later, just as we turned the sharp corner to descend the hill into Duddington, we overtook and wished good evening to Jack Yelverton, who was striding along in our direction.

He started suddenly, laughed nervously when I hailed him, and then kept on his way.

Had he walked from Stamford, I wondered.

But next second the suspicion grew upon me that he had kept a secret appointment somewhere on that bleak open road, and that the person he had met was Aline, the Woman of Evil.

Chapter Fifteen.
A Strange Assertion.

THE LOOK OF COMBINED alarm and surprise which Jack's face betrayed was sufficient to convince me of the truth. Aline was the woman from whom he had fled; and she had visited him secretly. She had, it was apparent, discovered his whereabouts, and rather than excite gossip by coming to call upon him in the village, had met him clandestinely at some point on the high road halfway between Stamford and Duddington.

Then I reflected upon all that he had told me on the previous night; of how fondly he loved her, and of the curious dread in which he held her. Were not my own experiences more extraordinary than those of mortal man? Were not the changes wrought in my rooms by her influence little short of miraculous?

Aline Cloud, although the most beautiful woman I had ever seen, possessed a potency for the working of evil that was appalling. When I thought of it I shuddered.

Perhaps Jack Yelverton had discovered this. Perhaps he, a clergyman, a worker in the holy cause, had found out what evil influences emanated from her, and on that account had held aloof. He had told me plainly that he had come there to escape her. Did not that prove that he had discovered, what I, too, had found out, that her influence was alluring, that in her hand she held the golden apple?

He had been entranced by her beauty, but fortunately her witchery had not been sufficient to allure him to his ruin. I remembered when, in a moment of madness, I had declared my love to her, how she had told me she could not reciprocate it. What more likely then, that she loved Jack Yelverton?

That night I sat alone thinking it all over in the small, old-fashioned sitting-room which had been my own den before I had left to live in London. What, perhaps, puzzled me most of all was the fact that Muriel possessed such intimate knowledge of Aline's actions and of my brief period of madness; and somehow I could not get rid of a vague feeling that she was aware of the truth concerning poor Roddy's sad end.

Oppressed by the knowledge of a terrible truth which he had sworn not to divulge, and hiding from a woman whom he feared, Jack Yelverton was in as strange a position as myself; therefore next day I called upon him to give him an opportunity of telling me how this woman had at last discovered him.

He, however, said nothing; and when I incidentally expressed my intention of returning to London, and a hope that his whereabouts would still remain a secret from the person whom he did not wish to meet, he merely smiled sadly, saying—

"Yes. I hope she won't discover me. If she does—well, I must move again. Should I disappear suddenly you will know the cause, old fellow."

These words caused me to doubt the truth of my surmise. His manner was as though he had not kept the appointment, as I had suspected, and indeed I had no absolute knowledge that Aline and this woman whom he held in fear were one and the same person. Thus I left him with my mind in a state of indecision and bewilderment.

I knew not what to think.

Through the close, stifling days of July and August I remained in London with but one object, namely, that of finding Muriel. She had disappeared completely, and with some object; for she had not only hidden herself from me, but also from her nearest relatives.

Through those hot, dusty days, which, in former years, I had spent at Tixover, I pursued my inquiries in the various drapery establishments at Holloway, Peckham, Brixton, Kensington, and other shopping centres, but with no result. She had not written to any of the "young ladies" at Madame Gabrielle's, and none knew her whereabouts.

Yet the unexpected always happens. Just as I was about to give up my search and return to Tixover to get fresh air, for August and September are pleasant months in the Midlands, I chanced one afternoon to be crossing Ludgate Circus, from Ludgate Hill to Fleet Street, when I suddenly overtook a figure that seemed familiar.

I started, drew back in hesitation for a moment, and then approached and raised my hat.

It was Aline Cloud.

"You!" she gasped, paling slightly as she recognised me.

"Yes," I replied. "But I'm not so very formidable, am I?"

"No," she laughed, in an instant recovering her self-possession as she took my hand. "Only you startled me."

I remarked upon the lapse of time since we had met, and in response she answered—

"Yes. I've been away."

I recollected her visit to Stamford, but said nothing, resolving to mention it later. It was about four o'clock, and in order to chat to her I invited her to take tea. At first she was unwilling, making a couple of vague excuses and contradicting herself in her confusion; but as I hailed a cab and it drew up to the kerb she saw that all further effort to avoid me was unavailing, and accompanied me.

During the first few moments of our meeting she had apparently been inclined to treat me with some disdain, but by the time we arrived at my chambers she was laughing lightly, as though the encounter gave her gratification.

She was dressed with more style and taste than before. Her costume, of some thin, bluish-grey stuff, was made in a style which few London dressmakers could achieve, and its ornamentation, although daring, was nevertheless extremely tasteful, and suited her great beauty admirably.

As she stood in my sitting-room pulling off her gloves I thought that she seemed even more strikingly beautiful than on the first night we had met, for her perfectly-fitting dress showed off her well-rounded figure, and her cream gauzy veil, drawn tight beneath her pointed chin, added a softness to her face which rendered it bewitching.

As her bright eyes fell upon me and her full red lips parted in a smile, I could scarcely bring myself to believe that this was actually the woman whose evil influence was nothing short of supernatural, the woman whose mission in the world was to supplant evil for good, and whose every action was enveloped in mystery impenetrable.

She lifted her veil and placed her delicate nose to the large bowl of red roses on the table. In summer our gardener sent me a box twice weekly, and as she sniffed their odour, I remarked—

"They are from Tixover—my father's place. It's near Duddington, on the Northamptonshire border. Do you know that country?"

"No," she responded quickly. "But the flowers are delicious."

I saw that she had no intention of admitting her visit to Stamford. There was a strange, indescribable fascination about her. She raised her veil, and turning to the mirror re-arranged her hair coquettishly with both her hands. Then, as her deep blue eyes again fell upon me calmly I felt that they penetrated to my very soul. The sunlight struggling through the smoke-dimmed windows fell upon her, enveloping her head in a halo of golden light, while the flashing of gems caught my eyes, and I saw upon her fingers two magnificent rings, one of rubies and the other of diamonds.

On the first occasion we had met she had been dressed shabbily, without any display of artistic taste, while today she presented a graceful, lady-like appearance, her richness of costume being devoid of that loudness which too often detracts from a woman's natural *chic*.

Simes brought in the tea, and seated in my armchair she took her cup and laughed gaily to me as she sipped it, declaring that at the moment we had met she had been contemplating entering a tea-shop, for she could not exist without a cup at four o'clock. The majority of men in London can usually go from luncheon to dinner on a whiskey and soda, but I must confess myself fond of tea. Therefore we took it in company, laughing and chatting the while. She appeared perfectly at ease, and our conversation was that of old acquaintance, until, when Simes had gone, I looked straight into her face, and boldly said—

"Aline, tell me truthfully. Why did you deceive me so?"

She met my gaze with a strange, determined look, answering—

"Deceived you! I am not aware that I have done so!"

"You told me that you lived with Mrs Popejoy in Hampstead," I said.

"And it was the truth. When I told you that, I did live there."

That was so. She had spoken the truth, and my accusation was so unjust that I was compelled to mutter an apology.

"But many things have occurred since we last met," I went on. "One event especially has happened which has oppressed and utterly bewildered me."

"What was that?"

"My friend, Roddy Morgan, is dead."

"I am aware of that," she responded, her face in an instant deathly pale. Although she possessed powers which no other human being possessed, she nevertheless was now and then unable to control herself sufficiently to preserve a perfect calm. In this alone did she betray that she was, like myself, of the flesh. Yet when I reflected how things withered at her touch, and how objects dissolved as beneath a magician's wand, I had often been inclined to believe that she was the incarnation of the Evil One in the form of a beautiful woman.

It was this feeling which again crept upon me as I sat there in her presence, noting her extreme loveliness. I did not love her now. No; I held her rather in fear and hatred. Yet she was still the most strikingly beautiful woman in all the world.

"Then you know how my friend died?" I said, in a rather meaning voice.

"It was in the newspapers," she responded. "I saw by them that you gave evidence."

I nodded in the affirmative, then said—

"You were here on that fatal morning, and you then told me a fact which has puzzled me ever since, namely, that my poor friend committed suicide at Monte Carlo months before. Do you not think you were mistaken, when you recollect that he died only half an hour after you left me?"

"What I told you was the truth," she replied. "I was present when he took his own life."

"At Monte Carlo?"

"At Monte Carlo!"

"Well, how do you account for the fact that for six or seven months afterwards he was here, in London, occupying his seat in the House of Commons, and mixing with his friends, when, if what you say is truth, he was then lying in a grave in the suicides' cemetery at La Turbie?"

"I do not attempt to reason," she responded, in a voice which sounded so strange that it appeared far distant, while the cup she still held was shaken by a slight tremor. "I only tell you the true facts. It was myself who identified your friend, and gave his name to the Administration of the Casino."

"And you say he killed himself because he lost everything?"

"That is what I surmise. Those who have good fortune at the tables do not generally seek the last extremity."

"But I knew nothing of his visit there. Even his man was in ignorance," I said. "I cannot help thinking that there must be some mistake. It must have been a man who resembled him."

"I know that he went to the Riviera secretly."

"Why?"

"Because he had devised some system which, like many others before him, he felt certain must result in large winnings, and he did not tell his friends his intentions lest they might jeer at him. He went; he lost; and he killed himself!"

"But he lived in London afterwards!" I protested. "I saw him dozens of times—dined with him, played billiards with him, and was visited here by him. He could not possibly have been dead at the time!"

"But he was dead!" she declared. "Strange though it may seem, I am ready to swear in any court of law that I was present when Roderick Morgan, the member for South-West Sussex, committed suicide in the Salle Mauresque at Monte Carlo. That fact can no doubt be established in two ways: first, by the register of deaths, and secondly, by exhumation of the body."

"But when Roddy was here in London, dining, smoking, and talking with me, how can I believe that he was already dead?"

"It was for a brief space that he came back to his own home," she responded, in that same far-away voice, turning her eyes full upon me. "And did not life leave him suddenly, in a manner which has since remained a mystery?"

"No," I answered determinedly, my mind fully made up. "Not altogether a mystery. The police have discovered many things."

"The police!" she gasped. "What have they discovered?"

"They do not generally tell the public the result of their investigations," I answered. "But they have found out that he received a visitor clandestinely half an hour before his death, and further, that he was murdered."

"Murdered!" she exclaimed, with an uneasy glance and stirring in her chair. "Do they suspect any one?"

"Yes," I replied. "They suspect his visitor; and they have discovered that this mysterious person who came to see him immediately before his death was a woman!"

Her lips compressed until they became white and bloodless, and the light died from her countenance. She tried to speak, but her tongue refused to utter sound, and she covered her confusion by placing her teacup upon the table.

"Have they found out who it was who called upon him?" she inquired at last, in a low, faltering voice.

"They have a strong suspicion," I said firmly. "And they are resolved that the one responsible for his death shall be brought to justice."

"There is no proof that he was murdered," she declared quickly.

"Neither is there any proof that he died from natural causes," I argued. Then I added, "Was it not strange, Aline, that you should actually have told me of my friend's death on the very morning that he died?"

"It was certainly a very remarkable coincidence," she faltered; after a pause adding: "If he has been murdered, as you suspect, I hope the police will not fail to discover the author of the crime."

"But you declared that Roddy was already dead!" I cried, dumbfounded.

"Certainly!" she answered. "I still maintain the truth of my statement."

"Then you do not believe he was murdered?"

She shrugged her shoulders without replying.

For an instant I gazed into those eyes which had once held me spell-bound, and said—

"The truth is already known to the police. Roddy Morgan was murdered by a woman, swiftly, silently, and in a manner which showed firm determination and devilish cunning. You may rest assured that she will not escape."

She started. Her face was blanched to the lips, and she sat before me rigid, open-mouthed, speechless.

Chapter Sixteen.
Rocks among Pebbles.

HER ATTITUDE CONVINCED ME of her guilt, yet what conclusive proof had I? None—absolutely none.

"Your photograph was found in his rooms. I found it myself," I said.

"Does that prove that I am untruthful?" she inquired, raising her eyebrows quickly.

I recollected the glove-button. But the gloves she wore were new ones, and all the buttons were intact.

There was a ring of truth in her denials, yet I was unconvinced. I saw in her answers careful evasion of my questions. First, I myself had found poor Roddy dead, and that he had committed suicide six months before seemed to me but a silly tale. Secondly, her strange actions were suspicious. Thirdly, her curious association with Muriel seemed coupled with the latter's disappearance, and her clandestine visit to Jack Yelverton intensified the mystery in its every detail.

"Of course, the mere finding of a photograph is no proof that you had met Roddy for six months," I admitted, recollecting Ash's statement that he had never seen her visit his master.

"Then why suspect me?" she asked, in a tone of reproach.

"I have expressed no suspicion," I said, as calmly as I could. "My surprise and doubt are surely pardonable under these curious circumstances—are they not?"

"Certainly!" she responded. "Nevertheless during our acquaintance I have, you must admit, been as open with you as I have dared. You professed your love for me," she went on ruthlessly, "but I urged you to hesitate. Was I not frank with you when I told you plainly that we could never be lovers?"

I nodded in the affirmative, and sighed when I recollected my lost Muriel.

"Then why do you charge me with deception?" she asked, stretching out her tiny foot neat in its suède shoe, and contemplating it. She seemed nervous and hasty, yet determined to get to the bottom of my suspicions and so ascertain the depth of my knowledge of the truth.

Detecting this, I resolved to act with discretion and diplomacy. Only by the exercise of consummate tact could I solve this enigma.

"Deception!" I said. "You must admit that you are deceiving me by concealing the truth of who and what you are!"

"That is scarcely a polite speech," she observed, toying with the lorgnette suspended from her neck by a long chain of gold with turquoises set at intervals. "What do you suspect me to be?" and she laughed lightly.

"According to your own confession," I responded, "you are possessed of an influence which is baneful; you are a worker of mysterious evil; a woman whose contact is as venom, whose touch is blasting as fire!"

"No! no!" she cried, starting up wildly and putting out her hands in imploring attitude. "I have done you no wrong—I swear I have not! Spare me your reproaches. A guilt is upon me—a terrible guilt, I admit—but I have at least spared you. I warned you in time, and you escaped!"

"Then you are guilty!" I cried quickly, half-surprised at her sudden confession. But, turning her eyes upon me as she stood, she answered—

"Yes, I am guilty of a deadly sin—a sin that is terrible, awful, and unforgivable before God—yet, it is not what you suspect. I swear I had no hand in the death of your friend."

"But you can reveal the truth to me!" I cried. "You shall tell me!" I added fiercely, as I approached her.

"No," she panted, drawing back, "it is impossible. I—I cannot."

She was confused, pale and flushed by turns, and terribly agitated. I saw by her attitude she was not speaking the truth. I was convinced that, even then, she lied to me. Because of that I grew furious.

"If you were innocent you would not fear to explain all you know," I cried in anger. "In every detail you attempt to baffle me, but you shall do so no longer."

She smiled a strange, tantalising smile, and leaning against the edge of the table assumed an easy attitude.

"Is it not the truth that you are a mystery to every one?" I went on heedlessly, at that instant recollecting the conversation between herself and the stranger in Hyde Park. "Is it not the truth that your character is such that, if the people of London knew its true estimate, you would be mobbed and torn limb from limb?"

She started, glaring at me quickly in fear.

"This denunciation is very amusing," she said, with a forced laugh.

"Amusing!" I cried. "I have not forgotten how your presence here had the effect of reducing sacred objects to ashes; I have not forgotten your own confession to me that you were a worker of iniquity, a woman endowed with an irresistible devastating force—the force of hell itself!"

"And even though I confessed to you, you now charge me with deception," she answered in a strained tone. "You offered me your love, but I was self-denying, and urged you to forget me and love Muriel Moore, who was as pure and upright as I am wanton and sinful. Did you take my advice?"

"Yes," I answered, a trifle more calmly. "But she is now lost to me."

"I am aware of that," she responded. "You tarried too long ere you declared your affection."

"Then you know her whereabouts?" I cried eagerly. "Tell me."

But she shook her head, answering—

"No, we are no longer friends after this denunciation you have today uttered. You suspect me of being a murderess; therefore I leave you to assist yourself."

"Do you actually know where she is and refuse to tell me?" I cried.

"Certainly," she responded. "There is no reason why her happiness should be again disturbed."

In an instant a fierce vengeance swept through my brain. This woman was of the flesh, for she stood there before me, her beauty heightened by the flush that had risen to her cheeks, her pale lips quivering with an uncontrollable anxiety which had taken possession of her, yet she was more cruel, more relentless, more ingenious in the working of evil, more resistless and invincible in her diabolical power, than any other person on the earth. All the strength, all the influence, all the ruling power possessed by Satan himself was centred within her.

I looked at the evil light in her eyes. She was, indeed, the incarnation of the Evil One.

"You hold the secret of Muriel's hiding-place and refuse to tell me; you openly defy me; therefore I am at liberty to act in whatever manner pleases me—am I not?"

"Certainly," she answered, slowly twisting her rings around her finger.

"Then listen," I said. "You told me once that you could not love me because you loved another. You spoke the truth, for since then that fact has been proved. Some time ago a man, honest and upright, who on account of his religious convictions had resolved to give himself up to labour in the interests of the poor, accepted a curacy in a poor London parish. He worked there, striving night and day, denying himself rest and the comforts he could well afford in order that the sufferings of a few might be alleviated. Into foul dens where people slept on mouldy mattresses upon the floor, where ofttimes a paraffin lamp was placed in the empty grate in place of a fire, and where hunger and dirt bred disease, this man penetrated and distributed food and money, endearing himself to those dregs of humanity, often the scum of the gaols, by his untiring efforts, his justice, and his kindness of heart. Men who were known to the police as desperate characters welcomed him and were tractable enough beneath his influence. He never sought to cram religion down their throats, for he knew that at first they would have none of it. So he went to work to first gain their hearts, and succeeded so completely that many a confession of crime was in the silence of those bare rooms whispered into his ear by one who was repentant."

I paused and glanced at her. Her arms had fallen to her sides; she was standing motionless as a statue.

"While pursuing this good work—work undertaken without any thought of the laudation of his fellow-men—there came into that man's life a woman. She came to tempt him from the path of righteousness, to dazzle his eyes with her beauty, and to absorb his love. He saw himself on the verge of a fatal fascination, an entrancement which would inevitably cause him to break his vow to God; and relinquishing his work for a time, he fled from her secretly. He wished to avoid her; for although he loved her, he knew that she had been sent into his life by the Tempter to rend and destroy him, for he, alas! knew too well that the evil influences in the world are far more potent than the good, and that the godly are as rocks among the pebbles of the sea."

I paused. Again our eyes met.

"And the rest?" she asked hoarsely, in a low voice.

"You know the rest, Aline," I said. "You know that the name of that man was John Yelverton, and that the woman of evil was yourself, Aline Cloud. You have no need to inquire of me."

"How did you know?" she gasped, trembling.

"That matters not," I replied, in as calm a tone as I could. "Suffice it to know that I have knowledge of the truth."

"And you know my lover?"

"He is one of my oldest friends," I answered. "He fled from you, but by your devilish ingenuity you discovered him and sought him out in the remote village where he had hidden himself. You travelled from London, and he was compelled to meet you clandestinely out upon the high road. By the evil spell you have cast upon him you are now hoping that he will return to London."

"And if I am?" she inquired, with a sudden boldness.

"If you are, then you may at once give up all hope that he will still remain your lover," I answered firmly. "When I have told him of the truth he will hate you with the same hatred in which he holds the Evil One."

"What, then, do you intend telling him?" she inquired.

"He is my friend, as Roddy Morgan was," I answered. "The latter died mysteriously under circumstances which were undoubtedly known to you, and I have resolved that John Yelverton shall not suffer at your hands."

"I do not intend that he should suffer!" she cried quickly. "I love him. I will be his helpmate, his adviser, his protector. I confess to you that I love him with as great an affection as I can love anything on earth."

"Did you not tell me once that even though you might love, your influence must nevertheless necessarily be that of evil?"

"Yes, yes, I know," she said. "The baneful power I possess is not of my own seeking. I suppress it so that it may not injure him."

"This mysterious power of yours injured poor Roddy. You cannot deny that," I cried.

She sighed, but made no answer. Her thin hands were clenched; she was desperate.

"Yelverton knows nothing of your inexplicable potency for the working of evil. But he must—he shall know."

"He will not believe you!" she cried defiantly. "You may tell him what you choose, but it cannot alter the love between us."

"Not if I prove that you were responsible for Roddy Morgan's death—that it was you who visited him during his valet's absence?"

In an instant she grew pale as death, and stood there quivering in fear. Her defiance had given place to abject terror, and she dared not utter a word lest she should betray herself. Holding her in suspicion, as I did, I was quick to note the slightest wavering, to detect the least fear as expressed in her flawlessly beautiful countenance.

"You may make whatever allegation you think fit," she responded, in a harsh tone. "It makes no difference. The man who loves me will not heed you."

"But he shall!" I cried, in anger. "I will not allow him to be victimised as poor Roddy was. Your very words betray you!" I burst forth again. "When you allege that he committed suicide six months before he died in London you lie!"

"I have spoken the truth," she answered, meeting my gaze with a calmness which seemed incredible. "Some day, perhaps, you will have proof."

"Why may not proof be given me now?" I demanded. "Why cannot you explain all, and end this mystery?"

"It is impossible."

"Impossible!" I cried. "Nonsense! You seek to conceal your evil deeds beneath a cloak of improbabilities, and fancy I am sufficiently credulous to believe them!"

"Surely heated argument is useless," she observed. "I love a man who is your friend, and you love a woman who is mine. Plainly speaking, our interests are identical, are they not? Your love is in hiding. She had a reason for fleeing from you, just as my lover's religious views caused him to endeavour to escape me. He knew me not, or he would not have endeavoured to hide himself from me. You, who know me better, are aware that from me there is no escape; that I spare not my enemies nor those who hate me. Before my touch men and things wither as grass cast into an oven."

"True, I love Muriel," I said. "She is in hiding, and you, if you will, can direct me to where she is." Aline, the mysterious handmaiden of evil, paused. Her full breast rose beneath her thin summer bodice and fell slowly, and for an instant her well-arched brows were knit as she thought deeply.

"Yes," she answered at length. "Your surmise is correct. I am aware where your love has concealed herself."

"Little escapes you," I observed, a strange feeling of terror creeping over me. "Sin is always more powerful than righteousness, and cunning more invincible than honesty of purpose. Why will you not impart to me the knowledge that I seek, and tell me where I may find Muriel? As you have very truly said, our interests are identical. I am ready to make any compact with you, in return for your assistance."

"Very well," she answered quickly, with a little undue eagerness, I thought. Then, fixing me again with her eyes, she said: "Once you gave yourself to me body and soul and implored me to love you. But I spurned you—not because I entertained any affection for you, but for the sake of the one woman who loved you—Muriel Moore."

"Then you knew Muriel?" I interrupted quickly, in an endeavour to at least clear up that single fact.

"No," she answered, "I did not know her. A reader of the heart, I was, however, aware that she was madly enamoured of you, therefore I was frank enough to urge you to reciprocate her love, and thus obtain felicity. Well, she has hidden herself from you, but you shall find her on one condition—namely, that you render yourself passive in my hands—that you give yourself entirely to me."

"What do you mean?" I gasped, holding back instinctively and glaring at her. "Are you the Devil himself that you should make this proposal which in the mediaeval legend Mephistopheles made to Faust?"

"My intentions are of no concern," she responded, in a strange voice like one speaking afar off. "Will you, or will you not accept my conditions?"

"But to give myself to you when I love another is impossible!" I protested.

"I make this demand not in any spirit of coquetry," she replied. "That you should be mine, body and soul, is necessary, in order that you should preserve the silence which is imperative."

"To put it plainly you desire, in return for the service you will render me, that I should utter no word to your lover of my suspicions?" I said, gradually grasping her meaning.

Again the glint of evil seemed to shine from those blue eyes, which changed their hue with every humour.

"Exactly," she answered, her slim fingers nervously twisting the golden chain of her lorgnette. "But you must become mine, to do as I bid and act entirely as I direct," she declared. "Unless you give me your word of honour to do this there can be no agreement between us. Remember that your silence will be for our mutual benefit, for I shall remain happy while you will gain the woman you love."

For a single moment only I hesitated. But one thought was in my mind, that of Muriel. At all costs I felt that I must discover her, for her disappearance had driven me to distraction. Never before had I known what it really was to love, or the blankness that falls upon a man when the woman he adores has suddenly gone out of his life. I may have been foolish, nay, I knew I was; nevertheless, in the sudden helplessness that was upon me, I turned and answered—

"I am ready to do as you wish."

Next instant I held my breath, and the perspiration broke forth upon my brow when I realised that my great love for Muriel had led me into an abyss of evil. Heedless of the dire consequences which must follow, I had flung myself into the toils of this mysterious woman whom I held in fear; a woman whose very touch was sacrilegious, and who was more fiendish than human in her delights and hates.

"Then it is agreed," she said in that strange voice which had several times impressed me so. "Henceforth you are mine, to do my bidding. Recollect that passive obedience is absolutely essential. If I command you will obey passively, without seeking to inquire the reason, without heed of the difference between good and evil. Do you agree to such conditions?" she inquired in deep earnestness.

"Yes," I responded, my mouth dry and parched. This speech of hers convinced me that she was possessed of some superhuman power which was as subtle as it was mysterious.

"Then having entered into the compact with me, first seek not to discover who or what I am. Secondly, say no word to my lover of the things you have seen or of your suspicions regarding me; and thirdly, rest confident that what

I have told you regarding your friend Morgan's suicide is the absolute truth. Seek not to argue," she went on, noticing my intention to interrupt; "remain in patience."

"But where shall I discover Muriel?"

She hesitated in thought.

"You wish to see her tonight—eh?" she inquired. Then, after a pause, she added: "Well, tonight if you go to Aldersgate Street Station, and remain in the booking-office, you will meet her there at nine o'clock."

"How do you know her movements so intimately?"

I asked in wonderment.

But she only smiled mysteriously. If it were the truth, as I now felt convinced, that she was possessor of a power supernatural, there was surely nothing strange in her knowledge of the actions of those beyond her range of vision. Had she not already told me that she was "a reader of hearts?"

Suddenly she glanced at the clock, declaring that it was time she went, drew on her gloves and re-arranged her veil.

As she stood ready to go I asked her for her address. But she only said that such knowledge was unnecessary, and if she wished to see me she would call.

Thus she left, and I stood again unmanned and undecided, just as I had been when she had left me on the last occasion, only I had now rendered myself helpless and passive in her hands.

I tried to shake off the gruesome thoughts which crept over me, but found myself unable. Already I seemed pervaded by a spirit of evil. The miasma of Hell was upon me.

That night I went eagerly forth to the Aldersgate Street Station of the Underground Railway. Time after time I passed through the booking-office, and out upon the long balcony whence the stairs lead down to the platform, until, almost on the stroke of nine, I caught sight of the woman I loved, neatly dressed, but a trifle worn and pale.

I dashed up to greet her, but next second drew back.

She was not alone. A man was with her, and in an instant I recognised him.

It was the thin, shabby-genteel man whom I had seen with Aline in the Park—the man who had urged her to commit some crime the reason of which was a mystery.

She was laughing at some words her companion had uttered, and brushing past me unnoticed took his arm as she descended the stairs, worn slippery by the tramp of the million wearied feet.

I hesitated in amazement. This shabby scoundrel was her lover. She had preferred him to me. A great jealousy arose within me, and next moment I rushed after them down the stairs.

Chapter Seventeen.
After Business Hours.

ALMOST AT THE SAME instant a train emerged from the tunnel and stopped at the platform. Following close behind Muriel and her companion, unnoticed among the crowd of foot-passengers, I saw them enter a third-class compartment; therefore in order to discover my love's hiding-place, I sprang into another compartment a little farther off.

At King's Cross they alighted, and it suddenly occurred me that the woman whom Ash had been sent by his master to meet at the Great Northern terminus might have been Muriel herself.

The pair ascended to the street, and after standing on the kerb for a few moments entered a tram car, while I climbed on top. I had been careful that Muriel should not detect me, and now felt a certain amount of satisfaction in tracking her to her abode, although I confess to a fierce jealousy of this shabby, miserable specimen of manhood who accompanied her. Up the Caledonian Road to the junction of Camden Road with Holloway Road they travelled, alighting in the latter road, and walking slowly along, still deep in earnest conversation, until they came to the row of shops owned by Spicer Brothers, a firm of drapers of that character known in the trade as a "cutting" house, or one who sold goods at the lowest possible price. It was, of course, closed at that hour, but its exterior was imposing, one of those huge establishments which of late years have sprung up in the various residential centres of London.

Before the private door a couple of over-dressed young men lounged, smoking cheap cigars, and within a watchman sat in a small box, like the stage-door keeper of a theatre.

Muriel and her lean cavalier paused for a moment, then they shook hands, and with a final word parted; he turned back City-wards, and she entered the door, receiving a rough, familiar greeting from the two caddish young assistants, who were not sufficiently polite to raise their hats to her.

I stood watching the man's disappearing figure, and hesitated. But even as I waited there I saw him emerge into the road and enter a passing tram. The reason I did not follow him was because I was too confounded in my feelings.

Muriel was my chief thought. I hated this man, and entertained no desire to seek further who or what he was. I knew him to be an associate of Aline. That was sufficient.

I noted the shop well, and the door at which my love had entered, then seeing that it was already ten o'clock, the hour when female shop-assistants are expected to be in, I turned reluctantly and took a cab back to my chambers.

At six o'clock next evening, I entered the establishment on a small pretext, and ascertained from one of the employés that they closed at seven. Therefore I smoked a cigar in the crowded saloon of the Nag's Head until that hour, when, together with a number of other loungers, I waited at the door from which the slaves of the counters and the workrooms, male and female, soon began to emerge, eager to breathe the fresh air after the weary hours in the stifling atmosphere, heavy with that peculiar odour of humanity and "goods" that ever pervades the cheap drapers'.

After waiting nearly half an hour Muriel at last came forth, dressed neatly in cotton blouse and dark skirt, with a large black hat. She went to the kerb, glanced up and down the broad thoroughfare, as if looking for an omnibus or tram, then, there being none in sight, she commenced to walk along the Holloway Road in the direction of the City.

For some distance I followed, then with beating heart I overtook her, and, raiding my hat, addressed her.

"You!" she gasped, halting suddenly, and looking into my face with terror.

"Yes, Muriel!" I answered gravely. "At last I have found you, though I have striven in vain all these months."

An expression of annoyance crossed her features, but next second a forced laugh escaped her.

"Why did you leave Madame's in the manner you did, without saying anything to me?" I inquired, as I walked on at her side.

"I did not leave of my own accord," she replied. "I was discharged because you kept me late, and I broke the rules."

"But you did not send me your address," I exclaimed reproachfully.

"I had no object in doing so," she responded, in a wearied voice, as if the effort of speaking were too much for her.

"You acted cruelly—very cruelly," I said.

"No, I scarcely think that," she protested. "I told you quite plainly that we could be but mere acquaintances in future."

"But I cannot understand you," I cried, dismayed. "What have I done to deserve your contempt, Muriel?"

"Nothing," she responded coldly. "I do not hold you in contempt."

"But you love another!" I cried quickly, recollecting her companion of the previous night.

"And if I do," she answered, "it is only my own concern, I suppose."

"No!" I cried fiercely. "It is mine, for I alone love you truly and honestly. This man you love is a knave—a scoundrel—a—"

"How do you know him?" she interrupted, regarding me in wonder. "Have you seen us together?"

"Yes," I replied, bitterly. "Last night I saw you with him. How long will you scorn my affection and trample my love beneath your feet? Think, Muriel!" I implored; "think how dearly I love you. Tell me that this shall not continue always."

"I am perfectly happy," she answered, in a mechanical tone, not, however, without noticing my hesitation. "I have no desire to change."

"Happy!" I repeated blankly. "Are you then happy in that low-class drapery place, where you are compelled to dance attendance on the wives of city clerks, and are treated with contempt by them because they think it a sign of good breeding to show capriciousness, and give you all the unnecessary trouble possible? In their eyes—in the eyes of those around you—you are only a 'shop-girl,' but in mine, Muriel," I added, bending nearer her in deep earnestness, "you are a queen—a woman fitted to be my wife. Can you never love me? Will you never love me?"

"It is impossible!" she answered in faltering tones, walking slower as though she would return to escape me.

"Why impossible?"

"I am entirely happy as I am," she responded.

"Because this man with whom I saw you last night has declared his love for you," I cried fiercely. "You believe him, and thus cast me aside."

She drew a long breath, and her dark eyes were downcast.

"What has caused you to turn from me like this?" I demanded. "Through the years we have been acquainted, Muriel, I have admired you; I have watched your growth from an awkward schoolgirl into a graceful and beautiful woman; I alone know how you have suffered, and how bravely you have borne the buffets of adversity. I have therefore a right to love you, Muriel—a right to regard you as my own."

"No," she answered hoarsely, "you have no right. I am alone mistress of my own actions."

"Then you don't love me?" I exclaimed despairingly.

She shook her head, and her breast slowly heaved and fell. The foot-passengers hurrying past little dreamed that in that busy road I was making a declaration of my love.

"You have cast me aside merely because of this man!" I went on, a fierce anger of jealousy rising within me. "To love and to cherish you, to make you my wife and give you what comfort in life I can, is my sole object. I think of nothing else, dream of nothing else. You are my very life, Muriel," I said, bending again until my words fell in a whisper in her ear.

But she started back quickly as if my utterances had stung her, and panting said—

"Why do you still persist in speaking like this when I have already given you my answer? I cannot love you."

"Cannot!" I echoed blankly, all my hopes in an instant crushed. Then, determinedly, I added: "No, you shall not thrust me aside in this manner. The man who declares his love for you shall not snatch you thus from me!"

"But cannot you see that it is because of our long friendship I am determined not to deceive you. You have asked me a question, and I have given you a plain, straightforward answer."

"You are enamoured of this cunning, lank-haired individual around whom centres a mystery as great as that which envelops Aline Cloud," I said.

Her lips compressed, and I saw that mention of Aline's name caused her uneasiness, as it had before done. There were many people passing and repassing, therefore in that broad artery of London's ceaseless traffic our conversation was as private as though it had taken place in the silence of my own room.

"Does the mystery surrounding that woman still puzzle you?" she inquired, with a calmness which I knew was feigned. Her fond eyes, which once had shone upon me with their love-light, were cold and contemptuous.

"Puzzle me?" I repeated. "It has almost driven me to distraction. I verily believe she possesses the power of Satan himself."

"Yes," she agreed. "If the truth is ever known regarding her I anticipate a strange and startling revelation."

"Ah!" I exclaimed instantly. "You know more than you will tell. Why do you seek always to conceal the truth?"

"I know nothing," she protested. "Aline is your friend. Surely you may ascertain the truth from her?"

"But this lover of yours—this man who now occupies the place in your heart which I once hoped to occupy—who is he?"

She hesitated, and I saw that she intended still to fence with me. Of late all her woman's wit seemed to concentrate in the ingenious evasions of my questions in order to render my cross-examination fruitless.

"He is my lover, that is all."

"But what is he?" I asked.

"I have never inquired," she responded with affected carelessness.

"And you have actually accepted a strange man as your lover without first ascertaining who or what he is?" I said in amazement. "This is not like you, Muriel. You used to be so prudent when at Madame's that some of the girls laughed at you and called you prudish. Yet now you simply fling yourself helplessly in the arms of this rather odd-looking man without seeking to inquire anything about him."

"I know sufficient to be confident in him," she responded, with a girlish enthusiasm which at the moment struck me as silly.

"If you are confident in him it is quite plain that he reposes no confidence in you," I argued.

"Why?"

"Because he has told you nothing of himself."

"It matters not," she responded in enraptured voice. "Our love is itself a mutual confidence."

"And you are perfectly happy in this new situation of yours?"

"No," she answered, vainly endeavouring to restrain a sigh. "Not perfectly. I'm in the ribbon department, and the work is much harder and the hours longer than at Madame's. Besides, the rules are terribly strict; there are fines for everything, and scarcely any premiums. The shop-walkers are perfect tyrants over the girls, and the food is always the same—never a change."

"Yet you told me a short time ago that you were quite contented?" I said reproachfully.

"Well, so I am. There are many worse places in London, where the hours are even longer, and the girls have no place but their bedrooms in which to sit after business hours. The firm provides us with a comfortable room, I must admit, even if they only half feed us."

Long ago, in the early days of our friendship, when she used to sit and chat with me over tea in my chambers, she had explained how unvaried food was one of the chief causes of complaint among shop-assistants.

"But I can't bear to think that you are in such a place as that," I said. "Madame's was so much more genteel."

"Oh, don't think of me!" she responded with a brightness which I knew she did not really feel at heart.

"But I do," I said earnestly. "I do, Muriel; because I love you. Tell me now," I added, taking her arm. "Tell me why you have turned from me."

She was silent a moment, then in a faltering voice, replied—

"Because—because it was imperative. Because I knew that I did not love you."

"But will you never do so?" I asked in desperation. "Will you never give me hope? I am content to wait, only tell me that you will still remember me, and try to think of me with thoughts of love."

"To entertain vain hope is altogether useless," she answered philosophically.

"Then you actually love this man?" I inquired bitterly. "You have allowed him to worm himself into your heart by soft glances and softer speeches; to absorb your thoughts and to kiss your lips, without troubling to inquire if he is worthy of you, or if he is honest, manly, and upright? Why have you thus abandoned prudence?"

"I have not abandoned prudence," she answered, a trifle indignantly, at the same time extricating her arm from mine. "I should certainly do so were I to consent to become yours."

I started at the firmness of this response, looking at her in dismay.

She spoke as though she feared me!

"Then you have no trust in me?" I exclaimed despairingly. "For one simple little piece of negligence you have utterly abandoned me!"

"No!" she replied, in a voice low but firm. "You have spoken the truth. I cannot trust you, neither can I love you. Therefore let us part, and let us in future remain asunder."

"Ah, no!" I cried, imploringly. "Don't utter those cruel words, Muriel. You cannot really mean them. You know how fondly I love you."

We had arrived outside Highbury Station; and as I uttered these words she halted, and without response, held out her hand, saying in a cold tone—

"You must leave me now. I ask this favour of you."

"I cannot leave you," I panted in the wild desire which possessed me. "You must be mine, Muriel. Do not let this man draw you beneath his influence by his smooth words and studied politeness, for recollect who he is. You are aware—therefore I need not tell you."

"Who he is? What do you mean?"

"I mean that he is in no way fit to be your lover," I responded, my lover's flame of passion unallayed. "When you meet him, test him and watch if he really loves you. Recollect that your beauty, Muriel, is striking; and that personal beauty is often woman's deadliest enemy. I have, as you know, always sought to protect you from men who have flattered you merely because you possessed a pretty face. I loved you then, darling—I love you now!"

A sigh escaped her, but without a word she turned and left me ere I could prevent her, and even as I stood I saw her walk straight across to the station entrance, where she joined the lean, shabby man who had been awaiting her to keep an appointment.

Her eyes, quickened by love, had detected him ere he had noticed her, for he gave no glance in my direction, but lifting his shabby silk hat he grasped her hand, then walked on by her side, while I stood lonely and desolate, watching him disappear in the darkness with the woman I so fondly loved.

I, faint soul, had given myself helplessly into the evil hands of Aline for no purpose. All was in vain. I had been brought near to hope's fruition, but Muriel had forsaken me. She had told me plainly that in her heart no spark of affection remained.

I stood crushed—hopeless—the past an inexplicable mystery, the future a grey, barren sea of despair.

Chapter Eighteen.
The Chalice.

EARLY IN SEPTEMBER MY chambers were insufferably hot and dusty. In the road below the eternal turmoil was increased every hour, as the presses of the *Pall Mall Gazette* turned out their various editions, which were loaded into the carts by an army of shouting men and boys. The club was deserted; most men I knew were out of town, and I felt utterly lonely and miserable.

A fortnight before I had received a letter from Jack Yelverton, saying that he had resigned the curacy of Duddington, and was about to return at once to St. Peter's, Walworth, he having been appointed vicar of the parish. I replied congratulating him, and expressing a hope that he would call as soon as he returned to town. But I had seen nothing of him. Had the offer of a good living proved too tempting to him, I wondered; or had he resolved to abandon the curious theory he held regarding marriage? I was intensely anxious to ascertain the truth.

Since that afternoon when I had met Aline at Ludgate Circus and been induced to relinquish myself into her hands, I had seen nothing of her. She had refused me her address, and had not called. Yet, strange to relate, I had experienced some delusions unaccountable, for once or twice there seemed conjured in my vision vague scenes of terror and hideousness which held me in a kind of indefinite fear which was utterly indescribable. To attribute these experiences to Aline's influence was, of course, impossible. Yet the strangest fact was that in such moments there invariably arose, side by side with the woman I loved, the countenance of the woman of mystery distorted by hate until its hideousness appalled me.

I attributed these experiences to the disordered state of my mind and the constant tension consequent upon Muriel's waywardness; nevertheless, so remarkable were the powers possessed by Aline that I admit wondering whether the distressing visions which arose before me so vividly as to become almost hallucinations were actually due to the influence she possessed over me.

I am no believer in the so-called mesmeric power, in hypnotism, or any of the quack influences by which charlatans seek to impose upon the public, therefore I philosophically attributed the visions to severe mental strain; for I had read somewhere that such hallucinations were very often precursory of madness.

Fully a month passed, from the night when I had vainly implored Muriel to give me hope, until late one afternoon Simes ushered in Aline.

So changed was she that I rose and regarded her with speechless astonishment. Her face was thin and drawn, her cheeks hollow, her eyebrows twitching and nervous, while her clear, blue eyes themselves seemed to have lost all the brightness and cheerful light which had given such animation to her face. She was dressed in deep black, and wore no jewellery except a golden bracelet shaped as a snake, the sombreness of her costume heightening the deathlike refinement and pallor of her countenance.

As she stepped across to me quickly, and held out her gloved hand, I exclaimed concernedly—

"Why, what has occurred?"

"I have been ill," she answered vaguely, and she sank into a chair and placed her hand to her heart, panting for the exertion of walking had been too great for her.

"I'm exceedingly sorry," I replied. "I've been expecting you for several weeks. Why did you not leave your address with me last time?"

"A letter would not have found me," she answered. "When I pass from sight of my friends I pass beyond reach of their messages."

I drew forth a footstool for her, and noting how wild and strange was her manner, seated myself near her. The thought that she was insane came upon me, but I set aside such an idea as ridiculous. She was as sane as myself. There was nevertheless in her appearance an indescribable mysteriousness. She bore no resemblance to any other woman, so frail were her limbs, so thin and fine her features, so graceful all her movements. No illness could have imparted to her face that curious Sphinx-like look which it assumed when her countenance was not relaxed in conversing with me.

And her eyes. They were not the eyes of a person suffering from insanity. They possessed a bewitching fascination which was not human. Nay, it was Satanic.

I shuddered, as I always did when she were present. The touch of that slim hand covered by its neat, black glove was fatal. This visitor of mine was the Daughter of Evil; the woman of whom Muriel's lover had said, that the people of London would, if they knew the mysterious truth, rend her limb from limb!

She put up her flimsy veil and raised a tiny lace handkerchief to her face. From it was diffused a perfume of lilies—those flowers the odour of which is so essentially the scent of the death-chamber.

"Well?" she asked at last, in that curious, far-distant voice, which sounded so musical, yet so unusual. "And your love? Did you discover her, as I had said?"

"I did," I answered in sorrow. "But it is useless. Another has snatched her from me."

She knit her brows, regarding me with quick, genuine astonishment.

"Has she forgotten you?"

"Yes," I answered in despair. "My dream of felicity is over. She has cast me aside in favour of one who cannot love her as I have done."

"But she loves you!" my monitress exclaimed.

"All that is of the past," I replied. "She is now infatuated with this man who has recently come into her life. In this world of London she, calm, patient, trusting in the religious truth taught at her mother's knee, was as my beacon, guiding me upon the upward path which, alas! is so very hard to keep aright. But all is over, and," I added with a sigh, "the sun of my happiness has gone down ere I have reached the meridian of life."

"But what have you done to cause her to doubt you?" she asked in a voice more kindly than ever before.

"Nothing! Absolutely nothing!" I declared. "We have been friends through years, and knowing how pure, how honest, how upright she is, I am ready at this moment to make her my wife."

"Remember," she said, warningly, "you have position, while she is a mere shop-assistant, to whom your friends would probably take exception."

"It matters not," I exclaimed vehemently. "I love her. Is not that quite sufficient?"

"Quite!" she said. Then a silence fell between us.

Suddenly she looked up and inquired whether I knew this man who was now her lover.

"Only by sight," I answered. "I have no faith in him."

"Why?" she inquired eagerly.

"Because his face shows him to be cold and crafty, designing and relentless," I answered, recollecting how this woman now before me had once walked with him in the Park, and the curious influence he had apparently held over her.

She smiled bitterly, and her eyes for a moment flashed. I saw in them a glance of hatred.

"And you still love Muriel?" she inquired quite calmly, repressing in an instant the secret thoughts which were within her, whatever they might have been.

"I still love her," I admitted. "She is my life, my soul."

She hesitated, undecided whether to proceed. She was wavering. At length, with sudden resolve, she asked—

"And you still have confidence in me?"

"In what way?" I inquired, rather surprised.

"That I possess a power unknown to others," she answered, bending to me and speaking in a hoarse half-whisper. "That the power of evil is irresistible!"

"Certainly!" I answered, glaring at her, so strangely transformed her face appeared. That glitter of hate was again in her eyes, which had fixed themselves upon me, causing me to quiver beneath their deadly gaze.

"You believe what I have already confessed to you, here, in this room?" she went on. "You believe that I can work evil at will—an evil which is overwhelming?"

"Already I have had optical illustration of your extraordinary powers," I answered, dumbfounded, drawing back with a feeling something akin to terror. "No doubt whatever remains now in my mind. I believe, Aline, that within your human shape there dwells the Spirit of Evil, its hideousness hidden from the world beneath the beauty of your form and face."

"Then if you thus believe in me," she murmured, in a soft, crooning voice, as one speaking to a wayward child; "if you thus place your trust implicitly in me, I will give you further proof of my power, I will fulfil the compact made between us. Muriel shall love you?"

"And you will use your influence to secure my happiness?" I cried, jumping up enthusiastically.

"I will cause her to return to you," the strange woman answered. "The affection she entertains for this man shall wane and fade ere another day has passed. At my will she will hate him, and again love you."

"Truly, I believe your power to be irresistible," I observed with bowed head.

It was on my tongue to confess how I had watched her walking on that night in Hyde Park with the man whom Muriel loved, but fearing she might be wrathful that I had acted as eavesdropper, I held my secret.

She smiled with an air of gratification at my words.

"Keep faith with me," she answered, "and you shall ere long be afforded illustration of a volition which will amaze you. The Empire of Evil is great, and its ruler is absolute."

If she could direct the destinies of Muriel at will, compel her to abandon this man with whom she was infatuated, and cause her to return to me repentant, then that, indeed, would be proof conclusive that she were something more than human. I had implored of Muriel to give me hope, and had used upon her all the persuasive power at my command to induce her to think more kindly of me, yet without avail. An influence which would cause her to return to my side must be irresistible, and therefore an exercise of the all-ruling power of evil.

"And when may I expect her to relinquish this man?" I inquired eagerly.

She rose slowly, a strange, rather tragic-looking figure, so slim, pale-faced and fragile that she seemed almost as one from whom the flush of life had faded. Her brows contracted, her thin lips twitched, and the magnificent marquise ring of turquoises and diamonds upon her ungloved hand seemed to glitter with an iridescence that was dazzling.

She raised her hand with an imperious gesture, describing a semicircle, while I stood aghast watching her.

"I have commanded!" she said a moment later, in that curious far-off tone. "At this instant the change is effected. She no longer loves that man who came between you!"

"And she loves me?" I cried, incredible that she could at will effect such changes in the affections of any person. Truly her power was demoniacal.

"Yes," she answered. "She will be penitent."

"And she will come to me?"

"Wait in patience," the mysterious woman answered. "You must allow time for the thoughts of regret now arising within her to mature. When they have done so, then will she seek your forgiveness."

"Why have you done me this service, Aline?" I asked, utterly mystified. "It is a service which I can never repay."

"We are friends," she responded simply. "Not enemies."

Then for the first time the terrible thought flashed upon me that by making the agreement I had made with her I might be aiding the murderer of poor Roddy to escape. She had set a seal upon my lips.

Next day was Sunday, and as Jack Yelverton had not called upon me, and I did not know his address, I suddenly, early in the evening, resolved to go down to Walworth and see whether I could find him.

Having no idea where the church of St. Peter was situated, I took a cab through Newington to a point halfway along the Walworth Road, that great artery of Transpontine London, and there alighted. Some of those who read these lines may know that road, one of the busiest in the whole metropolis. Even on a Sunday evening, when the shops are closed, the traffic in that broad thoroughfare never ceases. From the overcrowded districts of Peckham and Camberwell, districts which within my own memory were semi-rural, this road is the main highway to the City, and while on week-days it is crowded with those hurrying thousands of daily workers who earn their bread beyond the river, on Sunday evenings those same workers take out their wives and families for a breath of air on Camberwell Green, Peckham Eye, or some other of those open spaces which have aptly been termed "the lungs of London." Only the worker knows the felicity of the Sunday rest. People of means and leisure may talk of the pleasure and brightness of the Continental Sunday, but for the worker in the great city it would be a sad day indeed if the present custom were altered. It is now a day of rest; and assuredly rest and relaxation are required in the ceaseless, frantic hurry of the life of London's toilers. The opening of places of amusement would be but the thin end of the wedge. It would be followed, as in France and Italy, by the opening of shops until noon, and later, most probably, by the half-day working of factories.

The leisure of the English Sunday was well illustrated in the Walworth Road, that centre of lower and middle-class life, on that evening, as I walked alone until, by direction, I entered a narrow, rather uninviting-looking turning, and proceeding some distance came to a large, old-fashioned church with pointed spire, surrounded by a spacious, disused burying-ground, where the gravestones were blackening. The bell, of peculiarly doleful tone, was quite in keeping with the character of the neighbourhood, for the houses in the vicinity were mostly one-storied, dingy abodes, little more than cottages, let out in floors, many of their inhabitants being costermongers and factory hands. The old church, cracked and smoke-blackened, was a substantial and imposing relic of bygone times. Once, as was shown by the blackened, rain-stained tombstones in God's-acre, the residents in that parish were well-to-do citizens, who had their rural residences in that quarter; but during the past half-century or so a poor, squalid parish had sprung up in the market gardens which surrounded it, one of those gloomy, miserable, mean, and dreary districts wherein life seems so full of sadness, and disease stalks hand-in-hand with direst poverty.

I was shown by the verger to a pew well in front, and found that the congregation was by no means a small one, comprising many who appeared to be tradespeople from the Walworth Road. Yet there was about the place a damp, mouldy smell, which rendered it a very depressing place of worship.

As I had hoped, my friend, Yelverton, conducted the service, and afterwards preached a striking sermon upon "Brotherliness," a discourse so brilliant that he held his not too educated congregation breathless in attention.

At length, when the Benediction had been pronounced, and the congregation rose to leave, I made my way into the vestry, where I found him taking off his surplice.

"Hulloa, Clifton!" he cried, welcoming me warmly, "so you've found me out, eh?"

"Yes," I answered. "Why haven't you called, as you promised?"

I simply uttered the first words that arose to my lips, for truth to tell, I had a moment before made a surprising and unexpected discovery. As I had risen from my seat I saw behind me a tall, thin lady in deep mourning, wearing a veil.

I could not see the face, but by her figure and her gait as she turned to make her way out I recognised her.

It was Aline Cloud. She had come there to listen to the preaching of the man she loved. Once again, then, had she come into the life of this man who had fled from her as from a temptress.

The verger went back into the church, and my friend pushed to the door in order that whoever remained should not witness us, then answered—

"I've been busy—terribly busy, my dear fellow. Forgive me."

"Of course," I answered. "But it was a surprise to me to hear that you had left Duddington, although, of course, we couldn't expect you to bury yourself down there altogether."

"Well, I had this offer," he answered, hanging up his surplice in the cupboard, "and being so much interested in the work here, I couldn't refuse."

"It seems a dismal place," I observed, "a terribly dismal place."

"Yes," he sighed. "There's more misery and poverty here than even in the East End. Here we have the deserving poor—the people who are too proud to throw themselves on the parish, yet they haven't a few coppers to get the bare necessaries of life with. If you came one round with me, Clifton, you'd witness scenes which would cause your heart to bleed. And this in London—the richest city in the world! While at the Café Royal or Jimmy's you will cheerfully give a couple or three pounds for a dinner with a friend, here, within fifty yards of this place, are people actually starving because they can't get a herring and a pennyworth of bread. Ah! you who have had no experience in the homes of these people can't know how despairing, how cheerless, is the life of the deserving poor."

"And you live here?" I asked. "You prefer this cramped, gloomy place to the fresh air and free life of the country? You would rather visit these overcrowded slums than the homely cottages of the agricultural labourer?"

"Certainly," he responded simply. "I entered the Church with the object of serving the Master, and I intend to do so."

"And the lady who was once a parish-worker here," I said, with some hesitancy. "Have you seen her?"

"Ah!" he sighed, as a dark shadow crossed his thoughtful brow, and his lips compressed. "You alone know my secret, old fellow, you alone are aware of the torment I am suffering."

"What torment?" I inquired, surprised.

At that instant, however, the old verger, a man who spoke with a pronounced South London drawl, interrupted by dashing in alarmed and pale-faced, saying—

"There's been a robbery, sir—an awful sacrilege!"

"Sacrilege!" echoed Yelverton, starting up.

"Yes, sir. The chalice you used this morning at Communion I put in the niche beside the organ, meaning to clean it tonight. I've always put it there these twelve years. But it's gone."

My friend went forth into the church, and I followed until we came to the niche which the old verger indicated.

There was no chalice there, but in its place only white ashes and a few pieces of metal melted out of all recognition.

All three of us stood gazing at the fused fragments of the sacramental cup, astonished and amazed.

Chapter Nineteen.
The Result of the Compact.

"THERE'S SOME DEVIL'S WORK been performed here!" gasped the newly-appointed vicar, turning over the ashes with trembling hands, while at the same time I, too, bent and examined the fused fragments of the Communion cup.

The recollection of the miraculous changes effected in my own room was fresh within my memory, and I stood amazed. The agency to which was due the melting of the chalice was still a mystery, but had I not seen Aline, the Woman of Evil, leave the church?

It was apparent that Yelverton had not detected her presence, or he would most probably have referred to it. He loved her with an all-absorbing love, yet, like myself, he seemed to hold her in some mysterious dread, the reason of which I always failed to discover. His theory that the clergy should not marry was, I believe, a mere cloak to hide his terror of her. This incident showed me that now he had come back to his old parish she haunted him as she had done in the past, sometimes unseen, and at others boldly greeting him. That night she had sat a few pews behind me listening to his brilliant discourse, veiled and unrecognised in the half-lighted church, and had escaped quickly, in order that none should be aware of her presence.

But I had caught a glimpse of her, and knowledge of her visit had been immediately followed by this astounding discovery. Her evil influence had once more asserted itself upon a sacred object and destroyed it.

Truly her power was Satanic. Yet she was so calm, so sweet, so eminently beautiful, that I did not wonder that he loved her. Indeed, I recollected how enthusiastically I once had fallen down and worshipped her.

And now had I not a compact with her? Had I not given myself over to her, body and soul, to become her puppet and her slave?

I shuddered when I recollected that hour of my foolishness. This Woman of Evil held me irrevocably in her power.

"How strange!" I exclaimed at last, when I had thoroughly examined the ashes. I would have told him of Aline's presence, but, with my lips sealed by my promise, I feared to utter a word, lest I might be stricken by her deadly hate, for she certainly was something more than human.

"Strange!" he cried. "It's marvellous. Feel! The ashes are quite warm! The heat required to melt and fuse a heavy vessel like that would be enormous. It couldn't have been done by any natural means."

"How, then, do you account for it?" I inquired quickly.

"I can't account for it," he answered in a hoarse voice, gazing about the darkened church, for the lights had been nearly all extinguished, and the place was weird and eerie. Then, with his lips compressed for a moment, he looked straight at me, saying in a strange, hard voice: "Clifton, such a change as this could not be effected by any human means. If this had happened in a Roman Catholic church, it would have been declared to be a miracle."

"A miracle wrought by the Evil One!" I said.

And he bowed his head, his face ashen, his hands still trembling.

"I cannot help thinking," he said after a pause, "that this is a bad augury for my ministry here. It is the first time I have, as vicar, administered the Sacrament, and the after result is in plain evidence before us—a result which absolutely staggers belief."

"Yes," I said pensively. "It is more than extraordinary. It is an enigma beyond solution; an actual problem of the supernatural."

"That the chalice should be thus profaned and desecrated by an invisible agency is a startling revelation indeed," he said. "A hellish influence must be at work somewhere, unless," and he paused, "unless we have been tricked by a mere magician's feat."

"But are not the ashes still hot?" I suggested. "See here!" and I took up some of the fused metal. "Is not this silver? There seems no doubt that the cup was actually consumed here in the spot where the verger placed it, and that it was consumed by an uncommonly fierce fire."

Without responding, he stood gazing blankly upon the ashes. I saw that his heart was torn by a thousand doubts and fears, and fell to wondering whether he had ever had any cause to suspect the woman he feared of possessing the power of destruction.

Again he glanced round the cavernous darkness of the silent church, and a shudder went through him.

"Let's go, my dear fellow," he said, endeavouring to steady himself. "I'm utterly unnerved tonight. Perhaps the efforts of my sermon have been a little too much for me. The doctor told me to avoid all undue excitement."

"Keep yourself quiet," I urged. "No doubt some explanation will be forthcoming very soon," I added, endeavouring to reassure him.

But he shook his head gloomily, answering—

"The Prince of this World is all-powerful. The maleficent spirit is with us always, and evil has fallen upon me, and upon my work."

"No, no!" I cried quickly. "You talk too hopelessly, my dear old chap. You're upset tonight. Tomorrow, after a rest, you'll be quite fit again. You've excited yourself in your sermon, and this is the reaction."

He shrugged his shoulders, and together we left the church. I walked with him across to his lodgings in a poorish-looking house in Liverpool Street, facing the disused burial-ground. He had not entered upon residence at the vicarage, for, as he explained to me, his wants were few, and he preferred furnished apartments to the worries of an establishment of his own. As I entered the small, rather close-smelling house, I could not help contrasting it with Mrs Walker's clean, homely cottage in Duddington, where the ivy covered the porch, and the hollyhocks grew so tall in the little front garden. He took me into his shabby little sitting-room, the window of which overlooked the churchyard, and I saw how terribly dreary was his abode.

I remarked that the place was scarcely so open and healthy as at Duddington, but as he sank into his chair exhausted, he answered simply—

"My work lies here among the poor, and it is my duty to live among them. Many men in London live away from their parishes because the locality happens to be a working-class one, but such men can never carry on their work well. To know the people, to obtain their confidence, and to be able to assist them, one must live among them, however dismal is the life, however dreary the constant outlook of bricks and mortar."

With this theory I was compelled to agree. Surely this man must be devout and God-fearing if he could give up the world, as he had done, to devote himself to the poor in such a locality, and live the dismal life of the people among whom his work lay.

Yet in his acquaintanceship with Aline there was some strange mystery. His hiding from her, and her clandestine visit to Duddington, were sufficient in themselves to show that their friendship had been strained, and his words, whenever he had spoken of her, were as though he held her in fear. Mystery surrounded her on every side.

I sat with my friend for a long time smoking with him in that dingy, cheerless room. Once only he referred to the curious phenomenon which had occurred in the church, and noticing that I had no desire to discuss it, he dropped the subject. He was enthusiastic over his work, telling me sad stories of the poverty existing there on every side, and lamenting that while London gave liberally to Mansion House Funds for the relief of foreigners, it gave so little to the deserving poor at home.

Suddenly, glancing at the clock, he rose, saying that he had a visit to make.

"It's late," I exclaimed, seeing that it was after ten o'clock.

"Not too late to do my duty," he answered.

Then we passed out, and in silence threaded our way back through the narrow alleys until we gained the Walworth Road, where we parted, after I had promised to call soon and see him again.

When he had left me, I turned once to look after him. His tall, athletic figure was disappearing in the darkness of the slums. Truly this man, who had been my old college chum, was a devoted servant of the Master.

Several days went by, during which I reflected a good deal upon the strange occurrence at St. Peter's, and the promise made me by Aline. Would Muriel return to me? Was the influence possessed by the Woman of Evil sufficient to cause her to abandon her newly-found lover and crave my forgiveness?

She had told me to possess myself in patience, and I, in obedience to her command, neither sought Muriel or wrote to her.

A week passed. It was Saturday evening. I had been dining early over at the club, and on entering my chambers with my latch-key about eight o'clock, having returned there before dropping in at the Alhambra, I perceived through the crack of the half-open door that some one was in my sitting-room.

I held my breath, scarcely believing my eyes. It was Muriel.

Slowly she rose to meet me with a majestic but rather tragic air, and without a word stretched forth her hand.

"Why, Muriel!" I cried gladly. "You're the very last person I expected!"

"I suppose so," she said, adding in a low, strained voice, "Close the door. I have come to speak with you."

I obeyed her; then, returning to her side, stood eager for her words. The enigmatical influence of Aline was upon her, for I saw that to her dark, brilliant eyes there had already returned that love-light which once had shone upon me, and noticed how her sweet, well-remembered voice trembled with an excitement which she strove vainly to conceal. Her dress was of grey stuff, plainly made as always, but her black hat with a touch of blue in it suited her well, and as she sat before me in the chair wherein the mysterious Temptress had sat, she seemed extremely graceful and more handsome than ever.

"You have, I suppose, almost forgotten me during this long separation, haven't you?" she faltered with abruptness, after some hesitation. Apparently she had carefully prepared some little diplomatic speech, but in the excitement of the moment all recollection of it had passed from her mind.

"Forgotten you, Muriel!" I echoed, gazing earnestly into her soft, beautiful eyes. "When we last met, did I not tell you that I should never forget?"

Her breast heaved and fell; her countenance grew troubled.

"Surely it is you who have forgotten me?" I said, with a touch of bitter reproach. "You have cast me aside in preference for another. Tell me what I have done that you should treat me thus?"

"Nothing!" she responded nervously, her grave eyes downcast.

"Then, why cannot you love me, Muriel?" I demanded, bending towards her in desperation.

"I—I'm foolish to have come here," she said, in sudden desperation, rising from her chair.

"Why foolish?" I asked. "Even though you may love another you are always welcome to my rooms as of old. I bear you no ill-will, Muriel," I said, not, however, without bitterness.

A silence fell. Again she sighed deeply, and then at last raising her fair face to mine, she exclaimed in an eager, trembling tone—

"Forgive me, Clifton! Forgive me! I have come here tonight to ask you to have pity upon me. I know how I have wronged you, but I have come to tell you that I still love you—to ask whether you consider me still worthy of your love?"

"Of course, darling!" I cried, springing forward, instantly placing my arm about her neck and imprinting a fond kiss upon her white brow. "Of course I love you," I repeated, enthusiastic in my newly-found contentment. "Since you have gone out of my life I have been sad and lonely indeed; and when I knew that you loved another all desire for life left me. I—"

"But I love you, Clifton," she cried, interrupting. "It was but a foolish passing fancy on my part to prefer that man to you who have always been my friend, who have always been so kind and so thoughtful on my behalf. I wronged you deeply, and have since repented it."

"The knowledge that you still love me, dearest, is sufficient. It gives me the completest satisfaction; it renders me the most happy man in all the world," and still retaining her hand I pressed it warmly to my lips.

"Then you forgive me?" she asked, with a seriousness that at such a moment struck me as curious.

"Forgive you? Certainly!" I answered. "This estrangement has tested the affection of both of us. We now know that it is impossible for us to live apart."

"Ah, yes!" she answered. "You are quite right. I cannot live without you. It is impossible. I have tried and have failed."

"Then in future you are mine, darling," I cried, in joyous ecstasy. "Let the past remain as a warning to us both. Not only were you inconstant, but I was also; therefore on my part there is nothing to forgive. Let happiness now be ours because we have both discovered that only in each other can we find that perfect love which to the pure and upright is as life itself."

For me the face of the world had changed in those moments. A new and brighter life had come to me.

"Yes," she answered in a low tone, which showed plainly how affected she was. And raising her full, ready lips to mine, she kissed me passionately, adding: "You are generous, indeed, Clifton. I feared and dreaded always that you had cast me aside as fickle and unworthy a thought."

"No, no!" I said, my arm around her protectingly. "Think no more of that. Don't let us remember the past, dearest, but look to a brighter future—a future when you will always be with me, my companion, my helpmate, my wife!"

There were tears in her dark eyes, tears of boundless joy and abundant happiness. She had come there half expecting a rebuff, yet had found me ready and eager to forgive; therefore, in a few moments her emotion overcame her, and she hid her tear-stained face in her hands.

The prophecy of the Woman of Evil had been fulfilled. Yet at what cost had I gained this felicity? At the cost of a guilty silence—a silence that shielded her from the exposure of some mysterious, unknown guilt.

Such thoughts I endeavoured to cast from me in the dreamy happiness of those felicitous moments. Yet as I held Muriel in my arms and kissed her pale, tear-stained cheeks, I could not help reflecting upon the veil of mystery which surrounded the woman whose inexplicable influence had caused my love to return to me. In my sudden happiness there still remained the dregs of bitterness—the strange death of the man who had been my most intimate friend, and the demoniacal power possessed by the woman to whom I had unconditionally bound myself in return for Muriel's love.

The words I uttered caused her to hesitate, to hold her breath, and look up at me with those dark, brilliant eyes which had so long ago held me beneath their spell. Again her hand trembled, again tears rose in her eyes, but at last, when I had repeated my sentence, she faltered a response.

It was but a single word, but it caused my heart to bound for joy, and in an instant raised me to the seventh heaven of delight. Her response from that moment bound us in closer relationship than before.

She had given me her promise to become my wife.

Chapter Twenty.
One Man's Hand.

IN THE HOUR THAT followed many were our mutual declarations, many were the kisses I imprinted upon those lips, with their true Cupid's bow, without which no woman's beauty is entirely perfect.

From her conversation I gathered that the assistants at the great shop in the Holloway Road were treated, as they often are, as mere machines, the employers having no more regard for their health or mental recreation than for the cash balls which roll along the inclined planes to the cash-desk. Life within that great series of shops was mere drudgery and slavery, the galling bonds of which only those who have had experience of it can fully appreciate.

"From the time we open till closing time we haven't a single moment's rest," she said, in reply to my question, "and with nearly eighty fines for breaking various rules, and a staff of tyrannical shop-walkers who are always either fining us or abusing us before the customers, things are utterly unbearable."

"Yes," I said, indignantly, "the tyrannies of shop life ought to be exposed."

"Indeed they ought," she agreed. "One of our rules fines us a shilling if after serving a customer we don't introduce at least two articles to her."

"People don't like things they don't want pushed under their noses," I said. "It always annoys me."

"Of course they don't," she agreed. "Again, if we're late, only five minutes, in the morning when we go in to dust, we're fined sixpence; if one of the shop-walkers owes any girl a grudge he will fine her a shilling for talking during business, and if she allows a customer to go out without buying anything and without calling his attention to it, she has to pay half-a-crown. People don't think when they enter a shop and are met by a suave man in frock-coat who hands them a chair and calls an assistant, that this very man is watching whether the unfortunate counter-slave will break any of the code of rules, so that the instant the customer has gone she may be fined, with an added warning that if a similar thing again occurs she will be dismissed."

"In no other trade would men and women conform to such rules," I exclaimed, for she had often told me of these things before. "Who takes the fines?"

"The firm, of course," she answered. "They're supposed to go towards the library; but the latter consists of only about fifty worn-out, tattered books which haven't been added to for the past three years."

"I don't wonder that such an existence should crush all life from you. It's enough to render any one old before their time, slaving away in that place from morning till night, without even sufficient time for your meals. But why are you a favourite?" I asked.

She looked at me for an instant, then dropped her eyes and remained silent.

"I scarcely know," she faltered at last, and I scented in her indecision an element of mystery.

"But you must be aware of the reason that you are not treated quite as harshly as the others."

"Well," she laughed, a slight flush mounting to her cheek, "it may be because of my friendliness towards the shop-walker."

"The shop-walker!" I exclaimed in surprise, not without some jealous resentment rising within me. "Why are you friendly towards him?"

"Because it is judicious not to offend him," she said. "One girl did, and within a week she was discharged."

"But such truckling to a greasy, oily-mouthed tailor's dummy is simply nauseating," I cried fiercely. "Do you mean to say that you actually have to smile and be amiable to this man—perhaps even to flirt with him—in order to save yourself from being driven to death?"

"Certainly!" she answered, quite frankly.

"And who is this man?" I inquired, perhaps a trifle harshly.

"The man with whom you saw me on that night when you followed me from Aldersgate Street," she responded.

"That tall, thin man!" I cried, amazed. "The man who was your lover!"

She nodded, and her eyes were again downcast.

I sat staring at her in amazement. I had never thought of that.

"What's his name?" I asked quickly.

"Henry Hibbert."

"And he is shop-walker at your place?"

"Certainly."

"Why didn't you tell me this before, when I asked you?" I inquired.

"Because I had no desire that you should sneer at me for walking out with a man of that kind," she responded. "But now that it is all past, I can fearlessly tell you the truth."

"But what made you take up with him?" I asked, eager now to at least penetrate some portion of the mystery, for I recollected that night in the Park, when I had overheard this man Hibbert's strange conversation with Aline.

"I really don't know what caused me to entertain any regard for him," she answered.

"How did it come about?"

"We were introduced one night in the Monico. I somehow thought him pleasant and well-mannered, and, I don't know how it was, but I found myself thinking always of him. We met several times, but then I did not know what he was. I had no idea that he was a shop-walker. It was because of my foolish infatuation, I suppose, that I cast aside your love. But from that moment my regret increased, until I could bear the separation no longer, and I came tonight to seek your forgiveness."

"But what knowledge of this man had you before that night in the café?" I inquired. "Who introduced you?"

"A girl friend. I knew nothing of him before, and have since come to the conclusion that she knew him but slightly."

"Then was he, at this time, engaged in the shop in the Holloway Road?" I asked, feeling that this fact should be at once cleared up.

"I think so."

"Are you absolutely certain?"

"No, I'm not. Why do you ask?"

"Because," I answered reflectively, "because it is strange that you should have taken an engagement at the very shop where he was employed."

"It was he who gave me the introduction there," she said. "Only when I got there and commenced work did I find to my surprise that the man who had interested himself on my behalf was actually the shop-walker. He saw the look of surprise upon my face, and laughed heartily over it."

"Did you never seek to inquire how long previously he had been employed there?"

"No. It never occurred to me to do so," she answered.

"But you can discover now easily enough, I suppose?"

"Of course I can," she replied. "But why are you so anxious to know?"

"I have a reason for desiring to know the exact date on which he entered the firm's employ," I said. "You will find it out for me at once, won't you?"

"If you wish."

"Then let me know by letter as soon as you possibly can," I urged quickly.

"But you need not be jealous of him, Clifton," she said, seeking to reassure me. With her woman's quick instinct she saw that my anger had been raised against him.

"How can I help being annoyed?" I said. "The facts seem quite plain that he first took service with this firm, and then most probably obtained the dismissal of one of the girls in order to make a vacancy for you. He was in love with you, I suppose," I added, rather harshly.

"Love was never mentioned between us," she declared. "We merely went out and about together, and in business he used to chat and joke with me. But as for love—"

And she laughed scornfully, without concluding her sentence.

"And the other girls were jealous of you—eh?"

She laughed.

"I suppose they were," she answered.

"Was this man—Hibbert was his name?—an experienced shop-walker?"

"I think so," she replied. "But he was disliked on account of his harshness and his constant fining of everybody."

"Except you."

"Yes," she laughed. "I generally managed to escape."

She noticed the hard look in my face, as I pondered over the strange fact. That this man who was such an intimate acquaintance of Aline's was actually shop-walker where Muriel was employed added to the mystery considerably, rather than decreasing it.

"Why need we discuss him now?" she asked. "It is all over."

"But your acquaintance with this man who has evidently striven to win your love must still continue if you remain where you are," I said in a tone of annoyance.

"No," she replied. "It is already at an end."

"But he's your shop-walker. If you have refused to go out with him, in future he'll undoubtedly vent his spiteful wrath upon you."

"Oh no, he won't," she laughed.

"Why?"

"Because he has left."

"Left!" I echoed. "Of course you know where he is?"

"No, I don't," she replied. "He annoyed me in business by speaking harshly to me before a customer, and I told him plainly that I would never again go out in his company. He apologised, but I was obdurate, and I have never seen him since. He went away that night, and has not returned. His place was filled up today. At first it was thought that he might have stolen something; but nothing has been missed, and now his sudden departure is believed to be due to his natural impetuousness and eccentricity."

"Then it would seem that owing to a disagreement with you he left his employment. That's really very remarkable!" I said.

"Yes. Everybody thinks it strange, but, of course, they don't know that we quarrelled."

"And you swear to me that you have never loved him, Muriel?" I asked, looking straight into her upturned face.

"I swear to you, Clifton," she answered. "I swear that he has never once kissed me, nor has he uttered a word of affection. We were merely friends."

"Then that makes the aspect of affairs even more puzzling," I observed. "That he had some motive for leaving secretly there is no doubt. What, I wonder, could it have been?"

"I don't know, and it really doesn't trouble me," she replied. "I was exceedingly glad when he went, and now am doubly glad that I came and sought your forgiveness."

"And I too, dearest," I said, holding her hand tenderly in mine. "But, truth to tell, I have no confidence in that man. There was something about him that I didn't like, and this latest move has increased my suspicion."

"What suspicion?"

"That his intentions were not honest ones!" I answered.

"Why, Clifton," she cried, "what an absurd fancy! Do you think that because I broke off his acquaintance, he intends to murder me?"

"I have no definite views on the subject," I answered, "except that he intended to do you some evil, and has up to the present been thwarted."

"You'll make me quite nervous if you talk like that," she responded, laughing. "Let us forget him. You once admired that woman, Aline Cloud, but that circumstance has passed out of my mind."

"You must leave that place and go down to Stamford," I said decisively. "A rest in the country will do you good, and in a few months we will marry."

"I'll have to give a month's notice before I leave," she answered.

"No. Leave tomorrow," I said. "For I cannot bear to think, dearest, that now you are to be my wife you should still bear that terrible drudgery."

She sighed, and her countenance grew troubled, as if something oppressed her. This caused me some apprehension, for it seemed as though, even now, she was not perfectly happy.

I gave tongue to this thought, but with a light laugh she assured me of her perfect contentment, and that her regret was only of the past.

Then we sat together, chatting in ecstatic enthusiasm, as I suppose all lovers do, planning a future, wherein our bliss was to be unalloyed and our love undying. And as we talked I saw how at last she became composed in that haven of contentment which is so perfect after the troubled sea of regret and despair, while I, too, felt that at last I wanted nothing, for the great desire of my life had been fulfilled.

Suddenly, however, thoughts of Aline, the mysterious woman who had come between us so strangely, the friend of this man Hibbert and the secret acquaintance of poor Roddy, crossed my mind, and I resolved to gain from her what knowledge she possessed. Therefore, with care and skill I led our conversation up to her, and then point-blank asked her what she knew regarding this woman whose face was that of an angel, and whose heart was that of Satan.

I saw how she started at mention of Aline's name; how the colour fled from her cheeks, and how sudden was her resolve to fence with me; for at once she asserted her ignorance, and suggested that we might mutually agree to bury the past.

"But she is a mystery, Muriel," I said; "a mystery which I have been trying in vain to solve through all these months. Tell me all you know of her, dearest."

"I know nothing," she declared, in a nervous tone. "Absolutely nothing."

"But are you aware that this man, Hibbert, the man with whom you associated, was her friend—her lover?"

"What!" she cried, her face in an instant undergoing a strange transformation. "He—her lover?"

"Yes," I answered. "Did you not know they were friends?"

"I can't believe it," she answered, pale-faced and bewildered. Whatever was the revelation I had made to her it had evidently caused within her a strong revulsion of feeling. I had, indeed, strong suspicion that these words of mine had supplied some missing link in a chain of facts which had long perplexed and puzzled her.

"What causes you to allege this?" she asked quickly, looking sharply into my eyes.

"Because I have seen them together," I answered. "I have overheard their conversation."

"It can't be true that they are close acquaintances," she said in a low, mechanical voice, as though speaking to herself. "It's impossible."

"Why impossible?" I inquired.

"Because there are facts which have conclusively shown that there could have been no love between them."

"Are those facts so remarkable, Muriel, that you are compelled to conceal them from me?" I asked seriously in earnest.

"At present they are," she faltered. "What you have told me has increased the mystery tenfold. I had never expected that they were friends."

"And if they were, what then?" I inquired in eagerness.

"Then the truth must be stranger than I had ever dreamed," she answered in a voice which betrayed her blank bewilderment.

The striking of the clock warned her that it was time she was going, and caused me to recollect that a man would call in a few minutes to repay a loan I had given him. He was an officer—a very decent fellow whom I had known for years, and who for a few weeks had been in rather low water. But he was again in funds, and having met me at the club that afternoon he promised to run over at ten o'clock, smoke a cigar, and repay me.

I regretted this engagement, because it prevented me seeing Muriel home; but when I referred to it she declared that she would take a cab from the rank outside, as she had done so many times in the old days of our friendship, and she would get back quite comfortably.

She buttoned her gloves, and after kissing me fondly re-adjusted her veil. Then, when we had repeated our vows of undying affection and she had promised me to return and lunch with me next morning, as it was Sunday, she went out and down the stairs.

I was a trifle annoyed that, at the club earlier in the day, I had made the appointment with Bryant, but the sum I had lent was sixty pounds, and, knowing what a careless fellow he was, I felt that it was best to obtain repayment now, when he offered it; hence I was prevented from accompanying Muriel. But as it could not be avoided, and as she had expressed herself perfectly content to return alone, I cast myself again in my chair, mixed a whiskey and soda, lit a cigarette, and gave myself up to reflection.

Muriel loved me. I cared for nought else in all the world. She would be my wife, and after travelling on the Continent for a while we would live somewhere in the country quietly, where we could enjoy ourselves amid that rural peace which to the London-worn is so restful, so refreshing, and so soothing.

After perhaps a quarter of an hour I heard Simes go to the door, and Bryant's voice exclaim hurriedly—"Is your master in?"

"Come in, my dear fellow! Come in!" I shouted, without rising from my chair.

Next instant he dashed into the room, his face white and scared, exclaiming—

"There's something wrong down at the bottom of your stairs! Come with me and see, old chap. There's a girl lying there—a pretty girl dressed in grey—and I believe she's dead."

"Dead!" I gasped, petrified, for the description he had given was that of Muriel.

"Yes," he cried, excitedly. "I believe she's been murdered!"

Chapter Twenty One.
Silence.

"Murdered!" I gasped, springing to my feet. "Impossible!"

"I've just discovered her lying on the stairs, and rushed up to you. I didn't stop to make an examination."

Without further word we dashed down the three flights of stone steps which led to the great entrance-hall of the mansions, but I noticed to my dismay that although the electric lamps on all the landings were alight those on the ground floor had been extinguished, and there, in the semi-darkness lay Muriel, huddled up in a heap on a small landing approached from the entrance-hall by half a dozen steps. The hall of Charing Cross Mansions is a kind of long arcade, having an entrance at one end in Charing Cross Road, and at the other in St. Martin's Lane; while to it descend the flights of steps leading to the various wings of the colossal building. At the further end from the stairs by which my chambers could be reached was the porter's box, but placed in such a position that it was impossible for him to see any person upon the stairs.

I sprang down to the side of my helpless love, and tried to lift her, but her weight was so great that I failed. Next instant, however, a cry of horror escaped me, for on my hand I felt something warm and sticky. It was blood. We shouted for the hall-porter, but he was not in his box, and there was no response. He was, as was his habit each evening, across the way gossiping with the fireman who lounged outside the stage-door of the Alhambra.

"Blood!" I cried, when the terrible truth became plain, and I saw that it had issued from a wound beneath her arm, and that her injury had not been caused by a fall.

"Yes," exclaimed Bryant, "she's evidently been stabbed. Do you know her?"

"Know her!" I cried. "She's my intended wife!"

"Your betrothed!" he gasped. "My dear fellow, this is terrible. What a frightful shock for you!" And he dropped upon his knees, and tenderly raised her head. Both of us felt her heart, but could discern no movement. In the mean time, however, Simes, more practical than either of us, had sped away to call a doctor who had a dispensary for the poor at the top of St. Martin's Lane.

Both of us agreed that her heart had ceased its beating, yet, a moment later, we rejoiced to see, as she lay with her head resting upon Bryant's arm, a slight rising and falling of the breast.

Respiration had returned.

I bent, fondly kissing her chilly lips, and striving vainly to staunch the ugly wound, until suddenly it struck me that the best course to pursue would be to at once remove her to my room; therefore we carefully raised her, and with difficulty succeeded in carrying her upstairs, and laying her upon my bed.

My feeling in these moments I cannot analyse. For months, weary months, during which all desire for life had passed from me, I had sought her to gain her love, and now, just as I had done so, she was to be snatched from me by the foul, dastardly deed of some unknown assassin. The fact that while the electric lights were shedding their glow in every part of the building they were extinguished upon that small landing was in itself suspicious. Bryant referred to it, and I expressed a belief that the glass of the two little Swan lamps had been purposely broken by the assassin.

At last after a long time the doctor came, a grey-haired old gentleman who bent across the bed, first looking into her face and then pushing back her hair, placed his hand upon her brow, and then upon her breast.

Without replying to our eager questions, he calmly took out his pocket knife, and turning her upon her side, cut the cord of her corsets, and slit her bodice so that the tightness at the throat was relieved.

Then, calling for a lamp and some water, he made a long and very careful examination of the wound.

"Ah!" he exclaimed, apparently satisfied at last. "The attempt was a desperate one. The knife was aimed for her heart."

"But will she die, doctor?" I cried. "Is the wound likely to be fatal?"

"I really can't tell," he answered gravely. "It is a very serious injury—very. No ordinary knife could inflict such a wound. From the appearance of it I should be inclined to think that a long surgeon's knife was used."

"But is there no hope?" I demanded. "Tell me the truth."

"It is impossible at present to tell what complications may ensue," he responded. "The best course is to inform the police of the affair, and let them make inquiries. No doubt there has been a most deliberate attempt at murder. Your servant tells me," he added, "that the lady is a friend of yours."

"Yes," I said; "I intend making her my wife; therefore you may imagine my intense anxiety in these terrible circumstances."

"Of course," he replied, sympathetically. "But have you any suspicion of who perpetrated this villainous crime?"

I thought of that thin, crafty, bony-faced scoundrel Hibbert, and then responded in the affirmative.

"Well, you'd better inform the police of your suspicions, and let them act as they think proper. I've seen the spot where your friend discovered her, and certainly it is just the spot where an assassin might lie in wait, commit a crime, and then escape into the street unseen. My advice is that you should inform the police, and let them make inquiries. I only make one stipulation, and that is that no question must be asked of her at present—either by you, or by any one else. If you'll allow me I'll send down a qualified nurse, whom I can trust to carry out my instructions—for I presume you intend that she should remain here in your chambers until she is fit to be removed?"

"Certainly," I answered eagerly. "I leave all to you, doctor; only bring her back to me."

"I will do my utmost," he assured me. "It is a grave case, a very grave one indeed," he added, with his eyes fixed upon the inanimate form; "but I have every hope that we shall save her by care and attention. I'll go back to the surgery, get some dressing for the wound, and send at once for the nurse. No time must be lost."

"And you think I ought to inform the police?" I asked.

"As you think fit," the doctor responded. "You say you have a suspicion of the identity of the would-be assassin. Surely you will not let him go unpunished?"

"No!" I cried in fierce resolution. "He shall not go unpunished." But on reflection an instant later it occurred to me that Muriel herself could tell us who had attacked her, therefore it would be best to await in patience her return to health.

The doctor left to obtain his instruments and bandages, while Bryant, Simes, and myself watched almost in silence at her bedside. The kind-hearted old doctor before he went, however, asked us to leave the room for a few minutes, and when we returned we found he had taken off her outer clothing, improvised a temporary bandage, and placed her comfortably in bed, where she now lay quite still, and to all appearances asleep. From time to time in my anxiety I bent with my hand glass placed close to her mouth to reassure myself that she was still breathing. It became slightly clouded each time, and that gave me the utmost satisfaction and confidence.

After a quarter of an hour the old man returned, while a little later the nurse, in her neat grey uniform, was in the room, attending to her patient, quickly and silently, and assisting the doctor to cleanse and bandage the wound with a dexterity which had been acquired by long acquaintance with surgical cases.

With Bryant I retired into the sitting-room while these operations were in progress, and when I again entered my bedroom I found the lights lowered and the nurse calmly sitting by Muriel's side. Then the doctor assured me that she would be quite right for three hours, and that during the night he would look in again; and with this parting re-assurance he left, accompanied out by Bryant.

Through that night I had but little repose, as may be imagined. The long hours I spent in trying to read or otherwise occupy myself, but such was the intensity of my anxiety that times without number I went and peeped in at the half-open door of my bedroom, wherein lay my beloved, motionless, still as one dead.

A whole week went by. Two or three times daily the doctor called, but by his orders I was not allowed in the room, and it was not until nearly a fortnight had gone by that I entered and stood by her bedside. Even then I was forbidden to mention the circumstances of that night when such a desperate attempt had been made upon her life. Therefore I stood by her with words of love only upon my lips.

Ours was a joyful meeting. For days my love had hovered between life and death. The doctor had gone into that room and come out again grave and silent several times each day, until at last he had told me that she had taken a turn for the better, and would recover. The delirium had left her, and she had recovered consciousness. Then there came to me a boundless joy when at last I was told that I might again see her.

Not until ten more long and anxious days had passed was I allowed to speak to her regarding the mystery which was driving me to desperation, and then one afternoon, as the sunset, yellow as it always is in London, struggled into the room, I found myself alone with her. She was sitting up in my armchair, enveloped in a pretty blue dressing-gown which the nurse had bought for her, and her hair tied coquettishly with a blue ribbon.

She could not rise, but as I entered her bright eyes sparkled with sudden unbounded delight, and speechless in emotion she beckoned me forward to a seat beside her.

"And you are much better, dearest?" I asked, when we had exchanged kisses full of a profound and passionate love.

"Yes," she answered, in a voice which showed how weak she still was. "The doctor says I shall get on quite well now. In a week or so I hope to be about again. Do they know of my illness at the shop?"

"Don't trouble about the shop, darling," I answered. "You will never go back there again, to slave and wear out your life. Remain here content, and when you are well enough you can go down to Stamford and stay there in the country air until we can marry."

"Then you still love me, Clifton?" she faltered.

"Love you!" I cried. "Of course I do, dearest. What causes you to doubt me?"

She hesitated. Her eyes met mine, and I saw they were wavering.

"Because—because I am unworthy," she faltered.

"Why unworthy?" I asked, quickly.

"I have deceived you," she replied. "You are so good to me, Clifton, yet I have concealed from you the truth."

"The truth of what?"

"Of the strange events which have led up to this desperate attempt to take my life."

"But who attacked you?" I demanded. "Tell me, and assuredly he shall not escape punishment."

She paused. Her eyes met mine firmly.

"No," she answered. "It is impossible to tell you. To attempt a retaliation would only prove fatal."

"Fatal!" I echoed. "Why?"

"All that has been attempted is of the past," she responded. "It is best that it should remain as it is. If you seek out that man, there will be brought upon us a vengeance more terrible than it is possible to contemplate. Do not ask me to divulge the identity of this man, for I cannot."

"You will not, you mean," I said in a hard voice.

"No," she answered hoarsely. "No, I dare not."

"Then you fear this man who has attempted to kill you—this man who sought to take you from me!" I cried fiercely. "Surely I, the man you are to marry, have a right to demand this assassin's name."

"You have a right, Clifton, the greatest of all rights, but I beg of you to remain patient," she answered calmly. "There are reasons why I must still preserve a silence on this matter—reasons which some day you will know."

"Does this man love you?"

She shrugged her shoulders and extended her thin, white hands vaguely.

"And he is jealous of me!" I cried. "He attempted to kill you because you came here to me."

"Remain in patience, I beg of you," she said imploringly. "Make no surmises, for you cannot guess the truth. It is an enigma to which I myself have no key."

"The name of the man who has attempted to murder you is Hibbert," I observed, annoyed at her persistent concealment of the truth. "He is the man who was your lover. You can't deny it."

She raised her beautiful eyes for a moment to mine, then said simply—

"Surely you trust me, Clifton?"

Her question drove home to me the fact that my suspicion was ill-founded, and that jealousy in this affair was untimely and unnecessary. I, however, could not rid myself of the thought that Hibbert, this lover she had discarded, had attempted to wreak a deadly revenge. All the circumstances pointed to it, for he would know the whereabouts of my chambers, if not from Muriel previously, then from Aline, that woman whom once in my hearing he had urged to the commission of a crime.

"I trust you implicitly, Muriel," I answered. "But in this matter I am determined that the man whose hand struck you down shall answer for his crime to me."

"No, no!" she cried in alarm. "Don't act rashly, for your own sake, and for mine. Wait, and I will ere long give you an explanation which I know will astound you. To-day I cannot move in the matter because I am not allowed out. When I can go out I will find a means of giving you some explanation." Then, lifting her dark, trustful eyes to mine she asked again, "Clifton, cannot you trust me? Will you not obey me in this?"

"Certainly," I answered at last, with considerable reluctance I admit. "If you promise me to explain, then I will wait."

"I promise," she answered, and her thin, white hand again clasped mine, and our lips met to seal our compact.

Chapter Twenty Two.
To Seek the Truth.

THE DAYS OF MY love's convalescence were happy indeed. Most of the time we spent together, planning the future and gossiping about the past. Those were halcyon hours when we reckoned time only by the meals served to us by Simes, and we both looked forward to a visit to the old Lincolnshire town that was so very lethargic, so redolent of the "good old days" of our grandfathers.

Once she received a letter left by a man, and marked "private." In this I scented mystery; for she never referred to it, and when I inquired who was the sender she merely replied that a friend had written to her. This was strange, for none knew that she remained with me. We had thought it best not to tell any one until all could be explained, for a lady who lives in a bachelor's chambers is looked upon with some suspicion if no very valid excuse can be given for such a flagrant breach of the *convenances*.

The letter without doubt caused her much thought and considerable anxiety. By her face I detected that she was dreading some dire result, the nature of which she dared not tell me; and it was on that very afternoon that Jack Yelverton called to inquire after me, for I had neither written nor seen him since that night when the chalice at St. Peter's had disappeared into ashes.

He was stretched out in a chair smoking furiously, laughing more merrily than usual, and talking with that genuine *bonhomie* which was one of his most engaging characteristics, when suddenly Muriel entered.

They met face to face, and in an instant she drew back, pale as death.

"I—I didn't know you had a visitor," she exclaimed half-apologetically, her cheeks crimsoning in her confusion.

"Come in," I exclaimed, rising. "Allow me to introduce you," and I went through the conventional formality.

Upon Yelverton's face I detected an expression of absolute wonder and bewilderment; but seeing that she treated him with calm indifference, he at once reseated himself, and the pair recovered their self-possession almost instantly.

Puzzled at this strange complication, I spoke mechanically, explaining that Muriel was engaged to marry me, and that she had been ill, although I did not tell him the cause.

Yet all Jack Yelverton's levity had in that brief moment of unexpected meeting departed. He had become brooding and thoughtful.

I confess that I entertained doubts. So many things had recently occurred which she refused to explain, that day by day I was haunted by a horrible consuming suspicion that, after all, she did not love me—that for some purpose of her own she was merely making shallow pretence. I fear that the remainder of Yelverton's visit was a dismal affair. Certainly our conversation was irresponsible and disjointed, for neither of us thought of what we said. Our reflections were far from the subject under discussion.

At last the Vicar of St. Peter's made his adieux, and when he had gone I awaited in vain her explanation.

She said nothing, yet her efforts at concealment were so apparent that they nauseated me. I was annoyed that she should thus believe me to be one so blinded by love as to be unable to observe signs so palpable as those in her countenance. The more I thought it over, the more apparent it became that as Yelverton and Aline were lovers, Muriel, knowing Aline, would certainly be acquainted with him. If so, and all their dealings had been straightforward, why had not she at once welcomed him as a friend, and not as a stranger?

I saw that he was plainly annoyed at meeting her, and detected astonishment in his face when I announced my intention of marrying her.

I wondered why he looked at me so strangely. His expression was as though he pitied my ignorance. Thoughts such as these held me in doubt and suspicion.

With a self-control amazing in such circumstances, she reseated herself and took up some needlework, which she had that morning commenced—a cushion-cover intended for our home—and when at last I grew calm again and sat with her she commenced to chat as though our happiness had in no way been disturbed.

As the days went on and she rapidly grew stronger her attitude became more and more puzzling. That she loved me passionately with a fierce, all-consuming affection, I could not doubt. Not that she uttered many words of re-assurance. On the contrary, she heard most of my declarations in silence. Yet the heaving of her breast, and that bright, truthful look in her eyes, were signs of love which I could not fail to recognise.

During those nine weeks of Muriel's illness I heard nothing of Aline, and was wondering if she knew of my beloved's presence, or if she would again visit me. To her I had bound myself by an oath of secrecy, in return for a gift to me more precious than any on earth, yet the many strange occurrences which had happened since that first night at the theatre formed a puzzle so intricate that the more I tried to discover the solution the more bewildering it became.

Soon the dark-haired fragile girl who was to be my wife had so improved in health that the doctor allowed her to go for a drive, and in the days following we went out together each afternoon perfectly happy and content in each other's love. Those who have loved truly know well the ecstasy of the first hours in public with one's betrothed, therefore it is unnecessary for me to describe my feeling of perfect bliss and thankfulness that she was well at last, and that ere long we should become man and wife.

It had been arranged that Muriel should leave for Stamford in two or three days, when one morning, she having gone out with the nurse, and I remaining alone in my room, Jack Yelverton was admitted. In an instant I saw from his countenance that something unusual had occurred. His pale, unshaven face was haggard and worn, his clerical collar was soiled, his coat unbrushed, his hair unkempt, and as he seated himself and put out his hand I felt it quiver in my grasp.

"Why, what's the matter, old chap?" I inquired in surprise. "What's happened?"

"I'm upset, Clifton," he answered hoarsely.

"What's upset you? This isn't like your usual self," I said.

"No," he responded, rising and pacing the room with his hand to his white brow, "it isn't like me." Then, turning quickly to me, he added with gravity which startled me, "Clifton, I think I'm mad!"

"Mad! Nonsense! my dear fellow!" I protested, placing my hand upon his shoulder. "Tell me what all this is about."

"I've failed!" he cried in a voice of utter despair. "I've striven, and striven in my work, but all to no purpose. I've sown the wind, and the Devil has placed a bar between myself and the Master."

"How?" I asked, failing to grasp his meaning.

"I have made a discovery," he answered in a dry, harsh tone.

"A discovery!" I echoed.

"Yes, one so appalling, so terrible, so absolutely horrible, that I am crushed, hopeless, paralysed."

"What is it?" I demanded quickly, excited by his strange wildness of manner.

"No," he answered. "It is useless to explain. You could never believe that what I told you was the truth."

"I know that you would not willingly tell a lie to your oldest friend, Jack," I answered, with grave earnestness.

"But you could never fully realise the truth," he declared. "A sorrow has fallen upon me greater and more terrible than ever man has encountered; for at the instant of my recovery I knew that I was shut out from the grace of God, that all my work had been a mere mockery of the Master."

"Why do you speak like this?" I argued, knowing him to be a devout man, and having seen with my own eyes how self-denying he was, and how untiring he had worked among the poor.

"I speak the truth, Clifton," he said, a strange look in his eyes. "I shall never enter my church again."

"Never enter your church!" I cried. "Are you really mad?"

"The wiles of Satan have encompassed me," he responded hoarsely, in the tone of a man utterly broken.

"How? Explain!" I said.

"A woman's eyes fascinated me. I fell beneath her spell, only to find that her heart was the blackest in all the world."

"Well?"

"My love for her is an absorbing one. She is my idol, and I have cast aside my God for her."

"Why do you talk like this?" I asked reproachfully. "Has it not been proved to you already that you can marry and yet live a godly life?"

"Yes, yes! I know," he responded with impatience. "But to love Aline Cloud is to abandon the Master."

"Why?" I inquired, all eagerness to learn what he knew of her strange power of evil.

"I cannot explain, because there is a mystery which is impenetrable," he answered. "I shall resign the living and go abroad. I can no longer remain here."

"You will again fly from her, as you did when you went and hid yourself in Duddington?" I asked. "I can't understand the reason of your actions. Why not give me a little more explanation?"

"But I can't explain, because I have not yet fathomed the truth."

"Then you only entertain certain suspicions, and will act upon them without obtaining clear grounds. That's illogical, Jack—very illogical."

He pondered for a few moments, tugging at his moustache.

"Well, I hadn't looked at it in that light before, I must confess," he answered at last. "You think I ought to be entirely satisfied before I act."

"Yes, rashness should not be one of the characteristics of a man who ministers God's Word," I said.

"But the deadly trail of the Serpent is upon everything," he declared. "I can hope for nothing more. I cannot be hypocritical, neither can I serve two masters. Is it not better for me to resign from the Church at once than to offend before God?"

"For whatever sin you have committed there is the Great Forgiveness," I said calmly. "You are a believer, or you could not preach those enthralling sermons, which have already made you noted in ecclesiastical London. You are known as a brilliant, powerful preacher who can make the tears well in the eyes of strong men by your fervent appeal to them to turn from their wickedness and live. Think!" I said. "Recollect the men steeped in sin whom you have induced to come forth and bow before their God in penitence. Think of those men who have been saved by your ministrations, and then ask yourself whether there is no salvation for you?"

"Yes!" he sighed. "What you say is quite true, Clifton—quite true."

"Then if you abandon the Church you abandon faith in the generous forgiveness which you have preached, and exhibit to those who have believed in you a doubt in the grace of God. Surely you, Jack, will not do this?"

He was silent, with bent head, as he stood before me reflecting.

"Your argument is a strong one, certainly," he said at last. "But can I actually stand in my pulpit and preach the Gospel after the knowledge that has come to me?"

"Knowledge!" I repeated. "We found that knowledge to be a mere suspicion only a moment ago!"

"Yes," he admitted; "suspicion if you like. Well, that amounts to the same thing."

"Why don't you tell me all about it?" I urged. "What are these suspicions regarding Aline?"

I recollected my bond of secrecy, and it drove me to madness. If I could tell him all I knew, I felt that together we might combine to probe the mystery. As it was, my silence was imperative.

"It's my misfortune that I have not sufficient grounds for making any direct allegation. I love her still; I adore her; I worship her; but—"

At that instant, without warning, the door opened, and Muriel, bright and happy, burst into the room, bearing an armful of flowers. Next second, on recognising my visitor, her countenance changed, and she bowed stiffly to him, without offering her hand. Quick to notice this, I at once demanded an explanation, for the mystery had now driven me to desperation.

"There is some secret in your previous acquaintance with Muriel," I said, addressing Yelverton boldly. "Tell me what it is."

"Our acquaintance!" he faltered, while she drew back open-mouthed in alarm. The pair exchanged glances, and I saw that between them was some understanding. "What makes you suggest that?" he asked, with a forced laugh.

"You were acquainted before I introduced you the other day!" I cried, fiercely. "You can't deny that!"

"I have not denied it," he responded calmly. "It is quite true that I knew Miss Moore before our formal introduction."

"Then why did you not admit it?" I demanded, a feeling of jealousy rising within me.

"Simply because I had no desire to excite any suspicion in your mind, Clifton. That's all."

"Rubbish!" I ejaculated. "There's some mystery behind all this. Why may I not know?"

The Vicar of St. Peter's glanced inquiringly at Muriel, but finding no look of permission in her countenance, preserved a silence, which in a moment grew irksome.

Suddenly, however, Muriel, who stood near me, pale and excited, turned, and facing me, said—

"There appears to be a misunderstanding between you. It is quite true that I am acquainted with Mr Yelverton, and there is absolutely no necessity to deny the fact. We have known each other for a long time—ever since I was at Madame Gabrielle's. He was curate at St. Michael's, Rathbone Place, where I attended, and we were very good friends until—until—" and she did not finish the sentence.

"Until what?"

"Well, until an event occurred which transformed our friendship."

"What event?"

Again the pair exchanged glances. She was apparently trying to obtain permission from him to expose to me the whole truth. At that moment I felt assured that this woman I had so fondly loved was playing me false, and, after all, this popular preacher was her real lover. Certain circumstances appeared to point to it, for her confusion was apparent; she knew not what to admit, nor what to deny.

He shrugged his shoulders in dumb motion, as though he were careless, but this action apparently gave her confidence, and she turned to me again, saying—

"Any explanation you demand, Mr Yelverton will no doubt give to you."

"No, no," Jack cried, addressing her. "It's quite impossible. You know full well that I'm utterly in ignorance of the truth, and that you alone can explain, if you will."

She bit her lips, and endeavoured to recover her self-possession. Her illness had weakened her, and rendered her curiously nervous, so that the least emotion visibly affected her.

"Yes," I added, "you are concealing a secret from me, Muriel, and I, who am to be your husband, demand to know what it is. Tell me!"

"If you had asked me this a few days ago," she answered, after a pause, "I could only have given you a negative answer. But I have overheard Mr Yelverton's confession to you, and now that I am strong again, I am determined that neither he nor you shall longer remain in doubt regarding the mystery surrounding Aline Cloud."

"What is it?" I cried excitedly. "Tell us quickly."

"No," she answered, with a wave of the hand. "In this affair we must exercise patience, or those who are guilty will assuredly escape us. Besides, we have to ensure our own safety also."

"Our own safety!" Jack echoed. "What do you mean?"

"Have I not narrowly escaped death?" she asked. "If we are not wary, another attempt, perhaps more successful, may be made."

"You anticipate assassination because those who are guilty are aware that you are now in possession of their secret?" I cried. "Then let us act in union with care and discretion. What has caused you to preserve your silence until now?"

"Circumstances which rendered my secrecy imperative," she answered. "Until now I only entertained suspicions; but these have been confirmed, therefore to me the truth is apparent. In order, however, for us to solve the mystery, it is necessary that you should both obey me implicitly, without asking any questions, for to some of your demands I should be compelled to give false answers. Trust in me, both of you, and I will reveal to you something stranger than you have ever dreamed."

"We do trust you," we both answered with one accord.

"I'm ready to act in any manner you direct," I added.

"And you will not fear, even though a plot may be laid against your life?" she inquired with concern.

"I fear nothing while I have my revolver in my pocket," I answered, as coolly as I could. "Both of us are ready and anxious to carry out any plan you may form."

"But of what character is the plan?" asked the vicar, with natural caution.

"It's Friday today," she observed, disregarding his question. "Tell me when Aline will next visit you."

"On Sunday. She has written today saying that she will attend the service on Sunday evening."

"You will preach?" she asked.

"I don't know," he answered evasively. "I may be away."

"You mean that by that time you may have resigned and left the Church," I said quickly. "No, Jack. Don't think of such a thing. Muriel know? more than she has told us, and if she will assist us, I have no doubt that the mystery will be cleared up, and the guilty brought to punishment."

"Do you wish me to preach on Sunday?" Yelverton asked of my beloved.

"Certainly," was her response. "But, tell me—she never remains after the evening service, does she?"

"No, never," he replied. "By the time I'm out of the vestry she has always departed. It seems as though her quick, impetuous nature will not allow her to await me."

"Then preach on Sunday night, and leave the remainder to me," she said.

"You appear to know all her movements," Yelverton observed. "Where does she go usually after church?"

"Her destination is always the same—a secret one. But remain patient," she added, a strange look in her dark eyes, as though she were intent upon a fierce and terrible revenge. "You are her lover, and have discovered, as others have done, that she is possessed of a spirit of evil that holds you appalled in wonder. Her actions are truly astounding, yet the truth, when revealed, will be more startling and more bewildering than any of the strange things which have already happened."

"And you promise to explain everything?" I asked in breathless eagerness.

"No. I cannot promise that. I will furnish you with the necessary clue to the solution of the mystery, but even I myself know not all the facts."

Both of us tried to obtain from her some further information regarding Aline, but without avail. She remained absolutely mute, likewise refusing to reveal the identity of her would-be assassin. That she had met him face to face upon the stairs she admitted, but in response to my inquiries declared that the time was not yet ripe for the denunciation, and urged us to remain in patience.

This we did until at last Sunday night came. At about half-past six I accompanied my beloved in a cab to a small and very dismal little street in the immediate vicinity of St. Peter's, one of those mean, drab thoroughfares which abound in South London; and when at length the service concluded, we stood together in the gloom waiting for Aline's striking figure to emerge among the congregation.

At last she came, dressed neatly in black, her fair hair well coiled beneath a neat black toque, and in her hand her tiny prayer-book, with the ivory cross upon the cover. She walked straight in our direction without, of course, dreaming of our presence, but outside the smoke-blackened railings of the churchyard she paused for a moment beneath the street-lamp to glance at the little jewelled watch pinned upon her breast. Her lover's sermon had been a trifle longer than usual, therefore, on noting the time, she at once hurried away along the narrow little street towards the Walworth Road, in order, apparently, to keep some mysterious appointment.

"Come!" Muriel said. "Let us follow her!" And together we walked on, eagerly keeping her well in sight in the crowd of dispersing worshippers.

My heart beat wildly in those moments, for I knew we were upon the verge of some extraordinary discovery, the nature of which my beloved had predicted would be stranger than we had dreamed.

Chapter Twenty Three.
In the Shadow.

ERE WE HAD GAINED the Walworth Road, Yelverton, so breathless in his haste that he could scarce gasp "Good night" to the small crowd who saluted him as he passed, overtook us.

"Where is she?" he inquired.

"There—in front of us, standing on the kerb," I answered, halting in order to escape observation. "She's evidently waiting for an omnibus."

My surmise proved true, for a few moments later she entered one of those green omnibuses which ply to Camberwell Green, and the moment the conveyance moved off again Muriel, turning to me quickly, said—

"We must now lose no time, but take a cab at once to Herne Hill."

We therefore hailed the first four-wheeler, and in one of those most terrible of all conveyances which ply for hire in London—vehicles known in the vernacular as "fever-traps"—we made our way with much rattle and jolting along the Camberwell Road, past Camberwell Green, and up Denmark Hill.

The cab deposited us on the brow of the hill at the corner of that steep road, Red Post Hill, one of the few thoroughfares untouched by the modern builder, and together we descended Herne Hill until we came to a great old house standing back in its own grounds, with large trees around it, and approached by a broad carriage drive. It had undoubtedly been an important residence a century ago, but in the darkness I could discern that weeds had been allowed to grow upon the drive, that shutters closed the windows of the ground floor, that pieces of paper, straw, and other rubbish, the flotsam and jetsam of the street, lay upon the moss-grown steps leading to the front door, and the large board which announced that the desirable site was for sale "for building purposes" told conclusively how the neighbourhood had decayed until it was being gradually swallowed up by overgrown, overcrowded Camberwell.

The double gates rusting on their hinges were secured together by a chain and formidable padlock, but following Muriel we went to a small side door in the high wall, which she opened with a key, admitting us, closing it, and locking it after her.

Within the old tangled garden, where the shrubs, weeds, and flowers had grown wild and unpruned for years, all was silent as the grave. The old place, partly overgrown with ivy, which had almost hidden several of the windows, looked grim and ghostly in the gloom, for the moon was hidden behind a bank of fleecy cloud, and only shed a mystic half-light, which added to rather than decreased the sense of forlorn dreariness which oppressed one. By the aspect of the place it appeared as though it had remained untenanted for fully ten years.

As I stood with my two companions, in the deep shadow, preserving the strict silence which Muriel had now imposed upon us, I confess to entertaining some misgivings. There was a weirdness about the whole affair which I did not like, and I felt a foreboding of some vague evil which I could not define.

With a whispered word of caution Muriel crept forward, treading noiselessly on the carpet of weeds which had hidden the gravel, and skirting the house, swiftly approached a door at the side, evidently once the tradesmen's entrance.

"Hush!" she whispered, "make no noise. If we were discovered here it would be fatal to all our plans—fatal, indeed, to us!"

Noiselessly she opened the door with her key, while we stood behind her, scarce daring to breathe, and then we all three passed silently into a small, dark passage, down which we groped our way, after Muriel had again locked the door behind her.

I thought I heard a movement at my back like the swish of silk, but next instant reassured myself that it must be a rat disturbed by our intrusion. The place was silent as the tomb, for upon the passage were the remains of some old cocoa-nut matting, which deadened the sound of our footsteps as we crept forward to our unknown goal.

Jack whispered an inquiry to her, but gripping his arm, she answered—

"Not a word! While you are here speak not a word, nor utter any exclamation. Prepare yourselves for amazing surprises, but control yourselves so as to remain silent on witnessing them."

Suddenly she halted, passed her hands quietly over some panelling in the long, narrow passage which seemed to run the whole length of the house, and searched in the darkness for something she could not at first discover. At length she found what she sought, a small door, apparently concealed in the panelling, and through this we passed, down some winding stone steps where the air was foul and damp, and the walls seemed overgrown with fungi.

We were descending into a cellar. Was Muriel about to reveal to us the hidden evidence of some terrible crime? I shuddered, for the darkness was appalling. We could only feel our way lightly with our hands, taking care not to stumble nor to create any noise.

Of a sudden, I saw straight before me five circular rays of light which together formed themselves into a star, and as we approached we found that before us was a partition of wood, and that these round rays were of the light from a chamber beyond shining through what were apparently air-holes.

"Now!" whispered Muriel, hoarsely. "Utter not a sound, but look within!"

I placed my eye at one of the holes and gazed through. What I witnessed there held me dumb with terror. I stood rigid, open-mouthed, not daring to breathe. The scene was, as Muriel had predicted, stranger than any in my wildest dreams.

Chapter Twenty Four.
The Evil-Doers.

TRULY OUR GAZE ENCOUNTERED a scene of the most bewildering and terrible description. Within, was a spacious cellar-like chamber, the walls of which were hung with black whereon were curious devices in white, and around in sconces were burning candles of black wax. At the end, opposite where we stood, was a church Communion-table whereon burnt long, black candles, and before it stood a kind of low stool with a large cushion of black velvet upon it. All was black save the strange designs upon the walls, while the candles shed a curious mystic light upon the whole apartment, illuminating the central object so weirdly that our startled eyes were riveted upon it. This object, placed immediately over the altar, was nothing less than a great effigy of Satan, with a leering grin upon his ghastly features, holding in one hand an apple, and in the other a wine-bottle. In the eyes there burned a blood-red light, and the protruding tongue, as he laughed, seemed pointed as that of a serpent. It was hideous; and I heartily wished myself out of that noisome place.

Suddenly I saw something which paralysed me with terror. The effigy moved. What I had believed to be but a statue, bent down and uttered some words to a thin, pale-faced man who had at that instant entered by the door on the opposite side of the chamber.

"Look!" gasped Yelverton. "Look! It is living!"

But Muriel placed her hand upon his mouth, demanding that he should preserve silence and not risk our lives.

The newcomer spat into a marble bowl of water like that placed at the door of the Roman Catholic churches, whereupon Satan gave vent to a laugh so hideous that it sent a chill through me. Next second, some eight or ten others, men and women, entered, each expectorating into the holy water as sign of contempt for all things sacred.

With bated breath we watched. For several years there had been hints in the press of the establishment in London of a cult of Satan, but very few believed it. Yet here we were actual witnesses that Diabolism did exist among us. This age is indeed a decadent one, for according to the facts which had already leaked out the terribly profane doctrine of Satan consisted of a kind of reversed Christianity, it being inferred, from the condition of the world at the present time, that the mastery of the moment rests with the evil principle, and that the beneficent Deity is at a disadvantage. The Diabolists, therefore, while believing that the Deity reigns, declare that he is the author of human misery, and they therefore take sides with Satan in the cause of humanity. According to those who have come out of this cultus, the worshippers co-operate with Satan to insure his triumph, and they believe that he communicates with them to encourage and strengthen them.

Such, briefly, is the belief of the modern Diabolists, and such is the latest acmé of profanity established among the greatest and most civilised nation on the earth.

As we watched, our eyes strained to witness everything, we saw infamous rites performed, rites which caused us both to shudder in horror; yet curiously enough Muriel looked upon them calmly, without betraying the slightest fear. Those who assembled were, for the most part, well dressed, and present-ly the Evil One upon the pedestal reached forth his hand and rang a small bell. Next instant there entered two acolytes bearing a ciborium, which they placed upon the altar. Then, after repeating a prayer to Satan in Latin, in imitation of a Christian prayer, the worshippers with one accord fell upon their knees in adoration of the Evil One.

The scene was strangely weird, but utterly horrible, for on regaining their feet all formed a row and filed past the altar, each taking up a dagger, and as they passed stabbed the consecrated host within the casket. Then, at sign from the hideous man upon the pedestal, a Satanic liturgy was chanted, and a brazier was lit by the acolyte in the centre of the chamber, when each worshipper producing a crucifix spat three times upon it and cast it into the fire, while Satan laughed in triumph and they cried aloud to him in adoration. To witness such Pagan rites as these, where every element of Christianity was held up to ridicule, was sickening. A feeling of nausea crept over me when I heard these men and women anathematise the Deity, and the infamous and degrading ceremonies caused me to shudder.

Suddenly there was a stir among the members of this evil cult at that moment kneeling, for a woman slowly entered, veiled, followed by a masked man in a long, black vestment, bearing on the breast an effigy of Satan. A silence fell, deep and complete, for the woman in her flowing robes of black stood before the stool in front of the altar and raised her bare white arms above her head.

She was evidently the priestess of the cult, for I watched her stand before the stool, while the priest with the assistance of an acolyte brought out a huge crucifix of black and silver and placed it before her. Then he also produced a bag of black silk containing something which moved within, and deposited it at her feet.

When he had done this, and all was in readiness, she knelt upon the cushion, and placed her back as a reading-desk for him, while he went through the ceremony of the Black Mass, an appalling profanity impossible to here describe.

When at length this had been concluded, the woman rose and, bending, took from the bag the object that had been writhing within it. Eagerly we strained our eyes, and were amazed to see that it was a black cat. With a loud cry to Satan as ruler of the world, she took a long, thin dagger from her belt and plunged it into the animal, which expired almost without a struggle. Then, with a swift, dexterous movement she cut out the heart, and with its blood defiled the crucifix, an action which was applauded by the onlookers, now increased in number, and greeted with a loud laugh by the hideous representative of Evil at the end of that foul, terrible place.

Next second, however, a circumstance occurred which rendered our concealment impossible. The priestess with a swift movement tore her veil from her face, while the priest took off his mask.

The two faces revealed caused us to utter exclamations of surprise which at once rendered concealment no longer possible.

The priestess was none other than Aline Cloud, and the priest the bony-faced scoundrel Hibbert, whom Muriel had loved!

"We are discovered!" my love gasped. "Be careful, or your lives may be taken. These people are desperate."

Both Jack and myself drew our revolvers in an instant, and ere we knew how it occurred, a door opened, and we found ourselves within the Temple of Evil, struggling in the confusion which had been caused. The man who had posed as Satan, director of the cult, had sprung down to earth in a moment, shouting to some hidden person to close all egress and bearing in his hand the gleaming dagger with which the worshippers had stabbed the sacred elements within the ciborium.

Aline, when she had recognised us, gave a shriek and stood glaring at her lover, pale as death. Jack, tall, and strong as a lion, stood in the garb of the Christian Church within that foul den of the Diabolists and with a loud voice called upon them to remain quiet and listen.

But at that instant I saw in the eyes of Satan a dangerous expression, and with a curse he sprang at Muriel with his knife, and would have struck her dead had I not been quick enough to arrest the blow and point my revolver at his head.

"Would you," she cried, "attempt my life a second time? See!" and she pointed to me. "This man is my lover; and for your cowardly attempt to kill me you shall answer to him."

"And this was the man who attacked you?" I cried, as he flinched beneath my aim. "It is only what might be expected of a man who masquerades as the Evil One."

"You!" I heard Yelverton cry in a voice which showed how bitter was his regret, as he faced Aline, who in her long, black robe stood trembling and unsteady before him. "Then this is the truth," he cried hoarsely. "You are the priestess of Satan!"

"Ah, yes!" she cried. "But first hear me before you condemn me! And you, Clifton," she added, turning to me. "Hear me, and when you have listened try and regard me with sympathy and pity. I know I am unworthy of regard, wretched outcast that I am; but I have acted under compulsion. I swear I have!"

"Enough!" roughly cried the director of those profane rites, who had posed above the altar regarding all with satisfaction. "There has been treachery; and you, our brothers and sisters, must decide the fate of those who have dared to enter with the spy."

"Silence!" I cried, handling my revolver determinedly. "First let us hear the statement of this priestess of yours. The first person who lays hands on either of us pays for it with his life."

I was a pretty dead shot, and at that moment was desperate.

"Listen!" Aline cried, addressing Jack, "and I will tell you. Three years ago I was living with my father in Montgeron when I became acquainted with a man who one night persuaded me to go with him to a house in Paris, and there by his trickery I was initiated as a Diabolist. It was partly because of a passing fancy for him, and partly because of the mysteries surrounding it, that I became a member of the infamous cult; yet soon I hated the awful rites, and the revulsion of feeling within me caused me to embrace Christianity, so that when at length my father died, and I escaped from this man and came to England, I was received into the English Church. Then you know how we met, and I loved you. My father had left me fairly well off, and as atonement for my sin in worshipping Satan I devoted the greater part of my money to charity in the poorer districts of London. Suddenly, however, this man, who was one of the elders of the cult of Satan in Paris, found me in London, and a branch having been established here, he compelled me under threats of exposure to you of my association with this abominable sect, to return to them and become their priestess. Thus, powerless beneath his influence, I loved you and worshipped at your church, yet on each Sunday night compelled to come here and assist at the Black Mass of the Evil One. Can you imagine what my feelings have been? Can you fully realise the awful pangs of conscience when, fearing God as I do, I have knelt upon yonder cushion compelled to profane His name, because of my love for you and the fear that if you knew the truth you would cast me aside? Yes," she cried wildly, her face blanched and haggard, "I loved you, Jack!" and staggering forward she fell upon her knees before him in penitence.

"It is astounding!" he exclaimed. "Satan himself has sent you into my life, for you are his priestess."

"But tell me," I cried, addressing the kneeling woman. "Explain your object in so mystifying me, and how it was that at your touch any holy emblems were reduced to ashes?"

"It is part of our creed," she answered. "Each Diabolist on placing upon himself the Bond of Black takes an oath to steal crucifixes, Bibles, prayer-books, communion-cups, sacramental wine, or anything sacred to the worship of God, in order that they may be defiled or destroyed in the Temple of Satan. You have already seen the holy water, and the consecrated host, defiled, and each of the crucifixes burned in this brazier have been stolen by those who had destroyed them as offerings to the King of Evil."

"But mine was destroyed by fire—as was also the chalice at St. Peter's," I observed.

"No; in order to mystify those who follow Christianity the Diabolists have established a system by which the ashes of various objects burned in the brazier are afterwards supplied to the votaries of Satan, and when any sacred objects are stolen the ashes are substituted. Being carried in a bag of chamois-leather, they are warmed by the heat of the body, and hence, increased mystery is added by the ashes, when discovered, being warm."

"Then you stole my crucifix in order that it should be burnt here!" I exclaimed, amazed.

"Yes. The chalice, too, was melted in that brazier, as well as objects from the rooms of your poor friend Morgan."

"Morgan!" I cried, interrupting. "He was murdered! Tell us the truth."

"Yes," answered the unhappy woman, hoarsely. "He was murdered."

"Who was the assassin?" I inquired quickly.

"I do not know," she answered, looking boldly at me. "I myself have tried to discover, but cannot."

"But how do you reconcile your assertion that he died at Monte Carlo with the fact that he was assassinated in London?" I demanded.

"I felt assured that he committed suicide there, for I saw him carried out of the rooms dying. But, from further information which I have since obtained from the Administration there, I have found that he lay ill for some weeks in a hospital at Nice, and afterwards recovered sufficiently to be able to return to London. The Administration are always reticent upon the subject of suicides, and it was their refusal to give me any information when I applied on the day following the tragic affair that led me to believe that your friend had died and been buried in a nameless grave in the suicides' cemetery at La Turbie."

"Why did you so deceive me regarding your address at Hampstead?" I inquired. "Surely there could have been no necessity for doing that?"

"Yes, there was," she replied. "I was compelled to act as I did. In the house of Mrs Popejoy was a valuable ring belonging to the Pope which he had given to the Ambassador of France together with his blessing. This ring had been traced by the cult of Satan to this lady's possession, and it was arranged that I should enter the house as her companion and secure it. I did so on the night when you escorted me to that house, and the ring is now upon the hand of the chief of the order—the man yonder who personifies the King of Evil."

"Extraordinary!" I exclaimed when I had heard her explanation. "Your ingenuity at deception was truly marvellous."

"Yes," she answered, "but my actions were not my own voluntary ones. They were directed by the leader of the sect in whose power I have been held, unable to extricate myself for fear of exposure and a terrible denunciation. But it is all at an end now," she added in despair. "You have all of you witnessed my awful degradation, and how I have committed the deadly sins. For me what forgiveness can there be; for what may I hope?"

"Hope for the forgiveness of the man who loves you," I answered, glancing at Yelverton, who remained rigid and silent, his face white as death.

But she only burst into tears, and grasping her lover's hand pressed it to her lips, murmuring some broken words imploring pity.

"And you, Muriel?" I asked, turning to my beloved who was standing at my side shielded from the wrath of these angry people by my revolver. "How is it that you have been enabled to expose this most extraordinary state of affairs?"

"But for one thing I should never have dared to bring you here," she answered, looking at me openly. "I was jealous of Aline, because I thought you loved her, and was therefore content that she should suffer all the tortures of the mind which she has suffered, being compelled to bow before Satan and ridicule the Faith. I refused your offer of marriage because I believed you loved her, and in pique I allowed this man Hibbert to admire me. I—"

"Then you are a Diabolist yourself?" I gasped, dismayed.

"Yes. It was Hibbert who induced me to allow myself to become initiated. Truth to tell, I was curious to witness the strange rites of which he told me, but as soon as I found myself fettered by the Bond of Black I repented, and wished to come out of the terrible cult whose faith is in profanity and whose deeds are wickedness. Like Aline, I have been compelled to steal prayer-books, Bibles, and sacred objects, all of which have been defiled and consumed. I dared not tell you of my association with these Satanists, hence my constant silence regarding matters upon which you have desired explanation."

"But what caused you to so suddenly abandon Hibbert and return to me?" I asked, recollecting my curious compact with Aline.

"A discovery which I made—a revelation which, by Aline's instigation, was made to me," she answered. "I know full well how she bought your silence by promising that I should return to you. I came, and you believed, because of that, she was possessed of power supernatural. It is the object of every worshipper of Satan to cause the outside world to believe that he or she is endowed with a miraculous power by the Evil One, hence the manner in which ashes are substituted for the holy objects stolen. Aline, like myself, was compelled by the oath she had taken to impose upon you, upon Roddy Morgan, upon her lover, nay, upon every one about her, until they believed her endowed with power not possessed by any other living being."

"Yes," Aline interrupted, "what Muriel tells you is the truth. At my will this man Hibbert forsook her, and she returned to you because she was no longer jealous of me. And you believed that I committed the crime!" she said reproachfully. "You suspected that I killed the man who had been so kind to me."

"I certainly did believe so. All the evidence seemed to point to the fact that Roddy was killed by some secret means, and that the person who visited him was yourself. I found the button of one of your gloves there."

Slowly she rose to her feet, and seeing how grave was her lover's face she turned again to me, saying, in a tremulous voice—

"Yes, I know, it is useless for me to now conceal the truth. On leaving you that morning I went there and saw him. He opened the door himself, and I remained about a quarter of an hour. We had not met since I had seen him carried out of the rooms at Monte Carlo, and the reason of my visit was to ascertain whether what you alleged, namely, that he was still alive, was true. I fully expected to find that this man who was passing as Roddy Morgan was an impostor, but discovered that he was no doubt the same person with whom I had been acquainted at Monte Carlo. My aunt, with whom I was on the Riviera, liked him very much, and I confess that only by his attempted suicide was a match between us prevented. In that brief space, while I remained there, he again told me that he loved me, but I explained that I had now formed another attachment, a statement which threw him into a fit of deep despondency. His man was out, therefore he went himself into an adjoining room to get me a glass of wine, and while he was absent I stole a rosary from a casket, depositing ashes in its place. Then I drank the wine, and left him, promising to call soon, but giving him plainly to understand that although we might be friends, we could never again be lovers."

"And then?" I asked gravely.

"Ah! I have no knowledge of what occurred after that," she said. "I have endeavoured to fathom the mystery, but have failed. That poor Roddy was murdered is absolutely certain."

"You refused his love because of your affection for me, Aline!" Jack exclaimed, in a low, broken voice, for this discovery that she worshipped the power which he held in greatest hatred had utterly crushed and appalled him. Truly he had spoken the truth on that night in Duddington when he had told me that the Devil had sent her into his life to arrest the good deeds he was endeavouring to perform.

"Yes," she answered, looking up into his dark, grave face with eyes fall of tears. "You know, Jack, that I have ever been true to you. I have been forced to act like this; compelled to commit a profanity which has horrified me, and made to exercise the ingenious trickery which was born of the fertile resources of this man beneath whose thrall I have been held."

"It's a lie!" cried the hideous fellow who personified the Evil One. His very appearance caused us to shudder. "You are one of us—our priestess. Was it not you, yourself, who suggested to our brothers the Sacrifice of the Cat?"

"Yes," cried half a dozen voices, "it was Aline who suggested it."

"At your instigation," she answered boldly. "You first broached the subject and then induced me to suggest it. I've been your catspaw from the very moment we first met at Montgeron, and you took me to the Temple of Satan at Passy. From that day I have known not a moment's peace; the spirit of Satan has entered my soul, and I've existed in an awful torment of mind, like that prepared for the wicked."

Chapter Twenty Five.
Conclusion.

THE FACES OF THAT excited group seemed as demoniacal as the power they had worshipped, and about me I heard ominous words—words which caused me to grip my weapon resolutely. My arm was still around Muriel's waist, for I saw that another attempt would probably be made upon her, so incensed were they that she should have betrayed them. The cult of Satan worships in secret, hiding their infamous rites in underground temples—as well they may—and the votaries of the Evil One are under oath not to divulge the whereabouts of the Devil's dwelling-place or the character of their blasphemies and outrages, on penalty of death. Truly this religion of darkness, springing as it has done from the drawing-rooms of debased Paris, is a terrible and awful spectacle in our present enlightened age.

I glanced around. The doors were closed, and there were only two of us armed, while the daggers used for the piercing of the sacred element were gleaming in several hands. They now numbered nearly a dozen to each of us, and I knew that if we had to defend the two women we loved we should be compelled to fight desperately.

"Forgive me!" implored Aline, looking into her lover's face. "I swear that I have always loved you, and that I have been what you believed me to be, an honest woman. Tell me," she cried, falling again upon her knees before him. "Tell me, Jack, that you will forgive me, now that you know all."

"I do not know all," he answered, in a hard voice. "You confess to having visited Morgan immediately before his death."

"But I did not commit the crime!" she said wildly. "I am innocent—innocent!"

Some jeering laughter greeted this terribly earnest protest. Those around, mostly better-class people, judging from their dress and speech, now took a keen delight in her disgrace and grief.

"He was her lover, and she killed him when she knew that he had not died at Monte Carlo!" somebody exclaimed. "She wanted to marry the parson."

"It's untrue. I swear it is!" she cried. "We had flirted at Monte Carlo, but I had no thought beyond his friendship. When I left him on that fatal morning we parted the best of friends. Not until next day did I know of his strange death, then reported in the papers."

At the moment Muriel, who had remained silent and motionless, as if listening intently, suddenly disengaged herself from my embrace, and walking boldly forward, exclaimed in a loud, firm voice—

"Enough! The mystery of poor Roddy's death shall no longer cause your estrangement from your lover, Aline. Listen!" Then turning to me, she added: "You will remember that once, about eighteen months ago, when I was having tea one Sunday at your rooms, Roddy called, and you introduced us."

"Yes," I cried, suddenly remembering. "I had always believed that you were unacquainted, but I remember quite well now."

"A few days later I met him in Oxford Street, and from that time we were friends, although I saw but very little of him. One day, however, by a word I let drop, he suspected that I was connected with this terrible cult of Evil, and at once asked me to reveal some of its secrets, because he was about to ask a question in Parliament upon the subject, and wished to obtain reliable information. The asking of a question upon such a subject would, he knew, cause a great sensation, and if not armed with facts he must bring himself into ridicule. Well, I confess that I told him something of the rites, and afterwards, at his urgent request, brought him here by the secret way through which I brought you tonight. Unfortunately, however, his presence was detected, and his identity established; although at the time I had no idea that such was the case."

I noticed how the white-faced band of Satanists exchanged glances of fear as they listened to her words spoken clearly and fearlessly. She, too, glanced round at them with a look of hatred and defiance.

"The day on which he accompanied me here was," she continued, "three days prior to his death. I was in the habit of meeting him at railway stations of an evening and imparting to him various information until he knew almost as much of the ways and doings of the Diabolists as I did myself. We had an arrangement by which, if he was unable to keep an appointment, his man should come and bring me a letter with a blank sheet of paper, by which I should know that to keep the appointment was impossible. We met at railway stations for two reasons: first, because the Satanists should not discover my dealings with this Member of Parliament who would, in a few days, startle England with his statements; and, secondly, because you, Clifton, should not call and find me with your friend."

"Extraordinary!" I ejaculated. "Then the note taken by Ash to the King's Cross terminus was meant for you?"

"Certainly," she responded. "I, however, mistook the hour of our appointment, and having that day obtained information that the Satanists had discovered that he had been present, I hastened to warn him of his danger. Too
eager to wait and keep the appointment, and fearing lest harm should befall
him, I went straight to his chambers, arriving, I suppose, immediately after
Aline had left. The door was ajar, so pushing it open I entered. There were
strange sounds in the sitting-room, and in order to discover the reason of
them I slipped behind one of the bedroom doors to listen. Scarce, however,
had I done this when there were hurrying footsteps in the passage as a man
went out. I believed the footsteps to be yours, Clifton. Then when he had
descended the stairs I crept on into Roddy's room, but drew back horrified a
second later. I was too late. He was dying. I tried to rouse him, but he clutched
my dress so frantically that he tore it and held a piece of black chiffon in his
clenched hand. He had, I knew, been poisoned, and in the paroxysm his agony
was frightful. Powerless, I stood beside him for a few moments until the last
spark of life had left, then reproaching myself bitterly for my tardiness, I flew
from the house, fearing lest suspicion should fall upon me. I was witness of
that crime, and to ease my conscience I confessed to Mr Yelverton, then curate
at St. Michael's, all that I knew, although being a member of the Church, I
made no mention of my association with the cult. He knew the truth."

"Then tell me who was the murderer?" I cried.

"I believed the murderer to be my lover, Clifton Cleeve," she answered.
"But here, in this place, I overheard a confession, and discovered that the
man who committed the cowardly crime in order to conceal the existence of
this cult of Evil is the same who, having ascertained that I was witness of his
crime and might denounce him, afterwards sought to silence me also," she
answered; and pointing to the man who personified Satan, added, "It is that
man—Francis Vidit—the man under whose iron thraldom both Aline and
myself have been compelled to commit the profanity that has terrified us; the
man whose heart is as black with wickedness as that of the Evil One he now
represents. He is the murderer of Roddy Morgan!"

The villainous-looking fellow made a dash forward with a second knife in
his hand, but in an instant both Jack's revolver and my own were at his head
and he fell behind, flinching.

"Hold back!" I cried. "Drop that knife this instant, or by Heaven! I'll put a
bullet through you!"

At that moment, while he stood glaring at me, Muriel placed something to
her mouth and blew shrilly. It was a police whistle.

In a second the door was burst open, and an inspector in uniform, a detective and several constables, sprang into the room, creating a confusion utterly

indescribable. Their entry was so sudden that everybody stood dumbfounded.

In the detective I recognised Priestly, the man who had had in hand the
inquiries regarding Roddy's death, and in a moment saw how cleverly Muriel
had arranged the details of her revenge.

"Arrest that man!" she cried, pointing to the cringing ruffian before us.
"That man, Francis Vidit, I declare to be the murderer of Mr Morgan!"

Two constables stepped forward quickly, but the man whose Satanic garb
was so hideous, uttered a terrible curse, and with his face livid, turned quickly
and attacked the men with the knife in his hand. In his desperation he was
powerful as a lion, but in a few moments the inspector and the others had
overpowered him, and he stood before us held helpless within their grasp.

It was no doubt a smart capture, and the police owed it to Muriel's calmness and careful arrangements.

"Let my hand go!" the wretched man cried. "I want to get my handkerchief
to wipe my face. Don't hold me so tight; I shan't hurt you," he laughed with a
hoarse, hideous laugh, which sounded through the place.

Then, with a sudden twist, he freed his hand, and ere they could stop him
he had placed something in his mouth and swallowed it.

"You can do what you like with me now, you fools!" he shrieked wildly. "I
have no fear of you!"

"Look!" cried Muriel. "See his face! He has poisoned himself!"

All gazed at him, and we saw by the spasmodic working of the muscles
of his features that what she said was quite true. The agonies of poisoning
had already seized him, and his haggard face, fast swelling, was horrible to
behold. For a few moments he writhed in the grasp of the officers, while we
all looked on in silence, appalled at the frightful picture he presented; until
suddenly, with a piercing shriek, he seemed to stretch out his limbs rigid
and straight. Then all the light of a sudden died from his hideously distorted
features, and the men in whose grip he was knew by the dead weight upon
them that they held only a corpse.

No further need is there to dwell upon the ghastly events of that fateful
night, a night that will live within my memory for ever; nor need I describe
how we all four left that den of Satan in company with the police. Suffice it to
say that the self-destruction of Francis Vidit caused the disbandment of that
disgraceful Pagan sect which fortunately found so little support in Christian
England. Although the police were, by these revelations of Muriel's, made
aware of the existence of Satanism in London, the suicide of their head made
it unnecessary for any details of the *cultus diabolicus* to be given to the public
through the medium of the sensational Press.

At first the revulsion of feeling within me caused me, I confess, to hesitate whether to take as wife a woman who had actually been a votary of Satan, but on calmer reflection, as I drove back to Charing Cross Mansions with my loved one at my side, I saw plainly how she had been victimised and held powerless beneath the terrible thraldom of this murderer Vidit and his accomplice Hibbert, who had without doubt both carried on these practices with a view to gain the subscriptions of those who joined the cult. That she was pure, honest, and upright I had never doubted, and moved to sympathy when I remembered how bitterly she had suffered, I yielded to her entreaty to be forgiven, feeling convinced of her assertion that her suspicion that I was guilty of the murder of my friend was the cause of her casting me aside and acting as she did.

Just a year has now gone by, and it has been full of changes, for my father dying suddenly, Tixover Hall has come to me, and with Muriel as my wife we live in the old place in perfect contentment and happiness. Jack Yelverton, too, has modified his views regarding the marriage of the clergy, for Aline is now his wife, and in the good work among the poor of the dismal, overcrowded parish of St. Peter's, which he pursues with such untiring energy, she, once the priestess of Satan, is now his greatest helpmate. She is trying to make atonement for the flagrant sins she committed before God, and certainly if the ministration of His Word and righteousness of heart will atone for the profanity to which she once was forced because of her love for the man who is now her husband, then a great and blessed forgiveness will be hers.

The means by which poor Roddy's life was taken have remained an entire mystery until the other day, when Muriel explained how the man Vidit, being an expert toxicologist, once made certain experiments in that old house on Herne Hill, and from these it seemed clear that the poison—apparently one of those extremely deadly ones known to the mediaeval alchemists, a single drop of which is fatal—was flung suddenly into the eye of his victim while he spoke with him, causing instant blindness, general paralysis, and a swift, agonising death. It was the consequent discoloration of the eyes which had so puzzled the doctors.

We, however, in our blissful new-found joy seldom refer to those dark days when the shadow of evil was upon us. Happily they have passed, and are over, for Muriel has broken for ever that most terrible tie which held her aloof from God and man—the Bond of Black.